The Untamed

Anne Crompton

PINNACLE BOOKS   NEW YORK

THE UNTAMED

An original Pinnacle Books edition, published for the first time anywhere.

First printing, March 1981

ISBN: 0-523-41151-0

Cover illustration by Rod Dryden

Printed in the United States of America

PINNACLE BOOKS, INC.
1430 Broadway
New York, New York 10018

The Untamed

HISTORICAL NOTE

In the early 10th Century WENDZ ruled Bohemia as its first Christian duke; in some texts, king or prince. His state of health is not a matter of record. For reasons of state he married THE WICKED DRAGAMIR, daughter of a Magyar chief. Not trusting in her hasty conversion to Christianity, he gave away her first-born son to his mother, Ludmilla, to raise. He left Dragamir her next son, for reasons unknown.

LUDMILLA raised her grandson Wendceslas to be a saint, and later answered to Dragamir for this.

WENDCESLAS confirmed and broadened the influence of the Christian Church during his brief reign.

BOLESLAV, second son of Dragamir, conspired with her and obeyed her wishes, for a time.

NIKODEM is remembered—not by name—in a Christmas carol.

BISHOP NIKLAS is wholly fictional. Most Christian missionaries probably resembled the young man at the spring.

For story purposes time has been telescoped. The events of months and years transpire in days.

1

The Shrine

Bright plain, wide light. Spring flowers reddened the rolling land, which bumped and bounded under Belatruz's pounding hoofs. I saw small hands tangled in his windy mane. They were the hands of a little girl; of the child I used to be. My little heels drummed the war pony's sides. Strong-sinewed arms drummed the warpony's sides. Strong-sinewed arms circled me safely. I laughed, and leaned back against my father's breast. Boundless light poured from the far-arching sky. Red and purple and brown, the boundless plain reached to embrace the light.

I felt the wind. I felt my father's shoulder firm behind my head, and smelled Belatruz's warm sweat. Then, to my amazement, the world wavered. Without warning the plains buckled. Shot through with shadow the strong light faded. Alarmed, I cried out as my father's arms about me dissolved. And now where I had felt his shoulder I felt a stone. The vision crumpled and vanished, and left me alone in the dark; and in dread deeper than dark.

I had dreamed. But how had I dared to sleep? I jerked upright. Huddled on the stone ledge I shivered under the tattered horsehide. Gray light looked in coldly at the small, barred window. Outside a slow dawn was brightening to become my last morning.

The cell was yet dark, and cold with the damp of a hundred winters. No summer sun had ever warmed these dank stones. Rat-rustles troubled the silence; and far away, a hollow echo of footsteps on stone. Tensing, I listened. Were those footsteps coming nearer? I did not know when the guard would come to bring me before my son's high seat.

Closer rang the footsteps. I realized with relief that only one man was walking. Nor was he marching smartly; he shuffled, paused, then scuffed away, his echoes fading.

A little relaxed, I watched the dawn spread. How had I come to this last dawn? What implacable fate had led me step by step to this stone cell? I had always believed myself free. So decisive and independent I had been, the ignorant took me for a witch! Whom could I blame, then, but myself?

Briefly I considered that married monk, my husband. Certainly he was guilty, but so was I. For I had dealt with him on nearly equal terms; indeed, on an evil night I had forced him to accept my terms.

I thought of my father; he who had carried me before him on Belatruz, the savage war pony. As in my dream his encircling arms had dissolved, so in reality had his protection faltered and faded. Yet even so, the thought of him misted my eyes. Would his shrewd eyes mist, when my news reached him? Certainly not!

2

I blinked away his image and searched farther back in memory. The child in me rose, then, weeping with rage. That child hated my mother's memory. But as a woman I understood too much; no longer could I hate my mother with a whole heart.

Her hut was almost as rude and comfortless as this cell. I remembered waking, that Last Harvest morning, wrapped in lousy, scratchy blankets. I remembered myself small, perhaps five years old; barely old enough to know that today was Last Harvest, and tonight would be exciting.

My mother squatted at the stone hearth poking up a flame. At first I saw her as a dim shadow among shadows; humped and slight, and unusually active. Most mornings she shoved me out of bed first to build the fire. Surprised at this rare leisure, I lay in cozy-warm comfort pretending sleep; and watched through sly, slitted eyes as the reluctant flame mounted.

Now my mother's face leaned into light; pale and pitted, veiled with wisps of blond-gray hair. An unusual tension trembled in her thin, hunched shoulders. Behind her the wall rose curving, bound poles and straw and skins. Over her shoulder dangled our Corn Mother; the rude straw Goddess who hung in every village hut, even ours. Tonight, I knew, we would burn Her in the great bonfire and make a new Goddess from new straw. "And a good thing!" I thought, watching Her ragged swing and twirl. She was very tired. She was only two handfuls of straw bound to crossed sticks and wrapped in a scrap of linen; nothing like the beautiful Goddess in the

shrine. I wondered if we would save Her skirt for
the new Goddess; I hoped not. The new Goddess
should be all new. But linen was scarce.

Thinking this I forgot caution and opened my
eyes. My mother swung around to me. Her usual
gaze was a wide, blank stare. She would look
thoughtful, but few thoughts hid behind her cold
gray eyes. She was merely perceiving and absorbing,
at leisure. This morning her eyes were hard and
bright. Some frenzied thought hopped about in her
head; I could almost see it. This morning was decid-
edly different. Perhaps, I thought, Mother was excited about tonight? Yes, she was.

"Hurry!" she said. "Marya, hurry! It's Last Harvest. We don't want to start late, do we?" The words
held a strange menace. She began ladling gruel into
earthen mugs. Her thin hands shook, and the precious gruel spilled.

I noticed that she was dressed. Already she had
pulled on her gray linen shift, and knotted her ker-
chief. Now she gobbled her gruel fast, sitting on her
heels, watching the door-curtain as though at any
moment an enemy might yank it aside. Mother was
anxious, distracted, nearing an outburst of temper.
Prudently, I crawled out from my warm nest.

"Dress!" she ordered. I pulled my little shift out
from among the blankets and climbed into it. "Eat!"
I joined her at the hearth; but I could not gulp down
the hot gruel in great draughts, as she did. "Hurry!
Marya, hurry!"

I did not see this hurry. The fun was tonight, not
now. Tonight would be the bonfire at the shrine; the
tossing in of old Corn Mothers and binding of new

4

ones; the drum and pipe music, and circle dancing. I knew I might well have to sleep outside tonight; for after the dancing Mother might have visitors. But I did not mind. Visitors meant good food, maybe new linen; maybe even new skirts for ourselves and the new Goddess.

But all that was tonight. Today, this morning, I looked forward to nothing but work; a whole day's rough work. What was this earnest *hurry?* "Alright, don't eat. You can eat tonight, when we're safe. Now, hurry!"

The village street was full of hurrying figures. This strange morning no one paused to chat, no one even greeted his neighbor. Heads bent, hands grasping scythes like swords, people fairly rushed up the long street toward the shrine.

Our hut was the last, at the bottom of the street. Hurrying with the others, we trotted past better huts, made of wooden wattles; larger huts, with pole-fenced yards; and, at the top of the street, a few white-plastered houses where chickens scratched and clucked, and pigs grunted, watching us hurry past.

I knew all the neighbors who scurried through the morning mist. I knew the men who visited Mother, and the women who scorned her. Among their children I had a few friends. But no one looked at anyone, no one spoke. The silence was furtive, suspicious. A small fear tugged at my heart, and I tugged at Mother's dress. She brushed me away like a fly.

We came to the top of the street, to the shrine. The Goodess stood on a shelf under a wattled roof. She was wooden, painted rich red and blue. Her skirts and hair were plastered straw. She embraced a small straw goddess; Her beloved daughter, about to be torn from Her arms. This very night the little straw daughter would be tossed into the bonfire; and all the long winter the Goddess would mourn for her, as the earth mourned for the withdrawn sun.

This morning I noticed many little cakes left on the shelf. All who had extra meal baked Last Harvest cakes for the Goddess. I saw children I knew— not my friends—step up and leave their cakes, bowing in prayer for a quick moment. The little fear tugging at my heart squeaked alarm. I would have felt safer if I, too, could have left a cake with the Goddess.

We said our prayer, bowing hastily. At least, Mother prayed. I gazed up at the bright Goddess in awe and puzzlement. And then we were striding, trotting, running toward the rich neighbor's field where we worked.

Rolling fields surrounded the village. Each field was hedged from the next field; but this one stretched high on a mound, almost a hill; and I could look down over many hedges, and see many neighbors already bent to feverish work.

Mother urged me, "Hurry!"

She cut, I stacked. The field was not so great but that three men could have finished it by noon. But Mother lacked a man's reach; and my small legs took short steps. My arms could embrace only small sheaves. The corn was heavy, rough to my hands, rustling with grasshoppers. They leaped from the sheaves into my face and down my dress. Other days we had paused to laugh at this. Not today. "Marya, hurry!" When I lagged, Mother turned a gray, worried face over her stooped shoulder. "Hurry!" Straightening to ease my aching back I saw the lower fields full of bent backs. No one paused to drink, or to wipe the sweat from his or her eyes. But for the constant ringing insect-hum, the fields were silent. No one called to his neighbor, no one challenged or boasted. In the center of the silent fields the village waited, empty. No old woman limped down the street. No babies crawled, watched over by lucky girls. The empty village waited, the watching Goddess waited, I did not know for what. But I felt the waiting. Frightened, I stooped again to the cut corn.

The morning mists had long been burned away when Mother finally paused an instant, and sent me to the well. Always at noon I took our water-skin through the hedge to the well in the next field. Away from Mother, my fear relaxed. The sun hot on my shoulders, the brown stubble bruising my toes seemed natural, familiar. I almost forgot that this was somehow a very different day. Always I leaned over and looked down at the child in the well. This time, too, I passed precious moments greeting her. The child in the well was blond and sturdy. Her gray eyes were friendly, even trusting. I smiled down at her and she smiled back, cool and peaceful beneath the still water. I wished I could take her place!

The child in the well was pretty, like me. I knew I was pretty, Mother often told me so. She would stroke back my hair and smooth my eyebrows with

7

a sometimes gentle, dirty finger. "A pretty girl can always make a living," she would say. She herself was hardly pretty; her face was lined, her arms stringy. Gray showed persistently through her herbal hair-dye. Even so, she made us a living of sorts. Faint through the insect-hum I heard her calling. She sounded frantic.

I straightened; and noticed the nearby workers watching me. Working steadily, they yet peered up at me; and one man, a frequent visitor of Mother's, jerked his head meaningfully toward our field. "Hurry!" His gesture said.

Returning fear nudged me. I slung the water skin over my aching shoulder and scurried back through the hedge.

Now our pace was desperate. We worked sweat-blind, too fast. I dropped stalks that slower, more careful hands would have gathered. Mother strode far ahead of me. Finished with the cutting she worked back toward me, gathering. I noticed welcome shadows, a cool breeze; the sun was dropping.

Children dodged in and out of the hedge, making "Hurry" signs to me. Red-faced and stoop-stiff, they looked satisfied. Their work was done. In the near fields people straightened, rubbing their backs. Talk rose on the insect-hum, breaking at last the day's unnatural silence. Mother worked ever more desperately, making wild signs to me. I could not keep her pace. My shoulders throbbed, my legs buckled.

The man from the next field came to help. I think now that this was the finest, kindest deed I have ever witnessed. The Christians are famed for charity; but I have never seen Christian charity to match

8

this deed. The lucky, finished children came back through the hedge; but now they made no more signals. They stood and watched, some giggling, some grim. From all the farther fields people came trooping. They were all finished. Only we three worked on. Dimly I realized that this was what we feared.

Crawling through prickles I gathered the last corn. Distant voices rose louder, nearer. As I reached for the last handfuls a crowd of neighbors burst through the hedge.

I sat back on my heels and wiped sweat from my eyes with a trembling paw. The earth rumbled under my knees. A hundred boots pounded toward us. "Marya!" Yelled a woman. "It was Big Marya!" Someone else shrieked the man's name. But a big boy pointed at me. "She picked the last," he declared. "Little Marya."

The crowd, which had been making for Mother, swerved toward me. Men seized up hard-gathered sheaves and tore them apart, holding the straw high and wide. Open-mouthed, they yelled triumph and threat. Women screeched.

I scrambled up and ran for Mother. But she was drawing away from me. Her familiar face was strange, dead-white, pulled tight. The man held her by an arm and pulled her backward, away from me. Clinging together, they stared at me like strangers. I stretched my arms to her and ran hard. Her eyes had gone cold, but I had no other hope or refuge. I ran hard, but the crowd ran harder. They were grownups, with long strides. They caught me up and clapped armfuls of corn about me. Corn closed me in, blinded and smothered and choked me. I was wrapped in corn like a Corn Mother. I was lifted clear off the ground and carried and tossed.

Trying to cry, I nearly strangled. Now my mouth was full of corn, my closed eyes were bandaged in corn. Swooping and bouncing in the air I heard shouts, laughter, a wail that might have been Mother's. A drum boomed. Women shouted a harsh song. These were the happy sounds of Last Harvest; festive, fun-sounds; distorted now, as in a nightmare.

Panting, gasping for air, I scrabbled straw away from my face. I could breathe, now, through a hole in my package; and see a little, mostly stubbled ground whirling below me, and dancing feet; some in boots, some in rags, most bare. Flying, my straw package tilted; and I glimpsed through my peep hole a flash of red and blue. The crowd was dancing toward the shrine. Before the shrine stood the headman, resplendent in red-embroidered, clean white linen. Level sunlight glinted on the knife he held ready.

Close at hand women sang and wailed. Pipes trilled, the drum boomed so near the sound shook my small body like a heart-beat. Sky swooped across my peep-hole. Then I saw brown earth and the headman's boots rush toward me. (Even the boots were white, and richly embroidered.) I hit earth with a thump that knocked the breath out of me. Instantly the crowd fell completely silent. Drum and pipe and song and shout all ceased together. I heard the crowd breathe.

And still I did not know. I may not have seen this Last Harvest rite before; it does not grace every such festival. Or, seeing it, I may not have understood.

I drew rasping breath. Through the screech of indrawn air I heard another sound; a distant howl and rumble. Dozens of great drums beaten together might raise such a thunder. Through the straw I felt the earth trembling.

Something flashed by my peep-hole. The headman's knife stabbed earth by my nose and stood, swaying. Above me I heard screams, about me a rush of feet. The great drums came on. I was snatched back into the air. I bounded, I flew and soared, jostled and jiggled. Far below the earth rushed by, clothed in dark-flying dust, littered with corn and straw, spattered blood, a smashed bowl. The neighbors' cries dwindled, and died in distance. Men laughed and grunted, calling outlandish words to one another.

I thought I knew what had happened. Squirming in the dark straw I was sure of one thing. The mists of childish ignorance parted to reveal this one clear, understood fact. I had been bad. For this to happen I must have been wicked. This only happened to wicked children; children who lingered too long at the cool well; children who stole eggs from under neighbors' hens, and did not obey Mother; children who answered Mother with glib, fearful lies.

I had been so wicked that now I would never see Mother again. I would never see the village again, or the shrine, or my neighbors. Helplessly bundled like a trussed piglet, I was being carried away by the horse folk.

I knew the horse folk from song and story. They

were wild animals disguised as men. They had no homes and no language (though I heard them talking around me, now.) They had no gods and no morals. They rode fast, fierce beasts over the plains, and stole the fruits of labor from hard-working farm folk. Whoever objected was stabbed and trampled.

One service these wild beasts did the villagers; they carried off wicked, burdensome children like myself. I wondered why, if they did no work, they wanted children, good or bad? Once I asked Mother that. She shrugged. She thought most likely they ate them.

2

The Plain

Young Draga, who later became chief of the horse folk, rode alone across the plain. He rode his well-taught war pony; and his well-taught dog loped at the pony's heels.

In the noon heat they came to a secret hollow in the plain; a quiet green dip of land cupping a clear spring. Draga believed this spring to be his own secret; but he found that he was not alone here. Another young man lay prone in soft grass at the water's edge. He trailed a slim hand in the water, and his calm eyes followed the ripples.

He was neither tribesman nor villager. Draga had never seen his like before. Though he was young, the crown of his head was bald. Lower locks flowed, tangled, down upon the broad shoulders of his robe. His feet were bare to the warm grass. He bore no arms whatever that Draga could see; though a stout walking stick leaned against a bush; under the bush lay rope sandals and a flat wallet, probably empty.

The young man must have heard the thud of the war pony's hoofs, but he never looked up. He gazed into the water and trailed water with his fingers, and he watched it sparkle. He offered neither greeting nor apology to the young warrior looming above him, whose rippled reflection shadowed the spring. Neither startled nor frightened nor resigned, he simply ignored Draga.

Then Draga became angry. The fellow had no goods. Draga might have let him go, he might even have joked and shared dry meat with him; but he could not be ignored. Draga shouted to his dog, and threw out a hand in the young man's direction. The dog sprang to attack. Snarling it sprang, with ears laid back and white fangs bared. One great bound the dog made. Then it stood at the young man's shoulder, strangely uncertain what to do next. It whined, and looked back to Draga. "Attack!" Draga commanded. But the dog would not, or could not attack. It whined and wagged, growled and whimpered. Finally it sat down by the stranger, and rested its muzzle on his arm.

Draga was amazed. This dog had never failed him before! He kicked the war pony forward. "Attack!" He commanded with voice and knees and lifted spear. "Attack!"

The pony pranced forward, rearing to fall with heavy hoofs upon the stranger, who still did not raise his eyes. But coming nearer the pony side-stepped. Angrily it shook its mane and swished its tail, but it kept prancing away. Backing off, it pawed the ground in confusion. It could not attack.

Now Draga perceived that he was fighting magic. "Some magic he had," he told me years later; "he was some sort of shaman. There were strange gods with him. Well, his wallet was empty! Why should I

14

trouble myself? I rode away and left him; and after a time my dog followed."

I forbore to ask whether Draga had paused to drink, or to water his animals. That had certainly been his intention, and Draga always fulfilled his intentions; except, perhaps, that time. That was one of only two bafflements that Draga remembered in his old age. The young man at the spring puzzled him forever. And years later, I puzzled him for an hour.

As he led his men thundering toward the village that autumn evening, he saw the villagers grouped together in a tight circle. All backs were turned to the invaders; all eyes fastened hungrily on the bundle of straw at the headman's feet. So absorbed were these people, they never noticed Draga's band of shrieking horse folk till they dashed in among them. Swooping from the pony's back at full gallop Draga snatched up the straw bundle. He left what other loot there might be to his men; a little corn, a necklace, the headman's wallet. This bundle of straw must be worth more than all these; it might contain a village god, a jewelled talisman. Whatever it concealed must be the village treasure.

The raid was swift. Draga led his men rampaging down the one street and out across the fields, and so to the open plain. As the village dwindled behind them the galloping ponies slowed; the tribesmen drew together to laugh and boast.

Glancing back, Draga saw no village on the skyline. Autumn-brown plains spread quiet under the sunset. Draga halted. He swung down from the sweating war pony; there and then, under the en-

15

vious eyes of his men, he dived into the mystery bundle.

He drew forth no god, no talisman, no treasure; only a dirty child who stared at him through tangled blond hair; too frightened to cry.

I did not know my real danger. I knew only the terror of abandonment; of being smothered in straw and tossed and hurled through the air, and now surrounded by dark and hideous men who jabbered strange words, and who most likely intended to eat me. One of them held me in the air. His hard hands bruised my arms. He glared at me, scowling through the tribal scars that mapped his face. His thick black eyebrows twitched vigorously. His flared nostrils flared farther into hairy, moist caverns. The jabbering died away now, the men were silent. Only the ponies stamped and snorted, restlessly side-stepping. I feared the big beasts, which I had never seen before. I feared the ugly men, and especially him who held me. Choked by the heavy stink of leather, sweat and grease, I hung silent, like a straw doll, in Draga's hands.

A slow light dawned in his small eyes. He grinned. Crouching in the brown grass he brought my feet to ground. I stood shakily gaping, while Draga's big hand patted and lifted my hair. Murmuring, he raised a handful of it to the setting sun, then let it fall through his fingers. He leaned forward and spat in my face, and rubbed the spittle about with heavy fingers. The hand that gripped my shoulder gentled. Softly, Draga laughed.

The men laughed. The ponies whinnied, reared and shied. And in this heaving, shuffling circle of

16

laughter I was reborn. Heaven gave me a second chance. My small mouth opened and laughed with Draga and his men, even while tears of terror spilled at last down my cheeks.

In that sunset moment Draga took me for his pet; and I responded like any small, captive animal. Wherever he went I followed at his heels. Listening eagerly for his voice I learned his speech and promptly forgot my own. My short past became a misty dream for me; I lived happily enough in the waking world of the present.

All my life I had lived alone with my mother. Village mothers did not encourage their children to play with the whore's daughter; adults stepped around me. So my new aloneness among the dark children of the horse folk did not surprise me. I was well accustomed to stares and grumblings. But now my defense was secure. No longer need I rely on my mother to stand timidly between me and the world. Now I hid in the shadow of Draga the chief. He stood before me like a colossus; and I hooked my small fingers into his braided belt, and clung.

From the safety of Draga's shadow I peeped out upon the boisterous life of the horse folk. I watched women packing up goods and tents to move; and after a while I stole out and helped them. I watched children my age herding sheep; and soon I joined them. I learned to dodge for cover when warriors strode into camp with news of booty. If I came in his way then, Draga might kick me aside like a straw doll. But while drinking tea, mending tack or lolling in his tent he talked to me, as I have seen gentler men talk to their dogs.

17

I followed him everywhere. One day I followed him out of camp. Whistling through his teeth, Draga strode through a flock of sheep. Gray and brown and greasy, they trotted and bleated around us. To my eyes they looked big as ponies, their babble burned my ears. Their smell smothered me. I caught hold of Draga's tunic and held on; and so he brought me safely out of the flock, scarcely noticing.

The incessant bleating faded behind us. Now Draga swung over rough brown grass, striding from hillock to rock; while I scampered behind, watching out for thorns, sticky weeds and dung. We came among grazing ponies. Widely scattered mares and colts perked inquisitive ears at us. A foal pranced near, inviting me to play. The brilliance of his eye frightened me. Again, I grabbed Draga's tunic.

He stopped. I peered around him. Fifty paces ahead, a war pony faced us. It was solid black, chunky and alert. Its stance was a challenge. Even at that distance its smell seared my nose. It had staled the ground in all directions, and the earth breathed forth its stink. It wore no halter. Proudly it watched us, like some fearless wild beast; and seemed to dare us to move.

I shrank behind Draga and tried to stand small. Glancing back at our shadows I merged them, lest the monster notice there were two of us. Nothing in the world would attack Draga, I had no fear for *him*. But this fire-breathing monster would eat me in a gulp, I had no doubt.

Draga whistled through his fingers.

The monster stood on its front feet and kicked

18

the air. Swishing its tail, it bounded in circles, kicking. I wrapped myself around Draga's leather-clad knees.

Again Draga whistled. The beast spun to face us; snorted like a dragon; and rushed us.

I closed my eyes and clung desperately to Draga. The thunder of hoofs circled us. The coarse tail lashed my face. The air was heavy with horse stink. Stealing a peek, I found the round black barrel directly before me and a black hoof, white-striped, planted beside my foot. Grunting and squealing with pleasure, the monster was eating from Draga's hand.

Draga patted the bowed neck. Under his arm the creature looked straight into my terrified eyes. Snorting, it pushed forward. The huge, furrowed face approached mine. Blunt yellow teeth gleamed between drooping, drooling lips.

I knew better than to scream. I knew what Draga thought of white-gizzards. Pressing against him, I screamed.

Now for the first time Draga seemed to notice me. "Aha! So you're here?" He grasped my shoulder and peeled me away from him like a wet garment. "Come, meet Belatruz. You children must be friends. Tell you how you make Belatruz your friend; give him this."

Holding my shaking hand flat out, Draga placed on my palm a morsel of unleavened bread. The slobbering, toothy muzzle muttered wickedly over my hand. I thought my end had come. I squeezed my eyes shut, and felt Belatruz's warm moist touch as he picked the bread off my palm.

My fear was not simple ignorance. Belatruz was, indeed, a fearsome animal. Only Draga could handle him. He greeted all others with flattened ears and bared teeth; and, if they persisted, with flailing hoofs. He was the perfectly trained war pony; intelligently submissive to his master, hostile to outsiders. Years later, Draga sighed for him. "Never find one like old Belatruz again!" But we made a peace together, Belatruz and I. We had to, for we both belonged to Draga. We were his favorite pets. That very day I learned to stand apart from Draga, shakily alone before Belatruz; and he, after a few suspicious "whoofs!" learned to accept me. Later, gradually, we became friends.

Much later, I could go out on the plain and whistle up Belatruz myself. He would come trotting and stand for me, while I dressed him in his show-bridle with its swinging bone rings and amulets; and sometimes in the heavy saddle, of inlaid and lacquered leather, over a bright blanket. But these trappings were purely ceremonial. For serious purposes Draga rode bareback, like his men; and guided Belatruz with his knees, freeing his hands for weapons.

I remember the first time Draga lifted me before him to ride Belatruz. I leaned back against his hard chest. Safely circled by his arms I took the plains wind in my face. The wind was brisk up there. I had never seen the world from so high a vantage point. The far, purple horizon jiggled gently as Belatruz ambled out of camp. From a safe distance, away down there on the ground, mean dogs snarled and jealous children sneered. Outside camp we passed among the sheep; and I looked down upon their massed, wooly backs, at them jostling to let us through. From my grand height their bleatings sounded pathetic, rather than threatening.

Past the sheep we faced an empty plain. Belatruz snorted, his neck dipped and arched; and suddenly he was trotting. The horizon bounced as I bounced on his broad back. I clutched at his bouncing mane. I twined my hands in its greasy tangles and clung. And now we galloped free on the plain. Behind us the camp dwindled to a smoke-smudge, a low smear on the sky. Around us the light flowed wide; red and purple and brown, the boundless plain reached to embrace the light. Spring flowers reddened the rolling land, which bumped and bounded under Belatruz's pounding hoofs. Elated, I drummed my heels on his hot sides. I leaned back against Draga and laughed. My world of savage dogs and hard-faced children was pounded to fine dust by Belatruz's flying hoofs. I was safe with fast, fierce Belatruz. Always, I was safe with Belatruz; and the fiercer he showed himself, the safer I felt. He became for me an extension of Draga's protection. In case of danger in Draga's absence, I thought I could always creep in among the war pony's legs.

Like Belatruz, Draga was ferocious with outsiders. I soon learned to beware when his eyebrows twitched. His rising anger gave no other sign. He would sit calmly, his face almost impassive behind its mask of scars; and the envoy or the new recruit would talk on, innocently, till the storm broke. But our people took their cue from me. As long as I leaned against Draga, all was well. But if I noticed his eyebrows twitch, or felt a slight tightening of his

21

shoulders, I would scuttle away. Then women withdrew and men fell silent. The world awaited Draga's wrath . . . or laughter. A joke could blunt his anger. But once aroused—once he had leaped up scowling, hand on hilt—his rage roamed free as a wolf, knowing no border.

Anger could stir him to violence, but greed was the usual spur. When his scouts brought word of rich traders passing, he would summon his men with drum and wailing horn. Belatruz would be armed with leather on neck and flank. Sidestepping, tossing his tangled mane, he would paw and neigh as Draga mounted, eager as he. Among the swaying lances and lacquered shields Draga was distinguished by his black horse-tail plume. Even through the dust cloud raised by two hundred stomping hoofs, Draga's eyes would gleam like sun-struck spear points. Lighting momentarily on me, they would offer no gleam of recognition. At these times I did not exist in Draga's world.

When Draga raided a farm village we descended like vultures. With other children I ran past burning huts and around charred corpses to join the crowd milling about the heaped booty. Pushed to the outskirts, we hopped and jumped to look over grownup shoulders. There in the midst Draga presided. I glimpsed his face, and the earthenware pot he held up. Earthenware broke on trek; but while it lasted was a novelty. Draga destributed linen, clothing, corn, sometimes a bit of simple jewelry or a few bright-rubbed coins. I hopped from one foot to the other. His men satisfied, Draga might save me a scrap of ribbon.

Each man took his share from Draga's hands. Pushing his way out through the crowd he was instantly besieged by wives, old parents, unlucky friends. They pressed upon him, snatching, demanding, begging. Some men were glad to escape empty handed! Only the most sour-natured came out with all their winnings.

Running around the edge of the crowd once, I stumbled and fell headlong. The breath was knocked out of me. Sitting up dazed, I found a small village girl, about my age, lying beside me. Sprawled on her back, she held her face away from me. Twined in her black hair a smooth ribbon shone, green and red. This was my first glimpse of silk.

"You tripped me!" I shouted, angry with hurt. "You'll pay for that!" I grabbed the lovely, shining ribbon, and yanked. A tuft of hair came away with the ribbon. The girl's head rolled, and revealed her face. It was green. The open, staring eyes were dusty.

I stood up, clutching my prize. The other child had been stabbed and trampled. She lay strangely flat, not breathing. Around us feet shifted, turned and walked. Any moment, someone might bend down and snatch my treasure. I bunched it into my fist, and blood oozed out between my fingers. The silk was green; the blood was red.

I wiped my hand on the ground, and held onto my ribbon. The girl was a villager, she deserved to be dead; and I deserved my ribbon.

I felt more uneasy when Draga raided another tribe of horse folk. Listening to our men boast, I wondered about these foreigners, who were human beings like ourselves. How would it be to wake in the night and find the tent ablaze? Or to look at the point of a swift-descending dagger? I was thankful it was some other child who had watched the dagger plunge! As for me, I sat here safe with Draga, and tasted the mead in his skull cup.

While I was small he broke my bread with his own hard hands, and lifted the jug of mare's milk for me. Once I was ill. I lay in heat and dizzy dark, and breathing hurt. Then Draga fetched the shaman to dance over me and rattle his gourds and waft magic smoke through the tent. And as the fever cleared I saw Draga's face above me, smooth with kindness, smiling at my recovery. "Daughter," he called me then; "Dragamir."

He paid no such attention to his many real daughters. Now I realize they were surprisingly kind to me, considering that Draga seldom looked at them, and certainly never lifted one of them up on Belatruz! But among all my sisters I had only one true friend. That was my twin, Yolann.

They called us "the twins" because we were always together. We looked nothing alike. Yolann was plump, dark, a trifle hump-backed. Her small, homely face was scarred, her hair neatly braided; for she had a careful mother. I was pale, and my hair flowed free and tangled. Like two young fillies, one white and one dun, we raced through camp together, among drying racks, over dung heaps, between tethered ponies and gossiping women. Sheltered in the lee of a tent we built stick tents, and fashioned clay men and dogs to live in them. Yolann's mother made us baby-dolls of sticks and rags. For a day I nursed mine happily. Then I lost it. Nor did I ever search for it, or wonder in which dungheap it lay, or whether it cried for me. Yolann babied hers till it fell apart, and then her mother mended it. Wearily I watched her dandle it. Looking up from my clay men I saw them dark against the blue, far-arching sky—Yolann and her infant. Tenderly she bowed her head against the doll's rag head. Lightly her gentle hands enfolded its stiff stick body. Her love gave life; and even I could hear her baby's tiresome chuckles.

From the other side of the tent our brother Ruga whistled. He was looking for me. Boredom slid like a burden off my shoulders. I scrambled up. "Ruga's calling us. Come on!"

"Mmm, no. I want to feed Baby."

"Oh, come on, Yolann! Forget your dumb Baby, he's just a bunch of sticks!" Ruga knew much better things to do.

"Baby is hungry." Yolann said this so firmly, so like a grownup, that I gave up. I ran away around the tent, calling, "Ruga, wait for me!"

Ruga was about our age, eight or nine; but he was big, with a heavy, brooding face. His mother was Draga's favorite wife, and he owed his life to her charms; another child would have been quietly left behind on trek. For Ruga's tongue could not form words. Words of a sort came out, but they sounded wrong; they were like clothes turned inside out. To understand him one had to listen carefully. I listened carefully now as we trotted out of camp toward a flock of agitated sheep; but I could not

25

untwist the panting, writhing words. "Never mind," I called after Ruga, who had run ahead, "I'll do it!" Whatever it was.

The boys were riding rams. Ten or twelve young boys took turns on five rams. They would ride a few paces, laughing, clinging to the thick wool; while the animals bucked and circled, tossed their ridge horns and bleated rage. The ewes watched, confused; and sometimes a circling ram started an eddy in the flock; and for some moment all the sheep circled, bleating, together.

This was a favorite sport, but some of us were growing beyond it. I knew that Ruga had a hopeful eye on a certain small sorrel pony in the herd. But Draga kept putting him off. Draga regarded this son with contempt barely tinged with hope. Ruga was strong for his age, and skillful. He could shoot and thrust a lance as well as some grown men. But he could not speak clearly to Draga about the pony; and Draga was never one to listen patiently.

Ruga ran straight for the biggest ram, the one whose left horn curled into his ear. Another boy rode him, whirling in a storm of bleating ewes. Ruga seized the left horn and brought the ram to a skidding halt. "Yurn," he babbled at the rider, "Emme on, adim afore, yurn."

"It's not your turn," the boy replied, justly. "It's Sorbal after me. Let go!"

This little boy was a brother of ours, but his mother was dead. He was smaller than Ruga, and perhaps several years younger. In spite of all this he demanded his rights. "Let go, you blatherer!" he cried. Ruga dug his heels into the ground and hung on, dragging the ram's head low. The rider lost all patience. "I aid eggo!" He babbled, pretty fairly imitating Ruga's tormented speech. "It's my turn, 'ou 'ust came, eggo!"

Sorbal and his friends giggled. I giggled, myself. Ruga let go the ram's horn. He seized the rider around the waist and hauled him down. Kicking and butting, the ram rushed away in a cloud of dust. Sorbal and the others chased after it. No one noticed that Ruga was shaking his brother by the throat. As the dust settled I saw Ruga wrench the younger boy's neck with all his considerable might, and hurl him down. I heard the small, dull *thwack* as his head hit rock.

I stared in surprise. The little boy did not move. Blood seeped from under his head and dyed the rock. Ruga stood panting, looking down. He seemed dumbfounded. Sorbal came back, dragging the tired ram. His friends pushed it from behind. When they saw the boy on the ground in the slowly widening pool of blood, they let the ram go. We formed a silent circle around the still form. Now the rock was red, and blood was staining the sand around it.

Ruga looked around at us. He opened his mouth, but no sound escaped. Instead, he raised his hands to signal. Then, for the first time, he used the sign-language that later became his; a language we understood much more easily than his speech. "He angered me," was the message. "I didn't know the rock was there! Why did he anger me?"

I ran away, breathlessly, all the way back to camp and in among the tents. I leaped small fires, knocked over a toddler, kicked a dog in his ugly teeth. I ran straight to Yolann's mother, Barax; and buried my head in her lap.

Draga's young son was buried under a rock pile. Soon after, we struck camp and filed past this rock pile, leaving it alone under the sky. Another year I searched for it, half-heartedly, among spring flowers. I never found it.

No one teased Ruga after that. For his part, he never spoke. He adopted hand signals for conversation, and ordered Sorbal and his friends around with whistles and wordless shouts. They trailed him, admiring his strength and skill. Later, they admired his intelligence.

That was our last ram-riding. I was growing big; and Ruga went on immediately to better things. That same day Draga led him out among the herds and bridled for him the small sorrel pony.

Snow blew wild on the plains. Shrieking like warriors, frigid winds whipped snow against the tents. Invisible behind the blowing snow-curtain the herds huddled, motionless, rumps to the wind. In camp the streets were empty. Every tent was closed, curtains down, felts and skins held in place with stones. Even so, walls trembled, and snow blew in down smoke holes.

In a warm nest of rugs Yolann and I played knucklebones. We played for the flat, aromatic loaves Barax fried on her brazier. Wind might rattle the felt wall curving over us; snow might drift in and powder our hair, but we laughed, kneeling over the bones in the warm, flickering lamplight. When Barax had scooped up the last of the meal and moistened and fried it, she played with us. Chuckling, the lucky winner of a throw would dip her bread in honey and eat it slowly, teasingly. The brazier warmed us, the lamp and the body heat; but mostly the laughter warmed us so that we forgot the storm raging outside.

Sleepy at last, I peeped out through the curtains into snow-flailing blackness. I hesitated to stagger across three wind-sliced streets to the central tent. "That's as well," said Barax drawing me back. She closed the curtains. "It's time you move out of the central tent; are you Draga's daughter, or his wife?"

"Stay with us!" Yolann's black eyes were bright with welcome.

I slept in Barax's tent that night and the next. I moved in there, and the "twins" became inseparable. We were growing up, we must have been eleven or twelve; and Barax began to teach us tasks and chores. We learned to mend, patch and brew. We learned to spin the coarse wool of Barax's sheep. Yolann's home became my home, and her mother became almost my mother; almost, but never quite; for I remembered my mother's name, Marya Whore. I remembered her name and her face; sometimes in dreams it drifted by me; a thin, pinched face, framed by scraggly blond hair. It stared at me thoughtfully with cool, gray eyes. Sometimes in dreams Marya Whore drew away from me. Her gray eyes flashed with terror, she threw up her hands to ward off horror. From these nightmares I woke gasping for breath, smothered by a weight of sheepskin on my face.

I did not like mothers. The ones I knew were

harsh women, struggling to feed themselves and their brats by whatever means came to hand. If the children lived and grew they were satisfied, they hoped for no more than that. They gave life grudgingly, and kindness was a luxury. As for a foreign child like myself—pale, unscarred, blond—she should be thankful for every blow and kick withheld.

"I don't like mothers," I told Yolann. "I don't want to be one."

Yolann gasped, "You don't like *Mother*?"

"Oh, I don't mean Barax! I love Barax! But I don't want to be a woman. I don't want to do dull work and wait for a man to give me things. I want to ride out and grab my own booty!" I thought it must be wonderful to be a man; to ride free on the plain, and seize what you could by strength of arm and force of will. With all my heart I envied our brothers, who looked forward to this life.

"But you're a girl," Yolann pointed out, "and not even the shaman can make you a boy!"

For Yolann it was simple. She was glad to be a girl, she looked forward to womanhood. She had left her rag and stick baby behind with childhood; now she tended the babies of harassed neighbors and aunts. She dandled them more lovingly than their mothers did. She breathed wonderment over the softness of their skins, she marveled at the sweet innocence in their glossy eyes. "Oh, I want one!" she confided to me. "There's no treasure in the world like one of those!" I think she scorned the boys I envied, because this treasure would never be theirs.

I shook my head. "Not me!" I declared firmly. "If I ever have one I'll expose it." I must not be shackled to a whining infant; for how, then, could I ride out and grab booty?

But Yolann knew better than I. Our brothers' arms grew muscle-hard. Mine remained soft. I could shoot or throw as accurately as Ruga, but not so far. Dismayed, I discovered such new strength in his wrists that I no longer dared to wrestle with him. Newly awkward, my body sprouted small, soft breasts. "For a baby!" Yolann chortled, delighted. I groaned. And then one morning I woke in dull, uneasy pain, to find a snake of slithered blood on my mat.

"You are right," I told Yolann bitterly. "Not even the shaman can make me a boy!"

I must indeed become a woman. If I must do this, I thought I might as well do it right; I opened my ears to Barax's patient instructions; I watched and copied her gestures, from the deft twirl of her spindle to her languorous, heavy walk. It was like learning a new dance-step. Almost, I began to enjoy it.

"You twins are growing up," Barax noticed. She taught us how to make a cleansing paste from herbs and plaster it on our bodies. For a day we would walk about gingerly, cracking plaster at every step. Then in the evening we would peel off the paste, and with it all dirt, sweat, lice and itch. I have never enjoyed my body more than on those summer evenings when it emerged clean, fresh, faintly scented. Later I learned that not even the touch of silk, or of clean linen sheets could rival the delightful breath of evening air on herb-freshened skin. And when I lived a

31

soft life, almost removed from dirt and itch, this herb-cleansing remained my favorite luxury.

Barax showed us adornments. She taught us to make jewelry from seeds and pebbles, cosmetics from herbs. She showed us the mosses to gather for our bleedings, the teas to soften their miseries.

She liked to comb my hair. First she combed out the lice; then she spread the hair over her plump fingers, patting it, murmuring at the light upon it. "Draga loves this hair," she told me. "It shines like gold in sunlight. This is his luck charm. Always wear it smooth and shining, to remind him that you are his luck."

So, I was Draga's luck! That explained much that had been mysterious. I had certainly brought him good luck, then. Since he had found me in his bundle his riches had increased tenfold. His tribe had grown, other tribes had joined with him. Now he took impressive booty; no longer satisfied with the corn and flax of the farm folk, now he brought home silk and ivory and clinking coins. And this was all due to me! I said to Barax, "Let me see."

She handed me her bit of cracked mirror. With surprise and strange delight, I saw my hair glisten golden in a beam of winter sun. I must be a woman, yes; but I would be an unusually good-looking woman. And for the first time I saw that a good-looking woman might possess a certain power; a different power than that of the strong man, but comparable.

Barax nodded. "You see, it's like gold. Your looks saved your life once, Dragamir, it's time you

32

appreciate them. And you know, a pretty girl can always make a living."

I smiled; grimly, I hoped. "But what sort of a living is that—a baby a year!"

"Ah. Not necessary. Come nearer, children. Let me whisper."

And then Barax gave us her treasure, her jewel, her secret. She had taught us charms and teas to ensure safe childbirth. Now she taught us charms and arts to ensure no childbirth. "The charms are good," she murmured in our ears, "never forget them; but the arts are better. Never trust to charms alone."

This knowledge, Barax whispered, was not given to all women. She had it from her grandmother, whose grandmother was a shaman. "With these arts you can be as free as the men. You can decide your own fate. You can hold life in your hands, to give or refuse; and that Goddess whom women fear will have to ask your consent if She wishes to work in you!"

Wordlessly, we accepted the gift of freedom. We muttered no thanks—we were too dazed and startled. I wanted to slide my arms around Barax's warm bulk and hug her, but I hung back, abashed. Even now, remembering, I wish I had hugged her!

On a winter morning we woke to hear a frigid wind rattling the felts. Yolann and I snuggled together under a mound of sheepskins. I poked my nose out and smelled the cold. "Barax hasn't lit the brazier," I told Yolann.

"I know." Her teeth chattered.

"Lets us!"

"Why not?"

There was no reason why not, except that it was not our custom. Usually we lay warm abed while Barax blew up the embers, and fried the day's first handful of meal or mutton. With a sense of difference and adventure, I crawled out into the cold.

Barax lay huddled in sheepskin near the brazier. Bending to blow, I expected her to roll over and fix me with a dark, surprised eye; but she lay still, a mound of wool and spread hair. She did not move when the embers flared, and the tent warmed. She still had not moved when Yolann struggled up, talking loudly.

"No meal!" Yolann cried, "Nothing but tea! What do we do now? Mother, there's no meal." She knelt and shook Barax' shoulder. "Mother? Mother! Dragamir, look!"

I looked. I had seen green skin before, and dusty eyes. I ran across camp to fetch the shaman. I did not stop for a cloak, but ran out as I was into the bitter wind and never felt it. A deeper cold gripped me, an inward freeze. I retched as I ran.

As the shaman's tent came in sight I slowed. Timidly I hovered before the leather curtain. Need I face this magic man? Barax was dead. My hands still felt the clammy cold of her wrist. What could the shaman do now, but tell us she was dead? And we knew that. But how could Barax be dead? Last night she had laughed with us, talking faster than her spindle twirled. Yolann was waiting for me to fetch the shaman. What could I say to her, "I feared to ask him?"

I scratched on the curtain. The shaman called to

me to enter. Peering into the smoky dimness I saw him reclining, enjoying his morning tea like any ordinary human being. I quavered, "Bar . . . Barax . . . dead."

The shaman rose at once. He did not bother with cloak or shoes, he came with me barefoot. The wind was fiercer now, folk huddled indoors; hobbled ponies mumbled and turned rump to wind. The shaman's long hair flapped in the wind like a black banner. But he walked straight and firm beside me, while I humped and hugged myself, and bowed into the wind.

He agreed that Barax was dead. Cross-legged by the corpse he closed his eyes and swayed and sighed. Soon he began to mutter; and then to speak clear, soft words. He reported his vision as though it were happening then and there before him; though it had all happened during the night. "The soul drifts free . . . floats around looking . . . looks at you twins. It turns, it turns . . . drifts out there, through the wall . . . wanders. The soul meets another soul . . . yes, other souls. It forgets. The soul forgets to return. . . ." On a high note the shaman squealed, "Oh, too late! Aie, too late! The body is cold!" His voice sank to a whisper. "Cold . . . cold. . . ."

His eyes flew open. He grinned at us, friendly, matter-of-fact. "But you twins are grown girls now, you will manage. Do you have tea? Hot tea will restore your souls, girls—and warm my frozen bones!"

We grieved, We wept, wrapped in each others' arms. We tore our hair and our clothes, though we had no new ones; and we gave Barax our favorite baubles, and her own, to take with her under the rock pile.

But we strengthened each other, too. We were strong and young—fourteen or fifteen—and Barax had shown us the tricks of the trade life would hand us. "A pretty girl can always make a living"; and a not-so-pretty girl can do all right too, Yolann discovered. Neither did Draga let us starve. "The haunch is for Ruga," he would say, "the shank's for Sorbal. And give the twins the ribs."

I hesitated to put Barax's arts to work. I held back, waiting; though I did not know for what I waited. I wore my hair like a golden veil, as Barax had taught me; and I minced about camp with an exaggerated feminine gait. From the corner of my eye I watched men watch me, and I smiled to myself. I feared them little. I felt confident, like a young mounted warrior; though not eager for battle, I would not shun it.

This arrogance could have been dangerous. The tribe still considered me an outsider, if not a prisoner. But I did not see myself that way. I still felt as safe in Draga's shadow as when I rode Belatruz in his arms. I was his pet, his good-luck charm; and I thought I was his daughter.

So did the envoys of the city king.

They rode toward us through shimmering heat waves. From afar we watched the leader, a huge dark man who dwarfed his richly bedecked charger. Man and beast were heavy with riches—jewels and fabrics, sleek and shining. They came slowly across their heat-rippled, burned fields, leaving behind the stout city walls and the roofs beyond, which stood sharp against the hazy sky. The white charger labored under the heavy man and the rich hangings. Its head bowed low, it stepped carefully over the battle-dinted earth. Behind came mounted nobles, and a small army of hooded, unarmed men in white robes, riding mules. We girls tittered at that sight. Our giggles faded into the heat and left silence, save for the doleful boom of a big bell somewhere within the city walls. Behind the mounted crowd came a few armed foot-soldiers, and then a crowd of lesser men, roughly dressed, staggering under boxes and baskets. Seeing booty, the women around us smacked their lips.

We stood in silent groups watching the emissaries approach. Hundreds of us women and children watched from hummocks and knolls near the tents. Draga's tribe had swelled to such numbers that he could besiege a walled city now, destroy its farms and outlying villages, and force it to lay its wealth at his feet. Yolann and I stood together in a group of girls, friends and sisters. We all wore our best for this glorious occasion. Yolann wore the wedding dress of some wealthy village bride. I was decked in an eastern silken robe, with bright ribbons looped in my hair. We held hands as the slow procession neared. Both of us jumped when a horn wailed behind us. With much stomping of hoofs and rattling of quivers Draga and his guard rode out to meet the emissaries.

They sat very straight in their ceremonial saddles, with painted shields slapping at their sides. Bone and wooden rings clicked from a hundred bridles.

The war ponies pranced and arched their necks. They thought a battle was forward; and here and there an eager pony shrilled, to be answered by wailing horns.

Distinguished by his black plume, Draga rode at the head. He would never learn to draw back and wait while a second in command set the stage for him. After him rode his friends, battle-tried men his own age. The junior cohort in the rear was headed by Sorbal and Ruga. As they pranced by I let a proud sigh escape my excited breast.

The white-robed army wavered and almost broke. Even from that distance I could see fear in the shadowed faces and the doubtful gestures. Their leader turned back to them for a moment and they quieted, like a flock of nervous sheep whose shepherd takes command. Our guard trotted between us and them, and for a time we saw nothing but shields and shifting hooves and swishing tails, though we strained and craned to see more.

Rising dust clouded the heat waves. Out of this obscurity came Draga and the city leader, riding back toward us. Close behind followed the white-robed throng and the nobles, and behind these the servants stumbled, laden with the wealth that would buy their city's safety. The leaders passed close under our knoll, Draga riding proudly, the other glancing about uneasily. His black eyes were keen under his pointed hat. He passed so close to me I felt his presence, and was startled. Seeing him from afar I had thought him stupid, dull and tired. Close up he was still huge and slow; but his intelligence ran about lightly, like a spirit, free of his coarse body. He cast a sidelong glance upon our group and his eye caught mine. There was a strange power in his gaze. I shuddered, and Yolann pressed against me. "Lucky we don't have to meet him nearer," she muttered.

I knew what she meant. With intelligence and power I felt from that man a vigorous carnal interest. I had never encountered such before, or never so strongly; but I recognized it instinctively, as the hare recognizes the hound. I agreed with Yolann, that man was dangerous; and it was good that we would spend the rest of the festive day far from his company.

When the cortege had passed and Draga and his guests had entered the central tent, we were put to work. There were sheep to slaughter, sticks to gather. I held a struggling lamb by the hind legs while a wife cut its throat. I searched for weeds, sticks and dung through the scorched farm-fields around the camp—all in my silken finery, which was now bloodstained and stinking. My ribbons drooped, my hair straggled. But as dusk fell, and fires glowed and rich meat sizzled, a tough old wife came to me and said "Dragamir, you are to serve in the central tent."

"I? How do I rank so high?" I was appalled at the thought of entering the central tent and standing before the man in the high pointed hat. But even as I asked, I shook out my silk and vainly brushed at the blood-stains.

"Not to me you don't rank so high. Draga orders it. And you're to look good, too." The wife scowled at my silk.

39

"Come." Yolann pulled my arm. "You can wear my dress."

So I went to the central tent in the wedding dress of the rich village maiden, full-skirted, stiff with embroidery. I lifted the curtain and passed into lamplight and walked among sparkling silver dishes and hanging scimitars, on carpets so soft that my footfalls made no sound, and I stood before that man who was Bishop Niklas, high minister of the city king.

He looked up at me from his cushion, and his eyes were bright and appreciative in his heavy face. Again his virility reached out for me, though his plump hands lay in his lap. I shuddered, and smiled. Then Draga reached a hand to me and drew me down suddenly, surprisingly, beside him. "This is my daughter," he told the bishop. "This is the princess Dragamir."

Under the village bride's linen my heart thudded. My downcast face heated, I blushed with delight. "My daughter . . . the princess." I did not know what "princess" meant, but it sounded grave and beautiful and dignified. It was the word "daughter" I heard with joy, this was the word for which I blushed. I looked down at my lap and at Draga's gleaming leather leg, and the white horse-skin spread beneath. Joy melted my heart. I knew I was Draga's child, but now for the first time he had called me so in public, and before this very important person. Modestly I glanced up. Through joy-damp lashes I saw Bishop Niklas regarding me seriously, leaning forward to examine me . . . as he might examine a filly in the market. Around him, white-hooded faces watched attentively. I was the center of attention in the central tent. Never before had I felt important like this! Seldom had I felt so uneasy.

Draga laid a fatherly arm about my shoulders and drew me close. He smelled comfortingly of sweat and leather; I felt his warm strength flowing about me as it did when I was little. I leaned against him trustfully, like a child.

The men's conversation limped on in two languages. A small, bird-eyed interpreter sat cross-legged in the midst, tossing broken phrases this way and that. My attention wandered. Other girls came in to serve. I sat with Draga and was served. My sisters waited on me with raised eyebrows and suppressed grins. Offered mead and beer I drank both, gratefully. The rich food and drink, the heat of the tent and the day's labors overcame me. I drowsed, resting against Draga, his arm hard and reassuring about me. I must have slept.

When I woke we were alone. The lamps were burning out. Their last light, flickering high, showed me the tent empty, the pillows crushed and scattered. Draga sprawled beside me, snoring. A mead bowl, fashioned from some enemy's skull, tipped empty beside his open hand.

I rose shakily, holding my dizzy head. Outside the felt a pony stomped, a sentry mumbled. The night must be far advanced, the camp was so quiet. Cool night air was moving into the tent, and I did not wish to leave Draga uncovered. Bracing myself,

I pulled the white horse-skin free and draped it over his inert form. I should have known that Draga was never deeply drunk.

As I leaned over him his snoring abruptly stopped. He reached up and seized me.

"In a hurry?" He asked. His eyes opened swiftly, hawk-fierce. "Some young fellow out there?"

"No, no," I soothed him. "I will stay if you—"

"Any young fellow yet?"

I hung my head. I did not know what answer would please him, so I told the truth. "Not yet."

"Good." Draga released and patted me, then grabbed my wrist to hold me beside him. He sat up slowly, bracing himself on an elbow, shaking his head.

"I'll go get you water—"

"Go nowhere. Listen." I waited. Draga collected his powers quickly; words took longer. At length he said, "So, now you are a princess."

"I heard you say so."

"Know what that means?"

I shook my head.

"Means the daughter of a great man. King. Chief."

I smiled. "That I have always been!"

"Not like now. Listen. These names—king, bishop, prince—these are stories men tell each other. 'Chief,' now, 'chief' is real. The chief rides first, strikes first, speaks first. Men follow him. I am a chief." I nodded agreement. " 'Princess,' now. A princess wears a fine dress and walks with an air." Draga looked at me thoughtfully. "You will learn that air. Men bow to her, because their respect gives her power. You understand?"

I nodded, dumbly, though understanding was far from me.

"Now this Bishop Niklas, he respects you, Dragamir. He respects you mightily!" Draga laughed. At first his laughter was soft, then it mounted to a high giggle. He sobered; his eyebrows twitched. "So highly he respects you, he has gone home to his city king to suggest that said king wed with you."

My heart froze.

"This will be interesting," Draga mused. "Kings marry princesses to increase their power. This city king Wendz will wed a chief's daughter, and increase *my* power! Less to him, more to me!" He laughed softly to himself.

Cold dread seized me. Still hoping, I ventured to ask, "But why would a king make a marriage so . . . without advantage?"

Draga laughed louder. "He will do it, daughter! He will do it lest I break down his city walls and drag him by the heels! He will do it. And from that day, I get revenues. Not booty, revenues. Tax monies." He gazed fondly at me. "Truly, you are my luck!"

I snatched at a last hope. "His city does not seem so powerless. Can he not defend himself?"

"You see clearly. That city could easily defend itself. Ten years gone, I did not dare approach it! Hah! Ten years gone my luck was only beginning. You remember?"

"Not well."

"Wendz was powerful, then. Now he cannot defend his wealth." Draga spat, and stretched luxuriously among the crumpled carpets. But he kept his grip on my wrist.

"Why can he not? He has men, big horses——"

"Did you not see the white robes? His men are monks! His horses are mules! Wendz wallows in religion!"

Draga explained. Ten years before, King Wendz had listened to a traveling preacher. "Must have been like the shaman at the spring, the young fellow my dog wouldn't bite. One of those." This preacher had convinced Wendz of a new religion, and Wendz had convinced, or forced his subjects. Most of them were now Christians. Many were priests and monks, men withdrawn from the world, without women, family or wealth, who spent their lives praying to their god. "And without arms, let me add." Draga grinned. "This religion forbids most bloodshed. So Wendz will not fight for his wealth. For his god he might fight, but we make no quarrel of that. For wealth and power he dare not fight, his god would be angry!" Draga laughed. He laughed hard, and was sick. I held the skull bowl for him. Recovering, he wiped his mouth with the back of his hand, then hugged me fiercely. "And you, Dragamir! You are the soft key that opens the city gate to me! They say this Wendz lives without women, like a monk. But he needs an heir. Bishop Niklas insists he have an heir. You will bear him a son; and for this he will open his coffers. I shall leave him a pauper!" He sobered. "No, not quite. The richer Wendz grows from now on, the richer I grow. I will farm riches, not hunt them." Draga's gleeful voice trailed off into silence. He lay staring up at the silken hangings lit by the last leaping light. In his eyes I saw his future unfold in glory.

My own future looked bleak indeed. I had already seen enough of Wendz's city. It was walled. I did not know how to live within walls, and I had no wish to learn. Never to ride the plains again . . . never to laugh with Sorbal and Ruga! And this religious king who lived like a monk and feared bloodshed, what sort of man might he be? In my confused dismay my greatest sorrow went almost unnoticed. Never again would I ride with Draga.

The last lamp sputtered and died, and the tent was dark. Distant dogs quarreled. Sentries paced. In the darkness Draga spoke softly, as though in answer to my bitter thoughts. "Do not fret, princess." He let go of my wrist at last. "You lead a charmed life. I snatched you from death, that day we both remember. You do remember?"

"Yes."

"I was angry! You almost died twice that day! I had thought you were a golden talisman—and so you were! Then, you remember, you lived with me not as a slave, but as my child."

"Yes."

"And now you go to that walled city, not as a prisoner, but as its queen. Do not fret. You will eat meat every day, you will grow fat! You will wear silk and sleep warm, in a soft bed. Any woman would snatch at your fate!"

Any woman but I. I wished only to remain near Draga.

45

"And all Wendz will ask of you is a son! Draga-mir, some witch must have you in her kindly care!"

Staring into blackness I accepted these dark prophecies because I had no choice. I would live the wretched life that Draga described so exultantly. I would endure it far away from him, walled away from the plain. Thus I would serve him, linking his power to Wendz's wealth, bearing Wendz the heir he must have. I would do all this for Draga.

For myself, I would bear only the one heir, and never another child. Fervently I blessed the shade of Barax! By her kind wisdom I would live for myself; I would order my own fate. I would not be that city king's slave.

Never again would I be smothered as in straw, and carried and tossed and dropped where others willed, for their own purposes. This I vowed to myself.

My gown flowed golden about my ankles. A gift from the city king, it was the first new, clean dress I had ever worn. My skin marveled at its soft touch. Yolann combed my hair till it floated free and light, and even our dour sisters breathed delight at it. One looped long strings of amber around my neck, others held my hands and slid bracelets up my wrists, rings up my fingers. They looked at me with envious eyes; but I doubted that they would wish to stand in my place. I was the outsider, the expendable one. For this reason Draga had deceived the bishop, saying "This is my daughter, the princess." Not one of his own true daughters would he have sold to live within the walled city.

Standing at the curtain, hidden in its shadow, I could see across the camp to the walls and roofs of that city. Banners and hangings streamed in the light summer wind. The topmost windows of high buildings were jammed with spectators, and more spectators came jostling out of the gates every moment, hastening toward the camp, but hesitating, too. They looked with justified caution at our dark, bowlegged crowd, and at our bristling dogs. The few city folk I saw close by were fat, sleek and pale. Their faces were soft, their gestures round and gentle. Briefly, I thought of brightly dressed worms.

Loud and bustling, the camp was hot with ceremonial fires. Vats of beer and mead stood about, and folk helped themselves. Women staggered past my curtain; and children paused to be sick in the dust. Only Draga's guard were sober and alert, as he demanded; and he himself, striding toward me through the crowd, was resplendently armed. He bore his bright-lacquered shield, his horsetail plume bowed and bobbed, shimmering in the sunlight. He stopped in the entrance and looked me over, smiling through his hundred scars.

Over his shoulder I saw a procession leave the city. Bishop Niklas led on his white charger. Beside him ambled a black charger, whose thin, stooped rider was swathed in red. Sunlight glinted about his head, striking some metallic ornament. Around them came scores of white-robes, some on mules and others afoot. A few soldiers paraded on the outskirts. Over Draga's shoulder I watched my destiny approach and my mouth dried up. I could find no spittle to swallow.

Draga took my hand and led me out of the tent. My sisters followed, and outside the guard closed in about us. Stiffly I walked where Draga led me through the parting crowd. The instant we stepped forth, drums boomed, horns wailed, children blew whistles or their fingers. I waded through the noise, only half seeing the gaping crowd, only half feeling the dragging weight of my heart.

Ruga stepped close to me. He walked a few paces at my side and his thoughts reached to me, stronger than the words he could not speak. Of all the shifting, watching, laughing crowd he was the only one who would miss me, only he was sorry to see me go. Dismally, I knew I would miss him.

The crowd drew apart. Before us in an empty space stood a table, covered with golden cloth. Before the table stood Bishop Niklas, watching us come with heavy, hooded eyes. His mitre—the bishop's hat—shone white like sparkling stone. His wide enveloping robe was white, encrusted with brightness. I raised my chin and straightened my spine. Draga lifted my hand, and we proceeded with an elegant grace toward the table, Bishop Niklas—and the man beside him, half hidden behind his robe.

I saw immediately, with a sick stomach-shrinking, that the city king was older than Draga. His smooth brown hair was gray-flecked; and down his jeweled chest flowed a rich, gray-flecked beard. I had seldom seen a beard, and I stared at it, and at his thin hand stroking it. I could see the bones of that hand clearly, as though the pale skin were transparent.

Regally, Draga led me forward; we met beside the table; and the din abruptly stopped. Drums, horns and whistles fell silent, so did the near crowd. Loud conversations continued on the outskirts, fading away. Draga dropped my hand. I looked down at the city king's pointed slippers, and the hem of his red robe. I watched Draga's leather-shod foot advance as he spoke. Nearby the bird-faced interpreter alchemized words, turning one speech into another. Surprised, I found that I did not always need his services. In the city king's slow, soft speech I caught words with meanings; as when one sees a friend's figure dimly, through a mist, so I saw meanings in the king's words. I wondered where I had heard this speech before.

An angry tone crept into the guarded voices. The bishop's white robe swayed, his voice boomed darkly. I glanced up at Draga, beside me. His face was impassive under the all-concealing scars. But his eyebrows twitched, and his silk vest wrinkled over tightening muscles. Hope and fear leaped like twin fawns in my heart. Might it all end here? Might Draga shove me away, send me running back to the tent? How gladly I would tear off this clean golden gown! How gratefully I would pull on my own greasy rags and awake from this evil dream!

But Draga laughed softly, and beckoned to Birdface. The interpreter came up to me, bowing with wonderful respect. He was a small, pale man, a city worm. I wondered if I could take hold of him and throw him down. It did not seem unlikely.

Humbly he explained to me my bridegroom's one

demand. As the Christian king of a Christian city, Wendz could not wed a pagan bride. Before the marriage could take place I must be baptized Christian. Was I willing?

I looked to Draga. He made no move. His will remained unchanged.

"Ah . . . how do I become Christian?"

"A simple matter, lady. Bishop Niklas will pour water on your head and give you a Christian name."

I savored my new title. Very few women in my world were addressed as "lady"! Glancing once again at the impassive Draga, I nodded my consent.

Delicately, the interpreter took my hand and turned me toward the table. Bishop Niklas laid a slow, heavy hand on my neck and bowed my head over and down, down, till I could see only his white slippers under my nose. He must have had the water ready on the table. It sloshed startling-cold on my head, and ran down into my eyes. Still pouring, still gripping my neck, he intoned great, bell-like words over me; of which I heard only the last word, the name "Marya."

In that moment a new sound broke the restless silence around us. Grave and sweet, mens' voices rose as one. Men sang together, all the same clear note, their voices rising and falling in slow and doleful unison. The tune was mournful, the tone gentle; yet there was exultation in it. And to my innocent ears it seemed the voice of peace; of a calm, new life-way; perhaps even of love.

Bishop Niklas lifted his hand from my neck and I straightened, brushing stray drops out of my eyes. I saw the singers; a group of white-robes nearby.

Each clasped soft hands on his stomach and raised his eyes to heaven; and from his open mouth streamed the self-same note his brother sang.

Wendz's face moved close to me, and now I saw nothing else. His was a calm face, lined with years, but serene. The surprising beard hid the mouth. The eyes were quiet, gray, withdrawn. They searched my face without hope, or disappointment, or any kind of excitement. Under the magical sway of the strange music, under the gentle spell of Wendz's gaze, I thought "After all, this may be the birthday of a better life. This Wendz may prove an easy master; kinder than my father."

But in this I was mistaken.

3

The Palace

The city cathedral is like an immense dark cavern. When I first saw it men had been building it for ten years; and they are still building it today. Its building will likely continue while the earth stands. Seeing it for the first time I stood lost in amazement, as in a visionary dream.

Before me the carpeted aisle led like a long road to the far, high altar. Above, the ceiling vaulted into night. Nearer earth, massed candles blazed like daylight up and down the vast length of the cathedral. On the altar, heaped flowers blazed almost like candles at the feet of a huge, writhing giant nailed to immense crossed beams.

At the sight my knees buckled. I shut my eyes to fight rising sickness. The man was carved wood, but the agony was real. In the darkness of my closed eyes I saw a boy's head crushed against a stone. I felt smothered, bundled away from air. I slipped a finger between my constricted throat and my jeweled collar, and gasped. I must have swayed, for hands touched me from all sides; and a noble took my arm and held me upright.

Stiffening, I fought down the sickness and opened my eyes. But I did not again look up at the

53

nailed giant. Instead I dropped my gaze to a large
painting hung beside the altar. Red and blue and
gold, it nearly awoke a memory, as when one almost
recalls a dream.

A mother embraced her infant. Tenderly she
bowed her head against the baby's head; lightly, her
gentle hands enfolded his white-swathed body.
Bursts of golden light, mild suns crowned each holy
head. Holy they were, holy the picture was, it
strengthened me to walk forward that night down
the long carpet. In the flickering light of a hundred
candles the mother seemed to smile with grave sympathy. She knew me, she knew my story; and she
welcomed me.

I knew of her that she was the Holy Marya, the
god's mother. I fixed my eyes upon her, and I
walked forward through the whispering crowd. I
seemed to swim slowly through candlelight and
singing. In raised stalls along the walls white-robes
sang, bowing back and forth and to the altar, their
voices a mellow unity. Perhaps raised by the music,
my spirit seemed to float a little above my burdened
body. Dressed in finer, softer stuffs than I had ever
seen or felt, jewel-laden, I ached in every muscle.
My legs and back ached from lack of exercise. Rich
food stirred uneasily in my stomach. My head diz-
zied. I had not mounted a horse in ten days, since I
came within the city walls. To breathe clean air I
had' to climb to the palace roof, from where I could
see the farm lands and the plain beyond, widely
empty. Draga had packed up his tribe and departed
over the eastern horizon, leaving me here, deserted.
Dizzily, now, I moved on the noble's arm down the

long carpet toward the Marya, the candle-shimmering altar, and Bishop Niklas.

From halfway down the aisle I could see Wendz, seated near the altar. As he rose and went to await me beside the bishop, I glimpsed the woman who sat beyond his chair. I knew her face, sweet and gentle as the Marya's. I knew the pure white veil she always wore floating like a cloud about her white, bound hair and thin, rigid shoulders. Always she dressed simply; even tonight her gown was straight and unadorned. No jewels sparkled at throat or wrist. She sat straight and slim; and despite her years her back never touched the chair's back. As she watched me all but stagger toward her, kindness shone like a candle in her face.

That loving-kind gaze amazed and abashed me. With all my lonely young heart I wished to love this lady, and accept her love. Yet I feared her. She was a mother—Wendz's mother—and I distrusted motherly qualities. Seeing them openly displayed and combined with power frightened me. Longing to love, I was yet repelled. And so I feared Ludmilla more than her son, who waited for me now beside Bishop Niklas.

Ten days before, I had wed King Wendz in Draga's camp. That same night I had come back with him within his city walls. In the huge, soft bed with embroidered covers that Draga had foretold, I waited, that night, for him. Torn between dread and hope, I listened all night for his footfalls. He never came. Toward morning I dropped into a nervous doze. The next night and the next I waited, tense and fearful. Still Wendz did not come. I saw him only from a distance, or with Ludmilla in the palace garden, or at the sumptuous dinners that took place every night as a matter of course.

Walking with Ludmilla and me in the garden, Wendz taught me snatches of language; words and phrases I learned very readily. It was more like remembering than learning. A mist of forgetfulness seemed to thin, day by day; and very soon I could understand most of what he said, and answer a little. As soon as we could talk he showed me images; tiny paintings and statues of his gods. He showed me a miniature Holy Marya, and asked me to kiss it. This was a small gesture—easier than being sloshed with cold water before the watching world. I obeyed, and Ludmilla kissed me. Wendz looked pleased.

He was easily pleased with me, as a gentle man is pleased with a clever child. I learned quickly enough what he liked: a quiet face, a composed manner, reverence for his gods. I made my face a gentle mask and hid behind it. Only alone with Yolann was I myself.

Without Yolann I might almost have forgotten myself. Yolann came away with me to better herself, she said; but I knew she came for love. She slept in the antechamber between my room and the hall. Alone, we spoke our own language and laughed as we sewed, which was the only occupation allowed us. Ludmilla had assigned city maids to wait upon us, but we frightened them. They looked baffled at our foreign speech and disdainful of our manners, and our underclothes. We laughed at them and made a game of chasing them away. Left together, sometimes we were almost happy.

Yolann's face turned toward me now in the crowd. She smiled, rejoicing in my good fortune. I remembered where I was—staggering down the cathedral aisle to be well and truly wed; for now I understood that Wendz did not respect our camp wedding. That ceremony meant little to him, and nothing to his people. This ceremony tonight would be the wedding; and tonight Wendz would come to me.

I passed slowly by Yolann and the city maids, who gazed upon me with scornful envy. I passed the foremost monks; Wendz and Bishop Niklas stood before me, in front of the altar. The crucified giant hung above them. I dropped my eyes again as sickness lurched in my tormented stomach. The noble who had supported me withdrew, patting my arm to remind me to hold myself up. Stiffly I advanced and knelt carefully, slowly, before Wendz, as I had been instructed to do.

A heavy scent of incense drifted on the candlelight. Sick and faint, I did not see Wendz lift the small golden circlet from the altar; I only felt it set quietly down upon my head, where it weighed like a circlet of stone. Wendz reached down for my hand. I did not understand. He had to bend and take my limp hand and press it upward. Then I rose obediently and stood with him, hand in hand, while Bishop Niklas turned from us to face the altar. My head swam with incense, flickering light, the sweetness of a thousand dying flowers, the heavy odor of Niklas' stiff robes. Glancing away from the too-bright altar I met a pair of kindly eyes, a smile of happy possession. Sweetly satisfied, Ludmilla smiled upon us both.

From the wall opposite my bed the Marya icon smiled a similar smile as Ludmilla opened the bed with her own hands, and smoothed down the fine sheets. Her maids undressed me. I was too frightened to resist. Trembling, I slipped into the bed at Ludmilla's inviting gesture, and let her lay the silken coverlet over me, and arrange my hair on the embroidered pillows. She handled me like a doll, or a statue being set up for a ceremony. Her thin, shaky hands hovered about me, arranging every stray hair, every silken fold. At last she stepped back, smiling, gazing down at me with a sweet satisfaction that would have irked me, had I not been so terrified, and motioned to Yolann to open the door.

From the antechamber men's voices rose in a strong chant. Through the door came candles and torches, a cloud of light and in the light walked Wendz, the bishop, and their ever-present monks. I breathed shallowly, watching my bridegroom approach. He stopped near the bed and let two monks lift off his circlet and his crimson cloak; while another knelt to pull off his jeweled slippers. I wondered if they would strip their king as naked as I; what would these city people not do? But they left him his white shift. Still wearing this he climbed into the bed and lay beside me.

I have seen a tomb on which a stone warrior lay beside his stone lady. We lay like those two; not touching, not breathing, staring up into the dark beyond the torch light. Wendz's shift felt cold against my side. My foot shrank away from his foot. Once again, Bishop Niklas drenched me. He sprinkled us both, shaking water from his thick ringed fingers over the coverlet, muttering a charm. Ludmilla bent and touched Wendz's cheek with light fingers. They turned away. The whole troop of monks and maids turned away, and now they were carrying their candles and torches, their soft and cruel light, out the door.

Numbly I watched their retreating backs. I almost wished to call them back, to prolong this tense and aching prelude, even to begin again, with Ludmilla smoothing the sheets. My body feared this first invasion. My spirit feared extinction. Would I still be me, Dragamir, when next I rose from this bed? Or would I perhaps have been transformed into the submissive Marya Ludmilla took me for? Was there no help? Could nothing put off the dreaded moment?

The last candle departed. A dark hand closed the door softly. "Yolann!" I almost cried, "come back!"

Silently I awaited Wendz's first touch. Would he come at me carefully, or in a rush? I had seen no desire in his eyes, either this night or during the past ten days. Hopefully, he was in no hurry.

He made a sudden move. I started. But he had swung out of bed. I glimpsed him moving away, a white blur in the dimness. They had left one faint candle burning on a stand. This he extinguished with his fingers. Now he stood in blackness, an awkward gray splotch; and now I heard him padding softly back to bed.

He crept in beside me and breathed in my face.

59

He had a bad tooth. I inhaled decay with the smell of aging flesh. My heart shuddered. He began to mutter . . . I understood "Will of God . . . Christian heir . . . I will not hurt you, Marya. Marya, I will not hurt you." He laid cold hands on my shoulders.

Glad though I was of his repeated assurance "I will not hurt you," I was suddenly impatient. If we must do this thing, let us get it done! And some instinct murmured deep within me, "Not in this way would Draga approach a woman!"

Wendz's thin hands were cold on my shoulders, and only slightly warmer on my breasts.

Early in the evenings we rose from our mild entertainments. Board games were folded, charade costumes laid aside, musicians dismissed with a kind "goodnight." Then Ludmilla came gently to her son. On tiptoe she kissed his bearded cheek, while his lean hands patted her shoulders. This rite of love brought each day to its end. As though they would not wake to breakfast together on the morrow; as though they had not spent most of this day talking together; as though they met but rarely, mother and son embraced.

I marveled at this unembarrassed display of love. I marveled at all the kindness I found within these forbidding stone walls. Ludmilla moved gently. Her nearly constant talk was soft and friendly. She was courteous even to servants—even to the few pagan slaves.

For my part I saw no need of that much courtesy! After all, I was a baptized Christian. Before the watching world Bishop Niklas had pressed down my neck and doused my head with cold water; and I considered this magical humiliation a sacrifice, which had earned me a prideful place in this city world. "Sophie!" I would yell at my little pagan maid, "Clean this chamberpot before I throw it at you!" And Sophie would run to obey, cowering. She knew that I was perfectly capable of suiting action to word.

I enjoyed giving orders very much indeed. I who had always fetched my own water and fuel delighted now to lie among cushions and order Sophie up and down the steep stairs. "This room is chill, Sophie. Get wood!" "Tea for the lady Yolann—if it isn't hot I'll baptize you in it!"

The servants avoided me. Ludmilla noticed their nervous glances. She noticed how Sophie thinned and paled. One day in the garden she mentioned it. "My dear child," she said, "I was in the chapel, and the door closed; and I could hear you berating the slave as though you were in there with me! You are a new Christian, Marya, and a . . . foreigner; so perhaps you did not know. But Christians do not address one another in that manner."

Smugly I explained, "Lady, my Sophie is no Christian!"

I expected Ludmilla to nod, and forget the matter. I was surprised that she remained grave. She spoke now almost sternly. "Neither is your dear sister Yolann a Christian, but no one speaks that way to her! There is always hope for pagans, Marya, that one day they will accept baptism. Should your little Sophie be baptized, you might be amazed at

61

her stature in heaven! For God takes little note of worldly stature. Always remember, my dear, we Christians practice love. Charity is our most Christian virtue. If you cannot practice Charity for Sophie, at least practice Courtesy. Courtesy is Charity's younger sister."

I was young, and desperately eager to please. From that hour I practiced all the courtesy I could. City manners were new to me; and they were hard enough to learn, being in themselves quite senseless; what possible difference does it make who sits where, who speaks first, how one holds one's knife at table? Well, I learned these city manners. But now, I saw, I must learn a whole new dance! Christian manners were more difficult and less reasonable than city manners! I tried. I tried hard. And Sophie fattened again, and the color returned to her broad cheeks.

Ludmilla noticed me trying. She saw how hard I worked to be what she would have me be. And one evening, having kissed Wendz goodnight, she turned toward me. Kind-eyed as the Holy Marya herself, she came to me with outstretched arms. "Goodnight my child," she murmured, and planted a cool kiss on my forehead.

I stood dazzled. Ludmilla moved away. Wendz came to me with a crooked smile and took my hand. This was his night to come to my bed. Every third night he came and fumbled about disgustedly, revolting himself and me. I had been dreading this night; but now I forgot my dread. My heart swelled with joy. I was loved! I was an accepted member of this circle of love! Warm tears flooded my eyes so that I hardly saw Wendz's forced smile. I forgot, for the moment, that "We Christians practice love." It did not occur to me, then, that Ludmilla might be practicing Charity on me.

Joy-dazed, I let Wendz lead me off to bed. His sluggish, unwilling embrace repelled me momentarily, but then I remembered that this was the price I paid for love. Small coin, this, for the ecstasy of belonging! I turned to Wendz and gave myself freely; and Wendz seemed to respond. His body warmed and swelled and hardened; but later, when he rolled away and turned his back on me, I saw that his spirit revolted.

Lying carefully apart from him, I wondered. I had never known a man to scorn a woman's embrace as Wendz did. True, there were shamans who bought power with chastity. The Christian monks also did this. But Wendz was no shaman, he was not even a Christian monk! Wendz was a good, an excellent Christian layman. He prayed much. In a few moments now he would leave me and pad down the hall to the chapel, there to purify himself of me, and pray most of the night. He performed his state duties carefully, religiously. The poor did not groan beneath his yoke. His judgments were merciful, his decisions prudent. He was not a beloved leader, like my father; a certain cold remoteness in his bearing warded off love. But he was deeply respected. I myself respected him deeply, except in bed.

As if by accident, I allowed my hand to rest against his back. We had lain still and uncovered for long moments, now; but Wendz's back was still wet with thick, cold sweat. It smeared my hand.

Wendz shuddered at my touch and jerked away. Swinging his thin legs off the bed, he pulled on his robe.

In my mind a grave voice spoke. "He is not well." I watched him stoop, panting, to find his shoes. For him this was an effort. I remembered how he had dined that night; chewing slowly, picking over the rich food. Why, he had no more appetite for food than for love! And I had long wondered that he craved no exercise. Few men could have sat as patiently as he did, in high seat and garden, day after day! Never since our first wedding had I seen him mount a horse. He went abroad as little as I did, though he was bound by no cruel custom. "He is not well," I knew.

Pity awoke in my newly softened heart, but scorn hovered near. This man who could not love a woman who would not willingly ride a horse, who did not even relish his dinner—this man was my husband! Holy Mother Earth! How could I respect him? How could I serve him? He had bought me for peace and treasure, to bear him a son. Willing as I was, how could I do that by myself?

In my young pride I thought of this as of a deed that we, ourselves, must do. I forgot the Goddess. By Her power are children conceived, whether in a willing womb or an unguarded one; whether with the mother's knowledge or without it. The Goddess weaves secretly in the dark, drawing together the threads of life; and that very night, as Wendz's reluctant seed rushed upon a tide of unwonted vigor, Her divine hands caught up those threads. Even as he rose from the bed and turned to murmur a relieved farewell, the Goddess wove within me.

"You must forgive me, Marya," he mumbled, mightily embarrassed.

"Forgive you for what?" This time, I thought, there had been less to forgive.

"For . . . all this. It is not of my choosing, you know."

"Oh." I had hoped that this time it had been of his choosing!

"I cannot understand . . . and I have thought much upon it . . . why God chose this method to create souls for His glory! God knows I mean no blasphemy; but had I been God, I would have chosen a different way."

"I see." I tried not to laugh. "Wendz, had you been God, we would have had no bodies at all. We would all be pure spirits!"

"Indeed, so we would!" Wendz smiled an apology for his recent crudeness, and left me. I lay watching the candle, and pitying my cheated body. Instinctively I knew it was being cheated. Lovemaking should at least be enjoyable.

"Well," I consoled myself, "at least now I am one of the family. Ludmilla kissed me." I wrapped myself in that thought as in a light, soft blanket.

Ludmilla did seem to love me. Now I know that she was only practicing Charity, that most rare and lovely Christian virtue; but at the time I believed that she loved me, and I basked in that seeming motherly love. Gladly I learned whatever she wished to teach me: city manners and language, Christian morals, the wonderful art of letters. This we studied together in the garden, sitting under Ludmilla's rose-vines. She wished me to read hymns, prayers, the Holy Book, the stories of her gods. I enjoyed the learning. I found it freshening to exercise the mind, as I could not exercise the body. I enjoyed the act of reading, which came easier and quicker till I could read words almost as fast as hear them spoken. This gave me a wonderful sense of power! I liked to read; but I did not much like what I read.

In her bright, cool garden, where sun and shade wove patterns lovelier than Eastern carpets, where birds warbled and bees bumbled, Ludmilla sat, blind and deaf. Her ears were tuned to angel whispers. Her eyes were fixed upon an inward vision. Marking the place with a bony finger she would close the book, and murmur to me of the visions enthralling her. The Christ and the Holy Marya were more real to her than I was. She would not have been in the least surprised to meet them under the rosevine. Indeed, I myself sometimes glanced over my shoulder, half expecting to glimpse some haloed shadow hovering in sunshine, listening with a fond smile to Ludmilla's homesick murmurs.

Ludmilla was homesick for heaven. More than I yearned for the open plain, Ludmilla yearned for heaven. "Heaven is about us all the time," she whispered her precious secret to me, as Barax had once whispered hers. "God is here in this garden, with all His saints and holy angels; only we cannot see them, our eyes are blinded. Oh Marya! If we could only see God's glory with our earthly eyes we would never dream of sinning again!" I smiled. Of what sins could this pious old lady dream? She told me.

66

"No impatient word would ever cross our lips again. We would forget to enjoy our food, wine would not pleasure us. We would forget to love ourselves entirely, being wholly in love with God!" Maybe. There might well be a heaven I could not see, here in the garden. But for me, the garden I saw was enough. Why try to look beyond the rose?

"Sometimes," Ludmilla whispered, so low I had to lean to hear, "sometimes I catch glimpses of heaven. I am old, Marya, and God grants me these glimpses for my comfort. Once I saw Saint Agnes. I knew her by the white lamb she carried in her tender arms; symbol of her innocence. On her fingertips she showed me a crown of red roses; the souls of roses, Marya, glorious beyond imagining. But every rose carried a thorn."

As I listened, I glanced about the garden. I nearly saw Saint Agnes myself, a childlike goddess, a fairy, robed in sunshine. Ludmilla said, "She meant that I would wear that crown in heaven, you see; but not till every thorn had pricked me."

Though we could not see heaven, all of us baptized Christians hoped to go there. Ludmilla impressed upon me that baptism, while essential, was not enough. I must also earn heaven by my deeds; I must deserve to go there.

"But how can I deserve that?"

"By your Charity, Marya. There is no other way. Though you spoke with the tongues of angels, lacking Charity you would fail of heaven."

This I liked. For this one virtue I esteemed the soft city folk; that they spoke gently, and seldom laid rough hands upon one another. They gave to the poor. Their beggars were fat. Their monks and nuns even cared for homeless children and the childless aged. This kindness I loved and admired; and I thought the whole world would be better off for learning it. I amused myself by imagining a camp of horse folk, ruled by Christian Charity. In this camp women walked as proudly as men, children were courteously greeted. Even the dogs, I thought, waved friendly tails. Yes, the world would be better for following this Christian rule. But there were other rules, magical rules, that I found harder to accept.

To deserve heaven one must go often to the cathedral in the square. Merely to go there earned merit; merely to pass through the racket of hammer and chisel that accompanied its constant building, and kneel before the altar, where the sanctuary lamp flickered, proclaiming God's invisible presence. This earned merit, but not enough. One could not enter the Kingdom of Heaven unless one ate Christ's body, and drank His blood. Hearing this I drew back in horror. The city folk called my people cannibals, but they themselves were so! "It appears like bread and wine, dear," Ludmilla assured. "Not at all like eating flesh. It is a miracle. But I see that you do not quite understand this, yet." She decided that I should not join in this rite until I understood it. "To consume Christ unknowing, or unbelieving; that would be blasphemy!"

So when the congregation pressed forward to receive at the altar, I stayed in my place. Nobles and beggars, monks and servants, merchants and wives all went except me. I stayed behind with the pagan slaves, and a few sinners, while everyone else took his portion of divinity from the hefty hands of Bishop Niklas. I was almost relieved to be left alone and apart. Secretly I thought the god did not know his business, who left it in those hands!

"Listen earnestly to our good bishop," Ludmilla advised me. "He holds the key to heaven, that Christ gave St. Peter."

Astonished, I asked to hear that again. "Bishop Niklas can let me into heaven?" Or keep me out?

"He can best show you the road."

"But . . . but he . . ." I did not quite dare protest, "but he obeys none of your Christian rules!"

Ludmilla told me how Niklas first came to the city, a penniless, wandering preacher. "He was young then, and worn thin. His black eyes gleamed glory. Oh Marya, you should have heard Niklas preach, back then! He does not preach like that anymore. At first he preached in the markets, and in the square. We had no cathedral then, of course. Folk gladly gave up work and business to hear him preach! He was famous in the city before Wendz ever invited him to the palace. It was a midwinter feast, and we asked him to entertain us! I blush to think of it now, how we sat at dinner, eating and drinking, ready to laugh; and that humble man preached to us from the mummers' platform!"

Wendz did not laugh. He and Ludmilla listened open-mouthed, shocked and exalted beyond themselves. The nobles noted their reaction, and wisely stifled their own.

Niklas converted Wendz, and helped him to convert his city. "At first," Ludmilla admitted, "a certain force was necessary. I have taught you that Christians do not use force, but there are occasions . . . you see, it was a matter of salvation. Niklas had snatched us back from the brink of hell; and Wendz could hardly do less for the people in his care! For as you know, Wendz is more than a wordly king. Next to Niklas, Wendz is the shepherd of his flock. He could not allow his folk to fall into hell."

So Niklas whipped out a sword from under his preacher's robe, and silenced the snickering nobles. He convinced the rich merchants, and the hopeful merchants; and lesser folk followed suit, as they usually do.

Ludmilla sighed. "I sometimes wonder if . . . if Niklas' victories have been good for his soul. When he first came to us he was a truly spiritual young man. . . . It would be so terrible if Niklas were to save all our souls at the expense of his own! That is the one sacrifice we may not make for one another. But then, he is a good bishop. He shepherds the flock faithfully. Marya dear, forget what I said, I was rambling . . ."

I could not forget what had been said. I tried to imagine Niklas young, on fire with God; and suddenly I thought of the young man Draga had met by the spring. That young shaman must have been a Christian! Now I recognized the description: brown robe, rope sandals, tonsure—the man was a monk! His magic had been strong, his spirit magnificent. Could Niklas ever have been anything like him?

Pride was the chief Christian sin; but pride glowed unmistakable in Niklas' black eyes, shrunk now like pig's eyes among draped folds of fat. He had grown fat from his victories. While collecting souls for his god he collected riches for himself. Not all of his duties were spiritual. "It is most unfortunate," Ludmilla confided, "but it is true that government must sometimes deceive the people for their own good." Wendz had no need to sully his conscience with this deception. He had Niklas for mouthpiece and sword-arm. Taking much necessary sin upon himself, Niklas left Wendz blameless.

It was easy for me to see that Niklas was a humbug; I had only to compare him to the shamans I had known. But it was harder for the city folk to see this. Niklas shared with the shamans a high mastery of pomp. His sense for costume, for scene and mystery, rivaled that of the best actors. He used incense and music as a rich man's cook uses spice. I had to respect his art, and his unscrupulous ambition. From a discreet distance I respected Niklas; and I feared him.

When I first laid eyes on Niklas his lust had reached out to me. I felt it still reaching. From Yolann's gossip I learned that it was an active force. "Every night he sleeps with a different woman," she declared. I was uneasily aware of his gaze constantly following me; of his hot eyes watching me greedily from the very altar steps of his cathedral. I wondered that the pious crowd did not perceive this. I marveled that Wendz never remarked it, and even Ludmilla seemed unaware. Were they blind, or did they not feel the heatwaves? Even now that my rounding belly proclaimed the Goddess' work to the world—even now Niklas sent me his silent, urgent messages.

"He that looks after a woman with lust has already committed adultery with her in his heart," he thundered from the altar-step. Adulterers went to hell to burn forever, without a doubt. But even as the awesome words curled his lips, Niklas held me in his lecherous eyes. I glanced away; up at the wooden Saint Peter's golden key, or down into my lap, where the shadowed silk fluttered as my child kicked.

His first motion was an arresting delight. "He moved!" I cried to Yolann. "I felt him move!" For the first time I truly believed in his reality.

"That's your dinner moving," Yolann grunted. "They don't move that young."

But my child did. Often and oftener I felt his gently fluttering presence. As he strengthened, his tiny feet kicked more sharply, and his fists punched. "Feel that!" I pressed Yolann's hand to the spot.

"Yes, I feel something; like a tadpole in a pool. Hmm."

The Goddess wove within me; and before Her miracle the Christian miracles faded to fairy tales. Constantly I was amazed at myself, at the changes in my own nature. I had thought I owned myself; my thought governed my being. Now I discovered the Goddess owned me; my thoughts were Hers.

A softness entirely foreign to my nature invaded me. I had been proud of my father's ferocity. I had gladly watched his harsh, instant justice. Now I delighted in mercy. I nodded approval when Wendz handed down a dangerously mild judgment. Even

72

Ludmilla might shake her head, wondering if the offender would not offend again; but I smiled at Wendz. Always since my infancy I had defied the world, giving scowl for scowl. Now I found myself smiling at strangers, bowing pleasantly, wishing the world well.

I was most astonished that I no longer yearned to ride or walk. My body was grateful for rest. Like a bird quiet on its nest I sat by the hour in Ludmilla's window, sewing incredibly soft fabrics with incredibly fine thread.

Ludmilla taught me to make tiny garments as carefully as though a grown prince would wear them. "Your city babies are spoiled!" I laughed happily, holding up a finished baby jacket, embroidered and sewn with pearls.

"Ah, but this baby is a prince, dear. These garments only fit his station in life; though it is true, as he grows we shall teach him humility and simplicity; so that he can sympathize with his people, especially the poor. We must not forget the camel, and the eye of the needle!" Ludmilla laughed at my blank expression. "A camel is an enormous animal, Marya, a beast of burden. And Christ tells us that a camel can pass through the eye of a needle more easily than a rich man can enter Heaven." She squinted through the eye of her extraordinarily fine needle. "Therefore we use our wealth justly. You have noticed we make no display of grandeur. We show only enough pomp so that the city knows it has a ruler!"

No display! I glanced around the sunlit chamber. The stone walls were hung with bright tapestries.

Scented herbs matted the floor. On every wall hung icons: a Holy Marya, an ivory crucifix, a Saint Peter like the one in the cathedral, holding up a golden key. I glanced at the pile of baby clothes, soft as clouds, smooth as clean skin. "You see," Ludmilla murmured, "we live simply. Many well-to-do merchants live as well."

I wondered if she were teasing me, but Ludmilla never teased. Wit was not one of her many virtues. "No," I thought, watching her tranquil face bent once more to her sewing, "she has never lived in a tent. She has never brought all her goods out of one wallet. Perhaps she thinks she does live simply!" But if the camel-needle story was true, Ludmilla had no hope of heaven whatever! Her bed was soft. Her painted chests bulged with fine garments, which she very seldom wore. She never wore her jewels, either; perhaps she hoped to deceive her god. Her only vanity was the white veil constantly floating about her head, or tucked like a scarf about her stringy throat. She used it, I thought, as a declaration of purity and humility.

"Marya," she said softly, breaking in upon these thoughts, "last night I dreamed of your son."

Ludmilla talked continuously. Half the time I found I did not need to listen; I could nod and smile and think my own thoughts. But this time both her words and her tone commanded attention. I held my needle poised.

"It was not my first dream of him. This is a vision, it comes to me often. I think I should tell you, Marya, I think you should know. Always it is the same dream; a message from heaven."

Gently I punched the needle into the silk and folded the whole into my lap.

"I see a tall, broad young man. He stands facing me. His hair is golden, like yours. I see this because he stands bareheaded and barefoot, in snow. Snow falls around him, snow crowns him. He is wrapped in a dark mantle, but a holy light haloes him. In his hand, Marya, he carries a golden key—like Saint Peter's, yonder. A golden crown hovers over his head, not touching it. And in this hand he carries a lantern. Every night I dream of this man, Marya. He must be my grandson!" Ludmilla leaned toward me. Her pale, wrinkled face blazed with an excitement I could not share. "Your son will be a holy man of God, I know it! This is the meaning of the dream. The key means that he will open for others the gates of heaven. The lamp is illumination; the light of faith. Do you understand me?"

I nodded. Ludmilla's shining eyes held mine, but my mind raced away. "No!" I wanted to cry, "this is no child of mine who comes to you in dream! *My* child would come to *me!*"

"Now, as to the crown, Marya dear, prepare yourself. You are a new Christian, not firm in faith. This may be hard for you. Shall I tell you now?"

"Please."

"The crown means martyrdom. Your son will be a holy martyr, a crowned saint in heaven and a glorious example here on earth! How marvelous!" Ludmilla clasped her bony knees in ecstasy. "How wonderful to have a saint born here in our own city! As you know, my son Wendz is a good Christian soul, a fine Christian soul, but he was raised pagan, as I was. This prince will be baptized in infancy and will grow up Christian; and then he will die for the Faith! I know all this as surely as I know that we sit here together now!" In spite of her exaltation Ludmilla noticed my lack of enthusiasm. She hastened to add, "and he will be the saint of the horse folk too, of course! Amazing indeed, a saint from among the horse folk! Are not God's ways wonderful? But Marya, I think you do not believe me. You look so strange!"

I did believe her, that was my trouble. Ludmilla's dream held no delight for me. I had no intention whatever of bearing a son to become a saint, much less a martyr. Such men are of no value to the Goddess I served. She and I could think of no more sinful folly than that of dying—casting away the Goddess' bright gift of life—for the sake of an idea! But Ludmilla gloried in imagining such a pointless death. She saw it as a sudden, glorious translation to the golden heaven for which she yearned. I looked at her curiously, then timidly. Her face was tense with brightness. Somehow I must quench that light, or reduce it, before it bewitched my child.

"Lady," I said softly, "my child may be a daughter."

This was my dearest secret wish. Wendz needed a son. For this he had wed me, for this he had forced himself to act the lover's part. I, too, would rejoice to bear a son, for then I could rest. But in my deepest heart I hoped for a daughter; a sharer in mysteries; a Goddess incarnate.

Ludmilla's face crumpled, but only for a moment. "I know the young man with the lantern is your son, dear; and I think he is *this* child who lies within you this moment. I truly believe that his soul speaks to mine." More calmly, she asked, "What do you dream of him, yourself?"

How could I tell her? Smiling, I shook my head. "I have not your gift," I answered humbly. "To me he is only a forming child . . ."

Closing my eyes I looked inward to the forming child, and a river of fierce, sweet joy coursed through me. The child was alive. Life flowed to him or her through long streams of uncountable lives. His ancestors' names were forgotten; but they must have been strong women, bull-backed farmers, clever fighters; for each of them had lived on this rough earth long enough to give life. Now their life sheltered in me. Later it would flow away free, to divide and divide again into countless streams. Endlessly these streams would flow, while earth endured.

Even as I sat in the sunlight by Ludmilla's window, the child within formed soundlessly, molded by the Goddess. I did not know whether it was male or female; whether it yet had fingernails or eyelashes, or whether its small heart beat. The Goddess did all this. She shone within me like a quiet sun, radiating power. As a child I had nearly been sacrificed at her shrine. Now I lived gladly as a daily sacrifice to Her. Sweetness welled up from my depths, and warm tears rainbowed the sunlight.

"Marya!" Ludmilla cried, alarmed. I opened my eyes and found her leaning over me. This life I sheltered was partly hers. Hers was one of the streams that fed the river. She and I, different as we were,

77

were two drops mingled forever in the river. I smiled to her.

"I saw tears," she said softly.

I confessed, "Tears of joy."

Relieved, she sat down again. "Marya, do you know, dear, I love you better every day. Every hour we spend together you seem more human."

I started. Ludmilla explained, "You know, I dreaded having a daughter from among the horse folk. You understand, they do not seem quite human to the rest of us. I thought you would be . . . well, ugly. Scarred, like your dear sister. I feared you would be a savage, a cannibal; that's what they say of the horse folk. You can imagine how glad I was to find you so beautiful, so sweet, a real person . . . dear Marya!"

Taken completely aback, I stared at her. I held my tongue, but I wanted to cry, "Do not call me Marya!"

Alone in the dark I kept telling myself, "My name is Dragamir." I dreamed of flying over vast, free plains on Belatruz's back. Bright spring flowers reddened the land, I felt the strong wind in my face. Ludmilla would have called it a vision. In my heart I kept a shrine for Draga; and daily I remembered that my child was his grandchild. Someday my son might ride the plains with Draga, though I myself would never do so again. I wept to think of this, and felt noble and self-sacrificing.

Surprised, I remarked to Yolann, "We're still twins!"

Yolann chuckled, and patted her rounding belly.

"The father is young, but he's rich already. He imports for his father. Look what he gave me!" She threw open her chest and drew forth a length of red satin, and a silver cup filled with amber beads. "Remember, I came here to better myself."

"Mmmm. And a pretty girl can always earn a living." (But *Yolann*? In the *city*?) I asked, "But why a child? Does he pay enough for that?"

"Indeed no, the child is for me!" Yolann's eyes sparkled darkly. "Why should you be the only mother here? You know, sister, rich men or no rich men, this city is a trap!"

Dismally I nodded. I knew it well.

"Dragamir, do you never long to ride?"

"I did, before."

"I still do. I long to walk, even, across the horizon. In this city you see no horizon, just roofs."

"I know."

"And the nights are cold, lying alone."

"I know."

"What's wrong with your husband?"

"He is not well."

"I can see that for myself! What is the matter with him?"

"Am I a witch, to know that?"

"Well, anyhow, it will be a joy to cuddle with someone small; someone all mine. Dragamir, I am lonesome! My importer seldom sends for me now. Indeed, I have my eye on a new one. He's fat, but his cloak is sewn with pearls. Help me fold this."

"It's fine stuff." I rubbed the satin with light fingertips. "Draga would kill for this!"

"So would I, but I can get it easier." Yolann laid

the stuff away in the chest, and cushioned the cup in its folds. "You know, sister, these are rich treasures. But they are nothing compared to this treasure." Gently she patted her bulge of child.

I remembered the little Yolann saying, "There's no treasure like one of those!" Almost I heard her husky, childish voice; and for a brief moment I felt washed in sunlight that flowed from a far-arching blue sky. My eyes brimmed tears.

"What is wrong?" Yolann asked, puzzled and sorry.

"Nothing, sister. A memory. Why did you not tell me sooner?"

"You have been far away."

"Hah! No farther than the garden!" I envied Yolann her freedom. Whenever she chose she could walk down the stairs and out the door. She could travel the streets and alleys, she could mingle with beggars, merchants, soldiers. (I guessed she did not bother with monks.) Already she spoke a market dialect, different from the palace speech.

"Yolann," I said earnestly, "we must never part! Always we must be twins!"

She took my hands in hers and pressed them to her child. "We are twins now. Feel him move?"

Indeed, I felt the faint flutter through skin and wool. "That's your dinner moving!"

Autumn browned the garden. Naked, Ludmilla's rosethorns clicked together in a chilly wind. Ludmilla and I moved indoors, and sewed now at my hearth. Our work slowly filled the ornate, carved cradle in which the newborn Wendz had lain. Unknown to Ludmilla, I stored clothes there for Yolann's infant, too; hiding the rough wool under the silks.

Ludmilla leaned to rock the cradle. "Wendz was a good baby," she said dreamily. "He was so good, the nurse thought him unwell." She smiled to herself. Then she shuddered. A shiver ran through her thin frame, a dark wildness shone in her eyes. Instantly she recovered herself, veiling the emotion that had stood stark in her face: terror.

I asked her softly, "What are you thinking of?"

"I . . . well . . . I was thinking of Wendz's birth.

"Was the birth hard?"

"Very hard." Ludmilla turned her shoulder to me. She did not seem to wish to look at me.

"Did Wendz come feet first?"

"Nothing like that. It was only . . . he had such a big head! Marya, I nearly died. And had I died I should now be in hell, for as you know I was pagan, then." Shivers shook the old frame. "But God spared me to hear Bishop Niklas preach." Trying to smile, Ludmilla turned back to me. "Truthfully," she went on in a calmer tone, "while not even the most charitable Christian can say much good about your horse folk—cruel they are, and ignorant, and dirty—yet everyone knows they are brave. Courage is their one virtue. So I am sure that you, dear, will be much braver than I was! Perhaps it will be easy for you. You may have no trouble. But we do know that sons resemble fathers. We must pray."

Slowly, as last leaves dropped and first snow fell, I grew afraid. My beloved burden was heavy, and growing apace. Now hidden securely in my depths, how could it emerge into daylight without bursting me?

One night I sought Yolann's bed. "Can't sleep," I whispered, creeping in under her quilt. "Sister, tell me the truth. Are you afraid?"

"Naturally," she mumbled, barely roused from sleep. She did not sound ashamed to admit fear.

"You think about it too?"

"Naturally." Sighing, pushing and struggling, she rolled over and took me in her arms. Her warmth was comforting, like Barax's warmth. "But I remember what Mother said—you know, about breathing right."

"Yes." But would it work?

"And the teas. Dragamir, it's time we brew the teas."

"How can we find herbs?"

"I can buy them." Yolann had friends in the city alleys. Slightly comforted, I remembered that they could smuggle us anything we really needed from the outer world. "And tomorrow I'll steal us a chicken downstairs. Two chickens."

They were two pullets, one white, one black; alert-eyed, but paralyzed by their bonds, and the darkness of Yolann's basket. "Bar the door," she whispered.

Hastily I barred both doors. I knew well that no one must suspect what we did now. I was barely considered a Christian; and what might Ludmilla do if she found me sacrificing to the Goddess? I did not want to think.

Yet the sacrifice must be made. The Goddess within pushed at my heart and lungs. She pressed outward, threatening to burst me open. In her right hand she held life, golden like Saint Peter's key. But her left hand grasped pain and possible death. The sacrifice must be made, most certainly.

We knelt together at the hearth fire, whispering Barax's incantations. I drew the white pullet from the basket. She struggled in my hands, turning her head on her ruffled neck, looking fiercely into the flames. She opened her beak to squawk. Before she could make a sound I wrung her neck, and hurled the struggling corpse into the fire.

"Yours is black," I murmured, as Yolann lifted her chicken out of the basket. "What does that mean?"

Gravely she intoned, as though this were part of the ritual, "Night is black. Earth is black. The womb is black. You, Goddess, weave in the black dark." Her thumbs found the pullet's throat, but it managed a raucous cry before she killed it.

Silently we huddled, listening. We heard no footsteps or voices outside the barred doors; only a scurrying, as of rats. We wrapped our arms about each other, and watched the fire slowly consume feather, flesh and bone. Yolann poked the stubborn remains about, and heaped ash over suspicious-looking blobs. "No one will notice," she said finally. "I stole an ax, too. You can have it first, you will birth first." Gratefully I pushed the small kitchen ax under my bed. I breathed easier, now; and I saw by her smoothed brow that Yolann did, too.

I said, "I think She is content." I felt that She was.

"She's had her blood." Yolann rose, shaking ash

from her skirt. "We've done all we can do. Good thing your mother-in-law didn't come prying!"

Later, Ludmilla said to me, "It is time we pray together for a safe birth. Come to the chapel, dear; I have the blessed candles lit. Oh, and fetch your sister."

"If she will come."

"Pagan though she is, bring her along. I see that she, too, will soon need the Holy Marya's kindness."

I went to find Yolann. She shrugged. "Why not? Two medicines are better than one!" Holding hands we waddled into the chapel.

Ludmilla already knelt in prayer before the smiling wooden Marya. Blessed candles winked about the statue's feet. Half-turning, she motioned us to kneel beside her, which we did clumsily, pulling at our gowns and swaying on wide-planted knees. Now Ludmilla prayed aloud, pausing for me to mumble the responses. Knowing no responses, Yolann grunted tactfully. The candles flickered, the Marya smiled. I looked up at her indifferently. I had little faith in her power and none in her mercy, despite that everlasting smile. Why should these whining, groveling prayers move her? Thankfully I remembered the burned pullets, and the ax under my bed.

Watching her earnest, heartfelt petitioning, I thought how loving Ludmilla was, and how easily deceived. Even in my urgent need I felt ashamed to deceive her. I had yet to learn proper respect for the intelligence behind those bleary eyes; for the iron hidden in that heart.

* * *

In frigid darkness the Goddess came to me. I woke into a black, freezing night, and felt Her drawing near; Her presence filled the room, the palace, the city. The winter world was the Goddess. She held my spine in Her freezing hand, and squeezed.

Breathless I lay in her grip. She squeezed harder, harder, till I thought I could not bear it; of a sudden, then, She slackened Her grasp. I breathed again, and remembered myself. "I am Dragamir Marya," I thought, "and the Goddess works within me." I came clear, then. "Holy Mother Earth! This is the hour!"

I sat bolt upright, clutching the blankets to my shaking shoulders. I shivered all over, my teeth chattered. The cold power of the Goddess filled me to bursting. "I will burst," I realized, "soon or late I will burst. Let it be soon!"

Gratefully I remembered the ax under my bed. The thought of its keen edge comforted me. It would soon cut the pain. And the sacrifices we had made on the hearth—"Yolann!" I cried, "Yolann, it is now!"

Again the Goddess surged through me. Again She gripped my spine and the night swam black. But when I thought I could bear no more She relented. The pain drew away as Yolann opened the door.

"Sister, did you shout?" Oh, the comfort of that rough voice, speaking my own tongue! Yolann had pulled on a linen shift. She stood in the doorway haloed in candlelight, enormously pregnant, solid on wide-planted bare feet. I thought she looked almost a match for the Goddess, but the next pain-wave taught me better. We meet the Goddess alone; there is no help.

"Sister, it is now! Open the doors! Holy Mother, open all the doors!" My body felt the resistance of every closed door in the palace.

Calmly Yolann came forward. Candle in hand, she knelt heavily to look under the bed. "I thought the maid might have carried off the ax," she said, pushing herself up, "but never fear, it's there, sharp as ever. See now, I will open every door in this man-trap. Do not be afraid, sweet. Remember what Mother said. Breathe deep; yes, like that. Sleep between pains."

She lit a candle for me and went out, leaving her door and the farther door open. Great draughts of cold air swept into the room. Every door Yolann opened throughout the palace breathed new cold. The candle flickered and went out, but in my pain-trance I did not notice the dark.

Barax's instructions came back to me. I lay back and rested between waves of pain, I even slept. Barax had told us the truth, the pain never quite reached the promised agony. I would have died if it had, and that would not have served the Goddess' purpose; so She always withdrew in time. Dreaming in a trough between pain waves I felt myself covered and smothered, as in straw. Now I understood this dream, I remembered how I had nearly been sacrificed to the Goddess, and Draga had snatched me away. But he could not entirely save me; we are alone with the Goddess. Now She returned, demanding Her sacrifice. "Very well," I told Her, waking, "use me. I agree that You use me." I surrendered; and immediately I felt lighter, looser. The next pain was not so terrible. "I will live through this," I knew.

Lights—voices—a blur of candles, a torch; Ludmilla leaned above me. She had taken time to dress, her veil drifted across my face. "You are doing well, dear," she told me kindly, "Have no fear." I wished she had been Barax! Lovely Ludmilla was kind, her soft hands were comforting on my brow. But she knew nothing of the Goddess. The squat, homely woman who had mothered me would have known what to do, what the Goddess demanded. Ludmilla could only point to the painted Marya on the wall. "Pray to the Holy Marya," she advised me. "Blessed candles burn for you now in the chapel. The monks pray for you." Indeed they did; their doleful chant drifted down the hallway, through all the open doors. Then the Goddess returned and swept my mind away.

I cried for Yolann. "My sister," I begged the watching faces, "Let my sister in!" The room was full of faces; Ludmilla, her maids, two nuns—a man's face looked over Ludmilla's shoulder! Horrified, I tried to sit up. "What is he doing here? Throw him out!" For I was dimly aware of nakedness. The blankets had been pulled back. "Kick him out!" I realized that I was speaking my own tongue, but I could not think of the city words. I pointed a shaking, furious finger at the man's smoothly smiling face.

Ludmilla nodded soothingly. "Bishop Niklas must witness the birth, Marya. Your son will be a prince, you know; our Christian heir. This is our custom."

It was not my custom; but now I began to burst. "My sister!" I cried, and then, "Yolann! Yolann!"

That they understood; and the crowd parted to let Yolann come to my side. She knelt by me and gripped my hands. "Pull on me, Dragamir," she said quietly. "Brace your feet. Breathe light." Her face dissolved and became her mother's face, her voice carried authority. Panting, I obeyed her. For a long, long moment I burned, I burst. Then the women murmured. Bishop Niklas nodded, and left the room.

Yolann said softly, "You can let go." I let go of her hands. I lay limp and empty, wonderfully pain-free. I heard a soft cry.

The mists fled from around me. My sight cleared, I was aware. I knew that the maids were cleaning me and the bed, and laying decent covers. I listened to that new voice gaining strength, gasping, howling. Everyone smiled. Daylight entered the room. One by one the palace doors were closed, and the cold draughts ceased to blow. A maid built up a fire on the hearth. Insistently the new voice called. Listening, I felt my breasts tingle warm. Content with Her sacrifice, the Goddess bestowed now her sweet gifts: milk, and tender delight.

"Let me see him," I murmured. "Is he a son?" Not that I minded what he was. The city crown was only a dream, only one of those stories men tell each other. Life was real, the Goddess' gift. For me, it was enough that the child lived.

Only Yolann understood me, for I spoke my true

tongue. She turned to the others and spoke; and Ludmilla came to me with a bundle wrapped in clean white linen. She laid it beside me on the bed. Yolann helped me rise on my elbow, and stuffed cushions at my back. I looked down into the bundle.

He was pathetically small; yet large to have burst from my body. I could have covered his face with my palm. It was red with crying. I could not bear his crying, I must console him. "Come," I wanted to say to him, "This world is not so bad. Look, I love you. I will take care of you." I drew him onto my arm, close to my tingling breast. Immediately his mouth sought it; but Ludmilla stayed me. "Wait for that." Instead, I caressed his small, waving hand. I pushed a finger into it; and amazingly, the tiny fist tightened on my finger.

His crying died to a gurgle, and stopped. Soothed by my near warmth he gazed at me with wobbling eyes that had never seen light before. His mouth hung slightly open; so soft, so pink, I was reminded of a rosebud in Ludmilla's garden. I bent to feel his new breath against my cheek. Warm it came, soft, sure. My son was alive in the world beside me. We were alive together. And this was no dream, no story; this was the real gift of the Goddess.

My son slept on my arm. I drifted into a happy doze. I stirred when they lifted him away from me; but a soft hand caressed my hair, and drew the warm covers over me; and I sank into a serene sleep, a sleep of relief and joy; confidently expecting a happier awakening than I had ever known.

❋ ❋ ❋

I woke to broad, snow-bright sunlight. A leaping fire warmed the room. I pushed back the covers. Sitting up slowly, I found myself clean, and dressed in a new linen bedrobe, with my hair neatly plaited down my back. At once I looked to the cradle by the hearth. It was not there.

I could not have dreamed all that! I felt my stomach. No, it was no dream. The burden that had swelled there was gone. I gazed around the room. Something else was gone; the red and blue Marya was missing from the wall. In her place hung a hideous image of naked torture, an ivory crucifix.

"Yolann!" I called softly. "Sister!" At once the door opened, but it was Ludmilla who came in.

She minced lightly into the room, smiling cheerfully. Sunlight pierced her veil and her hair shone silver. "My dear child!" She greeted me lovingly, "What can I bring you? A heartening tea? Wine, perhaps?"

"My son!" I burst out discourteously. "I must see my child!" As I thought of him, of his pink rosebud mouth and wobbling eyes, my breasts swelled warm.

Ludmilla brought a chair and set it beside the bed. Very deliberately she sat down, smiling, in a ray of sunshine. "My dear," she said gently, "I must speak with you."

"Now? Lady, can it not wait? Or, speak to me while I feed my son." I indicated my full breasts. They were beginning to ache.

Ludmilla shook her head slowly. "It cannot wait. My child, what I have to say to you is of the utmost importance and demands your full attention."

I sighed. Well, I would give Ludmilla my full attention. Then she would bring me my son. "Lady, I will listen. Only say it shortly if—" I held back the forming words "if you can speak shortly. I am listening," I assured her.

Ludmilla clasped her hands prayerfully and bent her forehead upon her fingertips. She was silent for the space of a slow, reverent Ave. When she looked up the sweet smile was gone from her lips. Her eyes were sorrowful. Dread seized my heart. I started up, crying, "Is my son not well? Tell me quickly!"

She nodded. "Your son is well, Marya. You have a strong, healthy child, have no fear for him."

I sank back upon the pillows. Still fearful, I watched Ludmilla's mouth tighten, and wrinkles furrow her high forehead.

Slowly seeking the words that usually flowed in a steady stream she said, "Marya. Wendz and I do not believe that you are a true Christian. You see, we know about the sacrifice you performed on this hearth to God knows what pagan demon. You were frightened, we understand that. But a frightened Christian would have turned to God, and to the Holy Marya."

I was so relieved I laughed. Ludmilla wished only to preach. I need only listen attentively for a while, then she would bring back my child. "I am sorry," I apologized through my laughter.

Ludmilla raised her head high. Her nostrils contracted. "You laugh, young Marya. I very much fear that you will shortly weep. I would spare you if I could." Now I truly listened! "But my duty is to my son and his city; to God and His Church. In view of these heavy responsibilities . . . I am here to tell

you that . . . Wendz has considered well his duty
. . . he has decided . . . we have decided . . .
Marya. We have decided that you are not a fit
mother for the Christian heir."

I gasped. Fit or unfit, I was the heir's mother. He
and I and the Goddess had decided that last night,
and nothing could change it now. Maybe Ludmilla
meant that they were going to disown him? Declare
him *not* the Christian heir, and myself *not* Wendz's
true wife after all? Very well. I would not weep
much for that. I had no care for the city crown. My
son would still be my son, and I his mother. Almost
calmly I waited for Ludmilla to finish her speech.

"This is hard for me, child. I ask you to believe
me when I say that I desire only your good, and the
good of my grandson. You believe that I love my
grandson, do you not?" Ludmilla almost smiled a
bleak smile. "You believe that I am a woman, do
you not?"

I nodded, wondering.

"I am a woman like you, Marya. I was once
young like you, I bore my Wendz as you have borne
your Wendceslas." I accepted that. I felt a new kin-
ship with all womankind. Mankind, too, found a
place in my new compassion; for had not all men
been born? Every man I would ever meet had been
born on some particular day and hour to some
woman laboring in the grip of the Goddess. I smiled
my understanding to Ludmilla. She did not smile
back.

"So I know what you will suffer, my dear, and I
grieve for you. But take heart, it may not be forever.
If we could hope in your Faith . . . if we could

only believe that you would rightly raise our Christian heir . . ." She sighed. "Unfortunately we know otherwise. Left to your teaching, our little Wendceslas would grow up a savage, a pagan. You would doom his soul to everlasting damnation, and also, perhaps, the souls of his subjects. We are responsible, you see, not only for our own salvation, but for the salvation of all who come within our power." Ludmilla regarded me sadly, with heavy compassion. "We are responsible for your soul, dear, and believe me, we will try to save it!

"But for the time being we must be firm with you. You will think us cruel. This cruelty, dear, is true love. Only thus can we fulfill our hard duty to our Faith, our people, our God."

Holy Mother Earth! What would these people do?

"My son has appointed teachers for Wendceslas; pious men who will raise him in the straight and narrow path."

Very well, when the boy could speak and think they could teach him what they liked. But for now—

"And for now, during his tender infancy, we have given Wendceslas to a foster mother; a kind and pious woman. . . ."

Ludmilla continued to speak, but I did not hear. A *foster mother?* When my arms ached to hold him? When my breasts leaked rich milk? The woman could not mean it!

I burst out "Lady, I'll be Christian! I'll be what you want!"

Ludmilla shook her head. Milk stained my bedrobe. I leaned toward Ludmilla; I stretched begging hands. "I believe! I'll learn faster! I'll be good!" I cried like a beaten child. Ludmilla would not meet my eyes. Gazing at the floor, she shook and shook her head.

"Marya dear, Wendz and I have discussed this fully with Bishop Niklas. We have prayed over it all together, and we are all in full agreement." Bishop Niklas! This was his doing! "My poor child, we can do nothing else."

I rose in the bed, and tried to struggle out of it. I would have thrown myself at Ludmilla's feet. But I was weak. Old Ludmilla held me down in the bed quite easily, calling the while to her maids who waited in Yolann's antechamber. They came and held me, and one sloshed a medicinal tea between my teeth.

"There," said Ludmilla, standing back. "Now you will sleep. When you wake, dear, pray." She indicated the crucifix on the wall. "Rest now, child."

Finding no words for my desperation, I screamed. Ludmilla muttered instructions to her nodding, hard-faced maids and hurried out the door. Her white veil drifted behind her and fluttered in the doorway like a storm-swept cloud.

I wept for days. My breasts wept through their tight bandages. They ached, and hardened into hot lumps. Always in my mind was the image of my son's small face, the warmth of his new breath. They say that a warrior who loses an arm still feels that arm; its ghost remains with him, it can even itch. In the same way I felt my son beside me as I lay in bed.

Waking from a sad doze I thought he lay upon my arm. Joy flooded my bosom. Ludmilla had relented and brought back my child! I opened my eyes and found myself alone. Later, huddled at the hearth, I felt his dear weight in my lap. He seemed so real I cried out and grasped for him; but I grasped only my robe.

Awake, I imagined my child. Asleep, I dreamed him. In a dream of powerful sweetness I nursed him, loving the strong pull of his rosebud lips. Satisfied, he slept, and Yolann lifted him gently away and laid him in his cradle. She left us alone, and the dream turned dark. A wintry breeze from the window set the cradle rocking. All at once a lean, shaggy shape bounded in through the window. I lay horror-frozen, unable to scream or move. The window stood high in the wall, higher than six men standing on each others' shoulders could reach; yet a grim gray wolf leaped in from the winter night and stood at the cradle, drooling over my son. I tried to rise, but my body lay as if dead. The wolf snatched up my child in cruel-fanged jaws, turned, and soared out the window into blackness.

"Yolann!" I shrieked.

Yolann could not convince me that I had dreamed. I babbled and cried till morning, when Ludmilla came and leaned over me. Her slight, almost transparent hand trembled on my forehead. Her veil smelled of chapel incense. I struggled away from her to breathe. "No, my child," she assured me patiently, "there was no wolf. That was a dream, Marya, a dream Satan sent to torment you. I promise you, dear, your little one is safe in the lap of a good, kind woman. (True, she is only a farm wife. But God gives even such women sweet milk.) And how could a wolf leap in here? Look, dear, your window is high. You are in a city, Marya! There are no plains out there, this is no tent! You are safe in bed in an upper room in a palace in a city, and there are no wolves within . . . well, a day's journey. No, my child, there was no wolf. . . ."

"No wolf," Yolann agreed, shutting the door at last upon Ludmilla, "she herself is the wolf."

I drew myself up in bed and looked around at the clear winter morning. I knew that Yolann spoke truth: I had seen a true vision in my dream. The wolf I had seen was Ludmilla's soul. It had leaped free of her feeble body. It had cast off the mask of her sweet face, and in its own true form it had seized my child from me. I would never see him again. Even if I saw him in the flesh, he could be only an empty body. That wolf meant to devour his soul.

I wept in Yolann's arms. She sat down on the bed and held me tight against her swollen body, and I felt her unborn child kick and press against me. "Yolann," I gasped when I could speak, "I must find my son! She has him hidden somewhere in this palace. I will find him!"

"And I will help you," Yolann promised.

That same day I struggled out of bed. Leaning on Yolann, I explored the entire palace. Up and down the steep stone stairs we toiled. We looked into every open room and hall and closet. We knocked on every closed door. Startled faces looked out at us—

servants, nobles, monks. If they hesitated to open to us I showed them my dagger. I held my hand upon it the whole day; for I meant to seize my son where and when I found him, and none should stop me. The startled faces crumpled in fear. Doors opened. Silent, haughty nobles watched two crazed women, one swollen with child, one leaking milk, search their rooms. From the top of the palace down to the kitchens we searched every corner; and I would have limped out to the stables, but I burst out bleeding.

"Not even Ludmilla would keep her grandson in the stables," Yolann insisted. "Sister, we have searched this trap through and through, and he is not here. Come, I must get you back to bed. Don't fight me. Here, you!" she yelled at a kitchen maid, "help me get this lady upstairs!"

Naturally, Ludmilla heard the news fluttering about the palace. "Have you seen the savages? They threatened my lord with swords!" Scarcely was I imprisoned in bed with my feet on a cushion when she came swiftly in, her face as pale as her veil. "What ever made you *do* such a thing? My dear, you are fevered! They are bringing up chicken broth, they should be here now. Yolann, run see if they are coming! You must raise your feet more—yes, like that—but you need another cushion. Yolann, run and get a cushion from my room! They are bringing up herb tea, Marya, you will know what herbs they are—Yolann, do not let her get out of bed again! Call me at once if she tries it. We must take care of her, you and I—she is crazed, I have been watching for this, it is the fever. We must pray. Ah, here comes the tea. Yolann, run to the kitchen, hurry them with the broth—"

When she had gone we almost laughed. "They are bringing chicken broth, my child," Yolann mimicked bitterly, "and herbs picked by my lily white hands by moonlight and blessed by Bishop Niklas with the blood of a pregnant goat! Yolann, run to the cathedral, light all the blessed candles!"

"Why does she care?" I murmured. "Does she not wish me to die?"

"She wants another prince out of you. This one might—"

Yolann did not finish the thought. She did not say, "This one might die, he is only a human baby." Instead, she said, "She's right about this broth, Dragamir," tasting it, "it'll bring you back to life."

The broth did warm my body; and all day Yolann's rough comfort warmed my soul. But at night she went to her bed, and when I woke in terror I thought I was alone.

It was the chill hour before dawn. The fire was but a mass of glowing coals, radiating little light and no heat. But heat brooded in the room. A presence weighed upon me; formless, faceless, it breathed upon me. Darkness was its form, the thumping of my heart was its voice. It was the Goddess. She filled the room. Her hand pressed my throat. As She had gripped my body before, now She gripped my spirit. This pain, this tearing grief, was Her work in me. These were Her gifts to me: pain, misery, weakness.

I could bear no more. If I would live I must fight

back. I sat bolt upright, throwing off Her divine weight. Breathing hard, gasping defiance, I stood up on the bed. I struggled out of my woolen bedrobe and cast it from me. Sincerely naked I faced the Goddess, and addressed Her aloud.

"You!" I called to Her. I felt Her pause, listening. "You tried to kill me when I was young. You could have killed me three days ago, when I did Your work for You. And now You would tear my spirit, as You have torn my body? I tell You, You shall not do it! For I will live no longer as Your sacrifice! From this moment I live for me, Dragamir. I live no longer for You, I live for me. I am Dragamir, and I live for me!"

I stepped down to the floor and the floor was cold. I had forgotten, in the heat of Her presence, that it was winter. My searching hands found the robe tossed on the floor, and I climbed back into it, and went to stand by the glowing coals.

The Goddess drew away from me. I knew myself alone. The room became still and cold, and the first dawn light showed me the outline of snow on my window ledge.

Shivering, I wrapped myself tight in the wool robe. My sorrow and grief had gone away with the Goddess. She had picked up Her rejected gifts and carried them away with Her, and now my heart felt as hard as my bound breasts. I rejoiced, I exulted in its hardness. I was left alone with my pride, alone with my strength. "I am Dragamir," I whispered, "I am Dragamir, and I live only for me."

My being was empty. Love had drained away from it, like water from a shallow well. Now anger seeped in. Coldly I considered what those people had done to me. That simpering, saintly old woman with the heart of iron! What she had done to me no woman could do to another. She was in truth no woman, but a wolf-bitch. Always I would remember my vision! Ludmilla had carried my child away to her lair to devour him, and I had not found her lair. My child was lost to me forever. Lest my heart break I must not think of him. But I would avenge him!

And that mush-spined son of hers, who did her bidding as though she spoke for his god! He was my enemy, and I would have vengeance on him.

And the bishop; that wily, wolfish shepherd of Christians—he had incited Ludmilla to this deed. It was he who wanted a Christian heir—a bell-wether for his flock! He feared that my lamb might prove a wild ibex! He feared that my son might not listen to him as respectfully as his father listened now. So he had sent the wolf to snatch him away. I would have the bishop's blood.

I thought, too, of their god; the bleeding god who hung over the world, dripping blood on the world. This cruelty had been done in his name. And the Marya—sweetly she had mocked my empty arms! Painted on every wall, at the head of every stair, she had smiled down upon me as I rushed by, hand on dagger! But my day would come.

"I am Dragamir," I whispered. "I am a match for them all."

Days later in the cathedral I silently told the god, "I am a match for you." From afar I watched the baptism of a royal infant; a package of bright silks in Ludmilla's arms. She stood at the font, proud and triumphant; under her white veil her old head trembled with pious satisfaction. Her son stood beside her, resplendant in cloth of gold, quietly stroking his smooth beard, while Bishop Niklas poured cold water over the infant's soft head. The child squalled in protest. (Something moved in my heart. I spoke to it sternly, and it lay quiet.)

I raised my eyes, then, to the real enemy, the Marya. In the light of a hundred flickering candles she seemed to move. Tenderly she bowed her head against her son's crowned head. Lightly her gentle hands enfolded his body. Floating incense-smoke clouded her quiet face; and about her rose the monks' chant, a terrible, sonorous unity. When first I heard this monkish music I thought it beautiful; I thought it the voice of peace, perhaps of love. Now I knew it for a battle-cry. As warriors shout together, so did the monks sing together.

Silently I told the Marya, "You and I are enemies. You and I are at war. I will open your city gates, and my tribesmen shall ride in your streets. I will open your cathedral doors, and war ponies shall stable in your sanctuary. I will do this with my father Draga."

In the cloud of incense-smoke I seemed to see Draga mounting among his warriors. His black plume swayed, his eyes gleamed like spear points. He glanced down at me with recognition. At such times I did not exist in Draga's world. But when his ponies stomped in the cathedral, when the streets were littered with loot, then Draga would remember me. Then he would boast of me, "This is my daughter."

That night I dreamed of Draga. I dreamed of a bright plain, wide light, my small hands grasping Belatruz's mane, and Draga's hard warmth at my back. Happily I leaned against him, and his tough brown arms circled me.

We rode gently over rolling green land, toward water. Somewhere ahead was a spring. Immediately we were there, water rose cool in a cup of grass, reflecting the sky. But we were not alone. Prone in the grass a young man lay, trailing stubby, farmer's fingers in the water. Golden hair flowed bright upon the shoulders of his brown robe. I saw his wallet, empty, in the grass.

Draga raised a hand before my face. I felt angry breath swell his chest. He shouted, and a huge black dog raced forward at the young monk.

"No!" I cried, squirming against Draga. The harmless young man was beautiful, why should we see his blood? "No!" But Draga's arm tightened about me, hard as a chain.

Ears laid back, tail stiff, the war dog leaped. Mid-leap it dropped abruptly beside the monk, and whined. It would not attack. The monk never looked up. Quietly, he watched the rippled water.

Draga shouted again, and Belatruz reared high. "No!" I cried as we lifted into the sky and came down with Belatruz's hoofs on the young man's head. Again and again Belatruz reared and stomped, till the figure in the grass lay flat as unleavened bread.

I woke wide-eyed, with pounding heart.

4

The City

I despised myself. I shuddered to remember how I had striven for love, for approval; how I had tried to conform my own true face to the proper, accepted mask. Like a bitch puppy I had crawled and wagged. Believing myself loved, I had actually begun to love Wendz and Ludmilla. Now I saw that their kindness was Charity, no deeper than the painted smile of the Holy Marya. Behind her smile was nothing but wood and paint. Behind Ludmilla's hid a different woman: my bitter enemy.

After his baptism I never thought of little Wendceslas again. The wolf had devoured him. The infant who lay now in some pious village woman's lap was nothing to me; my son was dead. My old self had died grieving; and now a new young woman looked out of my eyes.

No longer did I pretend to be a Christian. I tore down the crucifix from my wall and slung it out into the hall; it was rescued, with horrified murmurs, by soft-footed servants. I heard them rustling about. I heard the terror in their muted exclamations and shook with silent laughter.

I never set foot in the cathedral, or in the chapel down the hall. There Wendz and Ludmilla prayed at night, opening their hard hearts to their god. Stealing down the hall at any hour of night I might glimpse lamplight through the half-open door, and see a cruciform figure kneeling rigid before the small altar. The sickly man and the old woman sacrificed their sleep and their joints, partly for me. I knew they prayed for my conversion, and, spying on their painful devotions, I sniggered.

Yolann and I prayed secretly at our hearth, and cast the few homely spells we knew. Yolann moved much about the city, and she warned me of my growing reputation. "Merchants call you 'the pagan lady,' " she reported. "To the poorer sort you are 'the savage.' "

This pleased me well. It must mightily embarrass Ludmilla and her son, and I rejoiced in their chagrin. This was my first revenge, a small one indeed. But soon I took another, much more serious revenge.

Wendz now had his Christian heir. Relieved of duty, he was delighted to be free of me. Weeks passed and Wendz never came near me. By day he looked at me askance, stroking his beard, no doubt wondering what evil spirit now possessed me. At night he prayed, or dragged himself to his narrow bed, where I am sure he rejoiced in his privacy.

But his prince was only an infant. Who knows whether an infant will live? Surely as many die as live! In the coming years the small heir must pass many tests; horses would kick, fevers strike, a plague might fall from heaven. The prince might lean too far out a window.

Did Ludmilla whisper in Wendz's ear? Or was it

that good shepherd Niklas who reminded him of his irksome duty? One evening after supper we heard a minstrel sing an old ballad. Sweetly he sang, and after each verse sketched a heart-softening melody with bow and string. I sat apart, as was now my custom, at the edge of the light. Hard though I was, I was yet young, and tears dimned the candlelight for me.

The ballad drew to its tragic end, the last pathetic note sank into silence. Even Wendz sighed. Ludmilla smiled, and dismissed the minstrel with a kindly nod.

We rose; Ludmilla kissed her son. No longer did she try to kiss me! She had tried it once, on my first evening downstairs after childbirth. I drew back and glared at her, singeing her with the muted blaze of my hate. She never tried again. But this evening, kissing Wendz's cheek, she patted his arm encouragingly.

Wendz stood there, thoughtful, after she left. With cold courtesy I awaited his departure. He straightened his shoulders and thrust out his chin in the stubborn way he had when valor was required. My heart sank as he turned toward me.

Slowly he came to me and took my hand. His hand was already slimy with cold sweat. Wordlessly, he led me out of the hall and up the stairs. Unwillingly we mounted the stairs together, dragging our feet. I am sure that our dread was equal.

But halfway up the stairs a thought nudged my mind. Brightening, I turned it over, looking at it from all angles. It began to glow like a lamp in my heart.

Why had I not thought of this sooner? Why had I not seen this glorious opportunity at once? Oh blessed Barax! When we left the stairs and turned toward my rooms I was smiling.

Wendz gave me a surprised, sideways glance. He murmured, "I am glad you are not angry."

"I? Angry? How should I be angry?" I simpered. "You are my lord husband, your will is mine!"

Wendz's astonishment was comical. I gave him no cause to doubt my submission. All was as before—or so he thought. Night after night he came to me, sighing, marshaling his pathetic forces for the assault. I smiled and yielded. I drew forth his sparse strength, I squandered his seed. Smoothly smiling, I closed my womb.

Ludmilla sent for doctors. Teas were brewed. Wendz drank powdered horn of unicorn and ate the ground bones of the giants of old. Bishop Niklas and Ludmilla conferred, whispering, shaking their heads. I walked past demurely, smiling; guarding my secret.

Nearly two years passed this way before they began to suspect. Then wary eyes turned in my direction. Could I possibly be responsible? Could a young girl know what Ludmilla and her ladies did not know? Could an ignorant savage baffle the Goddess—or, as they put it, the will of God? It was hardly possible! "Wendz, my dear," said Ludmilla, "we will try this new root from Asia. Pounded, it tastes bitter, they say; but one may add honey without harm."

Wendz neared complete exhaustion. Nightly I depleted his strength, and it was not replenished.

Sweats and tremblings overcame him. Often when he left me I heard him coughing in the chapel till his anxious mother, clucking like a hen partridge, sent him to bed.

Now Bishop Niklas and Ludmilla watched me uneasily. The servants drew away as I passed, more in outright fear than in respect. "Sister," Yolann warned me, "they whisper 'witchcraft.'"

I laughed. I teased my panting husband, "Why do you want another son? Your Christian heir looks healthy enough to me!"

A golden-haired toddler lived in Ludmilla's rooms. Usually cared for by maids, he yet spent much time with his grandmother. Passing her open door I might glimpse him playing near the hearth, building a palace from shaped wooden blocks; or was it a cathedral? Yes, it was. "Find the cross, dear," I heard Ludmilla say, "see, it goes on top of everything, like this." Carefully she placed the small golden crucifix on top of the tottering structure, and the child laughed to see the gold wink in the firelight. Indifferently, I passed by. It was all nothing to me.

On a summer evening I might watch them in the garden. From an upstairs window I could see the child leaning against the old lady's knee, studying the painted icons she held for him. Sunlight glowed on his bright, curly head and on his round, soft arms. Ludmilla's silver-gray gown glistened like the breast of a dove. Her grandmotherly voice drifted up to me, "and this, my sweet, is Saint Sebastian. See, he was only a boy, but he never denied Christ,

107

though the pagan archers used him for target prac-tice! Now, my pet, who is this one? Who?"

The fair head bent, the baby brows scowled in concentration. Triumphant, Wendceslas squeaked, "Saint Agnes!" And Ludmilla slipped a sweet be-tween his soft lips. No wonder the child was fat!

I never went near the small prince. Ludmilla might have called the guard if I had, and my pride would not allow that. But after all, I had no great wish for his company. He was no child of mine. I saw nothing familiar in him except . . . except sometimes, when we met in the hall, that grave, thoughtful stare. It reminded me of someone. Some-one had once gazed at me thoughtfully, like that, from wide, gray eyes. Neither Wendz nor Ludmilla used their pale eyes like that. Never had I seen that look among the tribes. The memory came from far, far back . . . those were the dull gray eyes of Marya Whore! Her stare had been sodden, despair-ing. Little Wendceslas' stare was childish, wonder-ing. But it was the same look. This was a thread of the Goddess' weaving, drawn through my body. Meeting my mother's eyes in the hallway my heart sometimes murmured rebelliously, but I subdued it. I learned to disregard this, to ignore it. We met in the halls and passed and went our ways; the child staring solemnly after me, Ludmilla and I in stony silence.

I returned to my rooms, and to the laughter, or whimpers, of Yolann's small daughter.

Yolann bore her a month after I lost my son. She bore her alone in the anteroom, with no fuss or noise, and only called me to help her oil and dress the little one. At first I heard the infant's quavering cry; and started up, frightened and angry, thinking the cry came from my own tortured heart. Grief repressed will cry out, I knew it even then. The firmer the lips, the louder the heart will weep. "Now I'm hearing voices!" I thought, alarmed.

Then I heard Yolann's urgent whisper. "Dragamir, come!"

I caught up my gown in both hands and ran to the anteroom. Red-wrinkled, the baby squirmed on the bed. Yolann had spread rags on the bed, and these were blood-slimed, like the floor. Crouched by the bed, Yolann was biting the cord.

Swiftly, silently, we worked together to clean up the child and Yolann and the rags; and set the little one to nurse. "Do not watch," Yolann advised me. Her sisterly concern warmed my heart; but I watched. I observed, and engraved each detail of the scene upon my memory: the soft action of the rosy lips, the happy wave of the tiny hand, the satisfied slumber. At last Yolann slept with the infant on her arm. I stood and looked down on them, nestled together in bliss. I seared my heart with the sight, as a doctor sears a wound with hot iron. I could not spend my life grieving. I could not avoid the sight of natural joy.

When I had quieted my heart enough, I lifted the baby away to the soft bedded chest, lest the sleeping Yolann overlie her. She cuddled warm in my arms, soft and infinitely lovable; but my scarred, closed heart gave no sign. I smiled approval to myself as I laid her down and went in search of lazy Sophie. "Hot meat broth for the lady Yolann, and quick, before I kick you downstairs."

Yolann's daughter lived with us. No one came and took her away, no wolf devoured her. She was no princess, her religion did not matter. We raised her in our own way. She wore homespun and cut her teeth on unleavened bread. I laughed with Yolann when she took her first wobbling steps. I sat up with her when fever struck, laying wet cloths on her hot little face and plump wrists. Together we smiled at her first words; and spoke to her slowly, clearly, our own true speech.

The three of us lived alone. We spun the rough wool Yolann had smuggled in. We played knucklebones and cooked our own meals, which our stomachs welcomed in place of the heavy palace food. More and more the servants left us alone. Sophie hid from us. Our language and our outlandish ways drew a circle of avoidance around us.

Only the golden-haired toddler down the hall seemed drawn to us. When we met, or stood together on public occasions, I always felt his wondering stare upon me. I never returned it. I looked away—heavenward, left or right, anywhere but into those wide grey eyes like my mother's eyes. I wished to forget that this child and I were in any way connected. Sometimes I did forget.

"Yolann," I asked once, "do you think Draga will ever return for us?"

"No, sister." Yolann bit off her yarn. "Draga will never come within walls. But I think he may send us a messenger; one of our brothers, maybe." She wrapped up her skein and stared longingly into the fire.

Of desperate loneliness my plan was born. Once born, it grew quickly; unfolding more and more exciting new dimensions. "After all," I murmured to Yolann, "I think I may bear Wendz his second prince!"

She started. "You'll give in to him? Why, has your heart finally softened?"

I chuckled. "That would please you, sister?"

"Yes, it would. You have had revenge enough. This hardness does not become you."

"Then I had better warn you that my heart has *not* softened. No, this is a plan; a beautiful plan for a beautiful, final revenge." I felt my face burning with excitement. Yolann gave me a most curious look.

"So you will give your husband his will—"

"To destroy him!"

"Might I ask—"

"No." Imperious, I rejected my sister. "You pity my enemies. Knowing the plan, you might betray me."

"Never that."

I knew Yolann would never betray me. Nonetheless, I felt safer alone with my plan, hugging it to me.

On a hot summer night I spoke to Wendz as he lay exhausted beside me. Sickly sweat drenched the sheet under him. I pulled away to the far edge of the bed where a faint breeze dried his slime from my flesh.

I did not beg or plead. I shed no tear. Knowing I

111

held the whip hand I stated my terms firmly. "You need a son, Wendz."

"Why else . . ."

"Why else would you be here with me. Exactly. You need a substitute heir, in case your Christian heir chokes on a chicken bone."

"You speak harshly, Marya." In the dark, I felt Wendz turn toward me in wonder. "No one would think Wendceslas was your son!"

"He is not my son, Wendz, he is your son." I stated that fact dispassionately and dismissed it. There was no mending the past, but the future was yet in my hands. I began now to mould it. "Well, I have decided to bear you the son you want—but only if I may keep him. You must vow to me that I myself shall raise him in these rooms; I myself, and not your mother."

Wendz stirred, and heaved a sigh. "I thought you were barren. Now you speak of bearing, as though you could choose."

"I can choose, Wendz. I have closed my womb to you. I can open it."

"Bishop Niklas told me that," Wendz answered slowly. "He said you were a witch." He shifted his sore weight on the bed. "He said you thwarted me deliberately."

"So I did," I admitted cheerfully.

With an effort Wendz proclaimed, "No woman has any right to defy the will of God." The words were pompous, but the circumstances robbed them of dignity.

"Who talks of God's will? We are talking of *your* will, Wendz! I have denied you, and I can continue to deny you till I wear you out. What is the matter? What is this illness that saps you?"

"No doctor knows."

"Well, though I am no witch I can see that you are failing. Before you fail entirely you want a son. I will give you a son—but only when you swear to me, as I said."

Wendz tossed from side to side. With an angry sob he brought out, "Very well. I swear that you may keep your next child to yourself."

"That is not enough."

"What more do you want, in Heaven's name?"

"You will swear this in the chapel, before your god. Bishop Niklas himself will witness it."

Wendz ground his teeth. "Very well. Tomorrow."

I had no need to say more, but I was enjoying my triumph. "For my part, I swear to you that this child will never be baptized! I know you call me 'pagan' and 'savage.' If I choose I shall raise my son as a savage pagan, and no one shall interfere!"

A mighty groan burst from Wendz's cold lips. "My son will fall into hell! With this vow I doom my innocent child! Marya—"

"Do not call me by that name again." I rose on my elbow. "I am a daughter of Draga the savage; my name is Dragamir. From this night I answer to no other name."

From wet hair to naked feet Wendz shuddered. Yolann would have pitied him. I waited, impassive, for his surrender. For a while he trembled in the hot dark. His misery shook the bed. At last he whispered, "Very well, Dragamir." Smiling, I lay down.

At the chapel door Bishop Niklas scowled upon

us. "What good is this?" he thundered at Wendz, ignoring me. "You will have no Christian prince! You will have a pagan tribesman! Holy saints, would you beget a child to feed the fires of hell? And to no worldly purpose, either?"

"My promise is already given," Wendz confessed.

"In the dark, in bed!" Niklas' oily lips curled. "That promise need not bind you!"

Quietly I stood aside and watched the struggle. Folding my hands demurely, I awaited the outcome with more curiosity than I showed. My mind was made up. If Wendz would not vow, then I should have to find some other way. My plan was laid.

Fortunately, Wendz could be stubborn. He thrust out his chin. "I have given the woman my promise," he insisted, "and she has given me hers. We have a bargain. You need not approve, Bishop. You need only witness."

"After all," Ludmilla put in gently, "Wendceslas is the heir. This poor child we are discussing will never come near the high seat. Even if he does, Niklas, we will trust you to guide him."

"Ah yes," Wendz agreed quickly. "We know we can rely on you, Bishop."

Muttering, Bishop Niklas gave way. We entered the chapel, then, and stood in a semicircle before the small tabernacle that gleamed in the light of a single sanctuary lamp. The narrow window behind the altar was closed, but summer light stole in through a crack in the shutters and lit the soft smile of the wooden Marya in the corner. Over Ludmilla's shoulder the statue smiled slyly at me. She seemed to know a secret that she did not intend to share with me . . . yet.

Bishop Niklas turned his back on the altar and faced us. Scorn and disapproval vivid on his face, he gestured to Wendz. Wendz took my hand, and held it as he would hold a snake. Clearly, slowly, he spoke his vow. The next child I bore, daughter or son, was to be mine.

"There," Ludmilla whispered, "now it is done, Marya— I mean Dragamir. You must be satisfied now, and fulfill your part of the bargain."

"No fear," I promised boldly.

For two years I had denied the Goddess. Now I invoked Her. Yolann stole more chickens from the kitchen, and we sacrificed together openly, not bothering to hide the evidence. We prayed that I might bear a son; and I counted more on Yolann's prayer than on my own. She was in favor with the Goddess, Who might bear me some grudge.

"Your mother-in-law knew, last time," Yolann remembered.

"Yes, and she took her revenge! This time, let her know!"

I no longer feared Ludmilla, or the city king, or the bishop. I held the whip hand. I walked proudly in the palace, and freely in the city; and my heart felt as hard and brave as the face I showed the shocked world.

Barax had once shown me my coming beauty in a cracked fragment of mirror. Now I owned a mirror; a shining lake bordered with carved leaves and flowers. It faced the window; and a candle in a tall silver stand illumined it farther.

This mirror told me that my beauty was now fully come. Like a mature rose it bloomed toward me from the cool mirror; as a little village girl had once smiled at me from the depths of a well. The mirror reflected no anger, no bitter sorrow; no loss or betrayal. It showed me only the pink of herb-rubbed cheeks and lips, and the golden sparkle of sun-rippled hair.

At this time I was nineteen or twenty; arrow-straight and slender, except where my new burden swelled. I bound my hair with amber pins and a bright veil. Sky-blue the veil drifted softly about my head. I never wore white. My veils were blue, green or scarlet. Let old Ludmilla wear white!

My new gown was red and black, heavily embroidered. My wedding jewelry sparkled in the mirror-light, bracelets and necklaces softly jingling. I carried my head high, I stood proudly before the mirror. I smiled at myself, at the glow and glory of me. Pregnancy only enhanced my beauty. The Goddess blessed me with new beauty at Her own cost; I meant to pay Her in no coin. The child I carried was my tool, a weapon for my war. I felt no love for it. I meant never to feel love for it. It lived and grew within me as best it could, formed by the Goddess, helped by no thought or care of mine. I cared only that it should be a son; for only a son could carry my sword. A daughter I would smother before Yolann could interfere. I would pay that evil Goddess in no coin whatever!

I smiled again at my young and charming reflection, and swept out the door. Proudly I descended the stairs and left the palace. I refused, now, to be bound by palace custom. I marched through the streets at will, alone, or with Yolann; and she did not need to tell me that men gazed after me. I felt their looks.

One who noticed me in the street, in the palace, at the Christmas banquet table, was Bishop Niklas. I never glanced his way across that silver-set table without catching his admiring eye. His gaze was constantly upon me; a dark, assessing gaze, cold, for all its lust.

I could not fail to respond somehow to Niklas' assertive virility. I was starved for virility. As soon as I knew my purpose was accomplished I had informed Wendz that I no longer required his weary attentions. Gratefully he had withdrawn to his apartment to pray, cough and spit his nights away. Wendz had never been any kind of a lover; I knew that instinctively, and from Yolann's ecstatic accounts of her affairs. I was a ripe young woman now, and I had never known love. For all the satisfaction I had known, I might as well be a virgin. Bishop Niklas' lust reached out to me with invisible arms, and I responded. My heart thumped a little faster. I warmed, and wondered. . . .

But I knew what fate awaited unfaithful noble wives. Bitterly I imagined how glad Wendz would be to burn me in the square—after his son was born.

He sat hunched in the high seat, pretending to taste the Christmas pork, goose and hot breads. He rarely touched even the ancient wine. Under the golden circlet his hair was white, his face a mass of wrinkles. He looked older than Ludmilla.

Ludmilla, smiling around at the company over her goblet, was my true enemy. By this time I understood that the sick Wendz had only done her bidding when he deprived me of my child. He always obeyed his mother, and not only in domestic matters. I heard her voice in many of the laws he proclaimed. That sweet old lady, simpering behind her everlasting white veil, ruled the city. For long moments I forgot to eat, watching her with delicious, agonizing hate.

Ludmilla and I were locked in warfare. She thought herself victorious, no doubt; but my ally lay curled, waiting, within me. Hers regarded me lustfully across the shining linen and gleaming silver. Bishop Niklas was Ludmilla's friend and advisor, and certainly my foe. If I would still my pounding heart and somehow feed my newly realized hunger, I must look elsewhere.

Half-seriously, I scanned the company. Red-faced nobles guzzled, slurped wine, tossed greasy scraps to the waiting hounds. They would likely approach a woman with the same rude gusto. I was sure their attentions would not be worth a burning in the square! Several of the young servants and pages standing behind the diners were handsome, even desirable. Erect, clean-faced, they watched the feast as if from a noble, disinterested distance. Their eyes slid over me and away. They saw that I was young and beautiful, but they dared not look at me frankly. And strangely, I did not dare look long at them. Some innocent strength in them daunted me;

118

some gift of young freedom that I had lost, or missed entirely.

In the gallery the musicians began to play. This "Christmas" was one of the great Christian feasts, the birthday of the god, and no effort was spared to brighten it. Falling at the death of the year, it reminded me of the midwinter feasts of my village childhood.

The death of the year is—hopefully—the birth of the new year. The villagers waited breathlessly, as the year died, to see whether the sun would stop its southern journey; would stand still, and turn its face again in our direction. And when the sun did, indeed, stop and stand, the village went wild.

To this day I remember midwinter with caught breath, a gasp of childish delight. I remember the evergreen wreathes that defied the snowy winds. "We live!" the evergreens whispered. "Life may sleep, but never die." I remember feasting, fire and song, dancing and gifts. I never gave or got a gift, but luckier children sported new clothes and new toys, carved or sewn. We learned new games, too, for midwinter snatched all the grownups out of our world. Gravity, sobriety and weariness were banned; and only children played and romped through the village, many of them big children, misshapen by hard labor and many childbirths. Everyone gambled, everyone sang. And winter seemed to draw back, dismayed, before our cheer. Later came the storms and fearsome cold; later, when the evergreens had been safely burnt. They were never allowed to wilt.

The city folk, too, hung green wreathes on their

doors and gave each other gifts; one would think they had turned farmers for the day. They, too, feasted and sang. And even solemn Ludmilla ordered the tables decked in green, and musicians to play while roasted stuffed pigs were brought in whole, their mouths stopped with honeyed-apples. She insisted, however, that all this festivity had nothing to do with the travels of the sun. "The sun goes and comes by the will of God," she declared. Christmas was God's birthday upon earth.

Lutes plucked sweetness, drum and tabor tapped excitement. I looked down the long table, passing over greedy face after drunken face, and found myself gazing into familiar, beloved eyes.

Ruga, Draga's son, answered my look with eager eyes that smouldered like coals. All the fierce intelligence to which he could give no utterance blazed there. Around those fiery centers his face, as young as my own, was already a map of tribal and war scars. He hunched like Wendz, but not from weakness. His was the hunch of the stalker, the lyer-in-wait. Ugly, aged beyond our years, Ruga radiated strength and resolve, energy and purpose. Beside his shouting vigor, Bishop Niklas' virility whispered, and fell silent.

I gazed long upon my brother. And Ruga answered my look with admiration and understanding. I beckoned to the page behind my chair. He leaned to listen, then skipped around the table to Ruga. His eyes on mine, Ruga listened to the boy; and nodded.

At midnight we met at my hearth. From the halls below sounded laughter, drums and pipes. Nobles and attendants still danced, though the king had long since dragged himself off to bed, and Ludmilla was by now at prayer in the chapel.

The three of us sat close by the fire. I held Yolann's hand and we feasted our eyes upon our brother's ugly face, which in the flickering soft light resembled Draga's. My heart yearned across the snowy plains to the camp where Draga now slept in his carpeted tent, surrounded by dung fires and stomping ponies. "Why did he send you?" I asked Ruga. "Did he send a message? Did he want to know about us?"

Ruga had a surprise for me. I expected a dumb-show, a puzzle of gestures; and I was sharpening my wits to interpret it. Instead, Ruga pulled from his wallet a small tablet and coal, and slowly wrote his share of the talk.

Draga had sent him with Sorbal to spy out the city, and learn something of its ways. The most useful of its ways was this art of letters; Ruga had quickly seen the virtue of this silent communication, writing. He had learned it from a friendly monk with all the speed of necessity, and now he talked to me freely, if slowly. "I never thought that game might prove *useful!*" Yolann remarked enviously. For I was nodding and smiling at Ruga's words, which to her looked like magical symbols.

"Has Draga a plan?" I asked Ruga.

"Plan for what?"

"Why, for taking over the city!"

No—Draga found his present friendly in-law status hugely satisfactory. He collected a trade tax from all convoys within a large area surrounding the city. With this wealth he had expanded his cavalry, hiring mercenaries—men not related to him by blood or fiction, men not even of his race. And with these forces at his command he was virtual chief of the hundred small tribes with whom he had used to spar. Draga was content, replete, though Ruga assured me that he had not grown soft. He rode as hard and long as before. He ate unleavened bread and mutton, he drank only mead. He looked younger than Wendz, who was actually younger than he.

I told my brother, "Well, I have a plan." He leaned toward me, thrusting his scarred face into ember-light. "I have told no one yet," I went on slowly, "not even Yolann, here; and I have no one else to tell, Earth Mother witness!"

Ruga nodded. His glistening gaze burned my face.

"Brother, you see that I am with child. If prayers and sacrifice mean anything, this child will be a son. If a king's vow means anything, this son will be a tribesman, unChristian; and he will rule the city in his father's place."

Ruga whipped up his slate and scrawled a question.

"You are right," I told him. "Wendceslas is the heir. Wendceslas will meet with an accident."

This was my plan, long considered, dreamed over, thought over, until it no longer shocked me. Once I had shuddered at the thought of an accident to Wendceslas—as though he were my child. Then, I had still confused the child who lived down the hall with my own baby son, whom the wolf-bitch seized. But later I remembered, and reminded myself, that the grey-eyed boy for whom I planned an accident was not my son, he was Wendz's son, Ludmilla's treasure. To me, he was no more than an obstacle.

Though I no longer shocked myself, I was amused to see shock work upon the others. Hunched to the fire, Ruga stared at me. Yolann drew her hand sharply out of mine and rubbed it against her skirt. The embers hissed in the following silence.

Ruga leaned back out of the light. Now I could not see his face, but I sensed from him a swiftly growing appreciation. Yolann rose and went to look at her sleeping child. When she returned she sat nervously, biting her hair.

"Ruga," I said at last, "my son will need guidance, more teaching than I can give him. You see how I am confined here, like a hobbled mare."

Promptly Ruga scrawled, "Trust me."

"And when my plan comes ripe, you will do what I cannot do alone?"

He underlined his answer.

"And you will rally Draga's forces for my son?"

Another underline, and, "Sorbal."

Long after the Christmas merriment downstairs had mumbled into silence, Ruga left us. Ruga never smiled, but he embraced us both, striking our shoulders with hard, hurtful hands—blows that he considered love-taps. We did not complain. We stood together in the dying hearth-warmth, newly conscious of our homesick sisterhood. Stalking away,

Ruga took with him the nostalgic smell of horse-sweat, grease and leather; a wild breath of the plains.

On a soft spring night I woke shivering, and felt my Enemy's approach. This time I did not fear Her. I lay quietly looking into the warm dark and let Her wrench and wring me. My teas were brewed, my sacrifices burnt. The ax under my bed was sharp. True, all the palace doors were shut; but what is a closed door to the Goddess? She smashes it with a breath!

I thought She would not harm me at this time, while we were allied in purpose. She did not know my plan! In the course of nature we would be allied for months to come; and I would slip easily, gradually, back into Her service. So thought my Enemy.

Toward the end I longed mightily to call Yolann. I yearned for a candle, for a warm, firm hand in mine. I bit my tongue. I must do this alone in the dark, face to face with the Enemy; for the child now slowly bursting me might be a daughter; useless to me, an incarnation for my Enemy. I was prepared for that. I had kicked away the blankets, but not the pillow; that I kept close at hand. Soft and thick, a goose-feather pillow, it could stop even a helpless adult's breath in moments.

Soft spring light filled the room when the child squalled. I twisted around to look at it. I had my son! I tossed the pillow away and gathered up the infant.

Sand could have run once through an hourglass while I tended my son. It was our first and last intimacy. I bit the cord. I oiled the soft, squirming body and bundled it in warm wool. I hesitated to bring the rose-pink lips to my breast, for I knew that this was the ultimate trap the Goddess set for women. Even cruel Ludmilla had not let me nurse the infant I was not to keep.

But then, was I never to know a moment's joy? Now was my chance; now, while Yolann slept, while the palace and the city slept. I drew the infant to me. He gaped at me like a caught fish, blinking and working his mouth. "Come now," I told him gently, "the world is not so bad! I will take care of you. I will—" I stopped in time. I must not promise to love him! "I will feed you, at least this once."

The touch of his lips was instant sweetness. He sucked strongly, waving his hands as I had seen Yolann's daughter do. Bitterly I had envied Yolann's delights! Now, while the rising sun tinted stone walls pink, I enjoyed my own. I sank into joy as into sleep. I wallowed in sweetness like a sow in a marsh. My Enemy smiled, thinking me trapped.

But She smiled too soon. My milk flowed warm for the baby, but not my love. That I witheld. Ambition, not love, stirred me. "We will do well together," I promised my child. "You will be city king, Boleslav, and I your advisor. We will rule together."

Boleslav slept. Soft and warm he lay on my arm while his first day brightened. I smiled at his huge, closed eyes. I fondled his feet, whose toes were small as my fingernails. His womb-soft skin held a coppery tint which I thought would darken as he grew. His hair curled wetly, thick and black.

The innocent creature was content to sleep, to breathe, to live. But I dreamed fantasies, the stories men tell each other. Over and over I whispered, "Boleslav, you will be city king!" I saw him, grown dark and tall, dispense justice from his father's high seat. I saw him ride the plains, galloping a war pony black as his plume.

The first hammer rang from the cathedral. The first bird to sing in the morning is soon answered by others; even so, this hammer was shortly joined by another, and another; while a chisel kept time among them. "Hear that?" I asked my sleeping son. He did not. He lay limp, breathing damp warmth against my ear. "That is the voice of your foe," I told him, "yours and mine. He builds and grows and spreads himself. He thinks he will conquer. But we will conquer, you and I."

The harsh-ringing hammers wakened my dreaming soul. If I cuddled this child longer I would love him, and love would weaken me, blunt my purpose. I caressed the tiny toes one last time and lifted my hand away. I wrapped up the sleeper like a bundle, and shouted for Yolann.

She ran in; at sight of the child her heavy face brightened. "But you should have called sooner!" she scolded. "It might have come to harm! What is it, sister, what is it?"

"It is a son. I call him Boleslav."

"What kind of name is that?"

"A name to remind him of his blood ancestors. One day I may tell him who they are." But not till he had served Draga as a royal grandson should! "Yolann, take him away to the cradle."

"That's all right Dragamir, you can hold him till I—"

"Take him now."

She leaned over us. "Did you count his fingers and toes?"

"I did."

"And he's all there?"

I smiled. All the health and vigor of the next city king was wrapped up in that bundle! Otherwise I would have wrung the infant's neck.

Yolann shook her head at me. "You have turned strange, Dragamir. I do not much like you this way." Tenderly she lifted Boleslav from my arm.

Her little daughter leaned in the doorway, sucking her thumb. Yolann clucked to her, "Come see the precious, come look at the plump partridge!" Some such drivel. The little girl followed her to the cradle. Still sucking her thumb she leaned over to inspect Boleslav. The expression on her small face was strange; an amusing mixture of surprise and disapproval. That, I decided, would be my own attitude to Boleslav from this hour; surprise that my Enemy had worked so well for me, and cold disapproval of any weakness that might dampen my purpose. I had borne Boleslav to be a tool, a weapon in my war. He would be that to me, and nothing more.

Yolann brought clean sheets, water, a comb. Sitting up, I said, "I think I have nice breasts."

"Lovely! Your son will never know hunger."

"I do not wish them pulled out of shape."

She laughed. "We mothers don't worry long about that!"

I said, "Yolann, Boleslav must have a wet-nurse."

127

In the act of spreading the new sheet over me, Yolann froze. From under her raised arm she stared at me, open-mouthed, while the sheet sank, crumpled, upon me. At last she bent to smooth it, shaking her head as though troubled by some evil vision. She said, "That was not you speaking, sister."

"Yes, it was. Boleslav must have a wet-nurse. You know I cannot soften, Yolann, I have a plan! If you won't help me find a nurse I'll tell Sophie."

"You mean that? You would do that?"

"I would, because I must."

"We don't want strangers here, city folk. If you are truly that hard-hearted I'll find you one of our own kind. But Dragamir, what is the matter? What do you fear?"

I laughed harshly. "This is not fear, sister, this is strategy!"

Strategy it was, and good strategy. I laughed in the Goddess' astonished face. I tossed back to Her the ball and chain She had hidden so slyly under the guise of sweetness and joy. I reminded Her, "I have vowed never to serve You again!"

But it was also fear. I had declared war on love, and now I feared nothing so much as love.

I told Boleslav, "Wendceslas is a sissy."

Boleslav wished to cross the garden and play Pagans and Martyrs with Wendceslas. From the shadow of Ludmilla's rosevine Wendceslas watched us anxiously. He must be a lonely child, I thought, to wish to play with one three years younger!

"He says he'll be the pagans," Boleslav pleaded. "He says I can be the martyrs because—"

I said firmly, "Wendceslas wouldn't know how to be the pagans! He can't aim a lance or an arrow." From across the garden the child's gray stare prickled my skin. He watched me, as always, with yearning. He knew that I was his mother, and that I was not to be approached. I could easily imagine Ludmilla's warnings: "Your mother is a wicked woman, dear; she is God's enemy. Do not speak to her. If she speaks to you, be polite. Then run." But there was no danger of my speaking to Wendceslas. He and his god were safe from me . . . for now.

"Anyhow," I said to Boleslav, "Wendceslas must stay in the southern garden, and you must stay in the northern garden, and that's the end of it. Look, here comes Uncle Ruga and the pony!"

Just in time, Ruga led a small spotted pony into the garden. Boleslav gasped a delighted "Oooo!" and forgot all about Pagans and Martyrs. Cautiously he approached the pony. Never before had he come so close to shifting hoofs or a suddenly swishing tail. Ruga beckoned him close. Taking Boleslav's small hand in his, he laid it along the pony's neck, then drew it down to pat the moist nose. The pony drooped, submissively. Ruga's patience surprised me. Well he knew how to introduce child and beast! He drew a wilted carrot from his wallet and offered it to the pony. Boleslav watched, entranced; and when Ruga held his fingers flat and laid another carrot on his palm he hardly winced. For a while Ruga helped him coddle the pony; then he stepped away and left them alone, face to face together.

I shot a quick glance across the garden. Pale Wendceslas was watching enviously.

"When will Boleslav ride?" I asked Ruga. His fingers sketched "Tomorrow."

While Boleslav gave the pony the last carrots I examined it. I was pleased to find it elderly, half-blind and pathetically docile. It had probably been hauling lumber till that morning. I said to Ruga, "I half-expected you to bring us a war pony!"

Ruga grinned. He brought out his slate and scrawled, "I have more faces than you know." That was true enough. I was still learning to appreciate Ruga's diverse talents. He was chief and strategist, warrior and scribe; and sly, kindly tutor to a boy of five.

At five, Boleslav was a bright, small warrior. Daily he had lessons with Ruga, or with me. Ruga gave me a small bow and made Boleslav a smaller one; and every day we shot at targets. Ruga taught the child to hurl a light lance, to fast, to sleep happily where he found himself; and I taught him the art of letters.

I introduced this rare art very early, so that Boleslav could communicate with Ruga. Later, it became surprisingly useful. We found that we could leave each other notes, write ourselves lists; when Ruga traveled he wrote us letters. (Often, of course, he arrived home before his letters did.) "I marvel," I said to Yolann, "that princes are not usually taught to write!" Yolann sighed. She had tried to learn with Boleslav; but it is hard to learn a new thing when one is mature, well past twenty.

"Wendceslas can read," Boleslav said.

"I am sure he can." Naturally. Ludmilla wished him to read the Lives of the Saints and the Holy Book. "But how do you come to know that?"

"Oh—I—well—" Boleslav had opened his mouth too wide, as he often did. By nature he was friendly and outgoing; caution came hard to him. Amused, I watched him cast about for a way out of his difficulty. He did not know how to lie. "Well," he confessed at last, "Wendceslas read me a story."

I fixed him with a cold eye. "I have told you to leave Wendceslas strictly alone," I reminded him. "I do not want you in his half of the garden, ever. I do not want you talking to him. I do not want you *looking* at him. Is that clearly understood?"

Boleslav sighed. "Yes, Mother."

"I am speaking to you seriously." I narrowed my eyes and tapped an angry-seeming foot. "What do you say?"

Boleslav hung his head. "Yes, lady."

We kept wide distances. The Christian family walked in the southern half of the garden, in the chapel, and in Ludmilla's apartments. Their rooms overlooked the garden; on hot summer nights, sweet, flower-scented air flowed through their windows.

We pagans lived in the northern garden, and in my rooms. Our windows over looked the square; we spun and knitted to the rhythm of hammer and chisel from the cathedral. The cathedral grew steadily under our noses; a poisonous mushroom, a noisy insult. Besides the endless clamor of building we heard every office the monks sang, every bell, every hymn. We wasted no opportunity to point out the

131

follies of the religion to our children, and I smiled when their sleep was broken by Christian bells and hammers. This taught them no love of religion!

In spite of the racket we were a happy family. Ruga strode in and out, bringing young tribesmen to meet Boleslav, or young sons of pagan merchants, eager for adventure. Sorbal brought heartening messages from Draga, ardently awaited. Sorbal haunted his brother like a pale shadow; standing alone he had his own vitality, but beside Ruga he shrank beyond notice.

Simply to escape from me, Sophie had got herself baptized; and then, a free woman, had taken service elsewhere in the palace. She was not replaced. So we were free to live in our own style. We slept on floor mats, and cooked mutton and flat bread. We spun and wove the coarse wool that Ruga smuggled in. Boleslav and his cousins kept the rooms lively. Always there was noise, cheerful or angry; loud games or quarrels. During those fifteen years (which later seemed to have been such golden years!) Yolann bore five daughters.

Yolann possessed the same art that I possessed, the blessed gift of Barax. She could have lain with every rich man in the city and piled up treasure without price or pain. But Yolann loved children. She was happiest nursing an infant at the hearth, or in the sun-washed garden. She used her art to ensure healthy children. She chose the fathers carefully, with an eye to vigor and good nature. She chose the birth times after consultation with astrologers. Her riches piled high, she bought new chests to hold them; and her daughters flourished like wildflowers.

Once I asked her, "Why do these city men desire you?" For by city standards Yolann was indeed ugly.

She laughed. "No problem. Sometimes a man needs a homely woman." I mused on that awhile. It might well be so. Yolann might bring a man a breath of plains wind, a scent of earth, that his slender, silken lady could not match.

The Christians down the hall were a quiet lot. Their household consisted of an elderly lady, an invalid, and a lonely boy. From the corner of my eye I watched Wendceslas grow tall and stocky. Broad in his flimsy, embroidered silks, he shuffled about the halls like a young bear. Sometimes, without thought, my heart would still lift at sight of his clumsy strength. How proud I could have been of such a son! But this one was not mine.

He was an intelligent cub, too. What Boleslav had let slip was true enough, he could read well at an early age. I often glimpsed him reading in the garden, or at a narrow window. Passing that way later, I might glance idly at the abandoned book; a tale of martyrdom, most like, or a sermon, or the Holy Book itself. Passing on, I might nod to myself. I piled information as Yolann piled treasure. It is wise to know the enemy.

In the way of manly arts, Wendceslas learned precious little. He fell off every horse he tried to mount. His arrow rarely hit the outside edge of the target. I made sure to point this out Boleslav, and we spent many happy hours laughing together in an upstairs window as Wendceslas sweated below. But his young mind was acute and well trained. Years

133

before his father died he was sitting in conference with his mother and Niklas, who now ruled the city.

Wendz probably loved his scholarly son, and he watched him with proud eyes. But I thought he was probably glad of his second son too, his extra heir; though he kept apart and away from him, even as I kept apart and away from Wendceslas.

Visibly, month by month, Wendz weakened. Reclining on a bed in the summer garden, shivering under a light blanket, he would cough and spit like a farmer, then doze like an old man. Spinning one morning at my end of the garden, I glanced across and noticed Wendz lying uncovered. The blanket had slipped to the ground. Wendz leaned over and plucked at the blanket, but he lacked the strength to pull it up. He rose on an elbow then, to call for help; but coughed instead. Glancing hopefully around, he caught sight of me. I saw hope die in his eyes. Across the garden I felt his despair.

Slowly I laid down my spinning, rose, and walked slowly across the barrier our custom had created. Crossing the southern garden I came to Ludmilla's rosevines, now past their bloom. The faded flowers looked no sadder than Wendz. Now I stood at his side.

Wendz watched me come every slow step of the way. His sorrowful eyes held mine. He said nothing. I do not think he could speak without choking on the phlegm I saw dribbling into his beard. He only watched me sadly, probably wondering if I came to help, or to gloat.

I had come to gloat. I had wished to look closely at his misery, while remembering his sins. Night

134

after brutal night this invalid had tormented me with his inept disgust. This invalid, commanded by his mother, had taken my newborn child away from me. This invalid . . .

I stooped and lifted the blanket. I shook the leaves and sticks from it and laid it softly over Wendz's trembling form. He struggled to thank me. In the end he managed a smile; and I fear that I smiled, myself, before I turned away. I was heartily ashamed of this softness, and hoped no one had witnessed it; but the helpless defeat in the man's eyes had called to someone within me, someone I no longer admitted to be part of me. She answered Wendz without my consent; and then she excused herself to me thus: "That man is not the true enemy."

"True," I told her silently, stalking back across the garden barrier, "but when we meet the true enemy, what will you do then?"

"Then I will be good," she promised. "I will hide myself away."

"Good. Let me see no hint of you, then!"

The following winter the high seat stood empty. Ludmilla gave judgment from a low chair placed beside it. Resting her arm on an arm of the high seat sometimes she patted it; as though it were her son's arm. Finding only polished wood under her fingers she would start, and turn to murmur with Bishop Niklas, who leaned over the back of the high seat. They would confer a moment, and Ludmilla would turn back to the assembly and pronounce "her" judgment in a clear, soft voice.

Spring returned to us, but Wendz did not. Now

doctors paced in and out of his rooms. Pausing outside I heard retching, the swift pad of hurrying feet, the burble of medicinal wines. I met an old priest scurrying up and down stairs; a gentle man whose very wrinkles shone with Christian Charity; that lovely virtue, rarer than gold. I was glad to see this man attending Wendz. It was time, I thought; Wendz deserved, and needed, a better confessor than the hypocrite. Then I caught myself. "Why do you care, Dragamir?" Carefully I answered, "At least Niklas does not whisper daily in the king's ear." Hah! Niklas had no need of the king's ear; he had Ludmilla's.

Ludmilla drifted sadly from high seat to sickroom. I noted with pleasure the fingerprints of pain on her papery old face. "You see, wolf-bitch," I chortled silently, "It is no easy thing to lose a son!" I hoped she remembered. I hoped she thought often, now, of how she had torn my son from me. Sometimes I stood in her way, forcing her to notice me and remember. At the last moment I would step aside; drawing my gown close lest it brush her. I feared the taint of grief. I feared the touch of any feeling, any emotion, for emotion is a strong weapon of the Goddess. I went always armed against my Enemy, and against all Her works.

Once after Wendz had closed his door, Bishop Niklas approached me. For years he had watched me, leering across the square, over the banquet table—even from the head of sacred processions. Then, on a fine summer evening, he came to me as I sat alone in the garden.

I heard a step behind my bench, a rustle of robes.

Turning, I found Bishop Niklas lowering his bulk to the bench beside me. He grinned at my amazement, a slow, dark grin. "Ludmilla will see us from her window," I said quickly. "As you know, her rooms overlook this garden."

"It matters little," he replied in his deep, deliberate voice. "She will believe I am here to convert you. See, I have brought something to aid that illusion." He produced from his robes a very large prayerbook, which he laid across my knees. His swarthy hand lingered beside the book.

I moved as far away as the bench would allow. Pride forbade that I should flee him like a timid maiden, yet the smell of him—incense and sweat—both sickened and drew me. I was constantly tormented by my brother's virile presence; I lived like a nun, and I feared myself, lost in the mists of Niklas' lust.

He hitched nearer along the bench. "Come, you have read my looks, lady, and I have read yours." He turned a page of the prayer book, and squeezed my knee.

I pushed the book. It fell at our feet, and Niklas' exploring hand appeared, revealed to the world. He snatched it away, scowling, and shot a glance upward at Ludmilla's window. The window stared blankly back. No white veil shimmered in its dusk.

"Why play this game? You are as eager as I. Do you not feel the blush that brightens your face? Look, you are pinker than yonder rose!" Niklas laughed, and bent to retrieve the fallen book. "Now let me show you this evensong; *our* evensong."

I pushed the book back and faced him frankly. "You are right. I am eager."

"And waiting for me!"

"No."

His bushy eyebrows rose. "Waiting for whom, then?"

"Bishop, I wait for no man." Angrily but quietly, I told him, "You and I are enemies. You know quite well that we are at war."

He laughed; good-natured, pushing back his gray curls, he laughed. " 'War' is a rather grandiose term for it, lady. I grant you, we have not been friends. But that may come. In the meantime, do you think it wise to rattle your sabre at me? If we were indeed 'at war,' who do you think would win?" I swallowed my indignation. I knew I was blushing furiously. Niklas leaned forward till his stomach pressed his knees. Sweat darkened his glossy cheeks. "You would do better to placate such an enemy as I. Now, this evensong—"

"Niklas, listen. I am not one of your city women. You cannot browbeat me, or buy me."

"You are not human?"

"I am . . ." I drew myself up, " . . . a princess of the horse folk."

Niklas sniggered. "Between ourselves, lady—between you and me, eh, and no eavesdropper—I never knew the horse folk acknowledged princesses!"

Even angry and stirred as I was, I had to smile. Niklas and I were much alike; had we not been bitter foes we might have been friends. I said "Niklas, I have taken a vow. I shall always live for myself alone; never again will I risk bearing a child."

Niklas started, as if greatly surprised. "Risk? What risk? You would take no risk with me, you are a witch!"

"What?"

"Certainly, everyone knows that. The whole city talks of your science. It is well known that you open your womb, or close it, at your will." Slowly he smiled, an ingratiating smile. "My love presents you with no threat whatever. Lady, I offer you what you yourself desire . . . and peace. Maybe friendship, eh?" Smiling, he studied me. Calmly the summer evening blessed the garden around us. Birds sang in the bushes. Kind shadows dappled Niklas' heavy, wistful face. Almost, on that golden evening, I might have considered his offer of peace. My lonely soul cried out for human contact. Niklas' lustful aroma misted my brain. The affair he proposed would be quick and discreet, and would leave no scars. Nor could Niklas seek to trap me, try as he might; for he would trap himself. Had we sat longer, silent, in the resounding birdsong, I might have weakened.

But Niklas moved too soon. He opened the prayer-book once more across my lap; and I looked down into the sweet, maternal face of the Holy Marya.

My enemy's arm crept about my shoulders. The touch of a serpent would have been more welcome. This soft voice now murmuring darkly in my ear had once advised Wendz, "Safeguard your Christian heir. The pagan woman must not raise him in her evil ways." All that had followed—the division of the household, the barrier of silence, the breaking and hardening of my heart—all this was the doing of the fat lecher now licking my ear.

I leaped up. "I will learn no evensong, no hymn or prayer from you!" If Ludmilla sat near her window she certainly heard my cry. "And do not come to me again like this! I warn you, Bishop, I will . . . I bite!" And picking up my gown I fled from Bishop Niklas, and from the dusky garden.

But I had not lied to Niklas. Truly, I took no chances. Though my husband sickened and Ruga's stirring presence goaded me unbearably, I lived aloof, pure as any Christian saint. There was always the matter of the fire to consider; I knew myself watched. One move, and my enemies would have me chained to a stake in the square. But the danger I had mentioned to Niklas was closer, more real. Arts or no arts, charms or no charms, the Goddess is powerful. I strongly suspected that Yolann's fourth child arrived unplanned. And another child might drag me back into the Goddess' world of feeling. I knew that children are delicate treasures, and death lies in wait; yet I never doubted that Boleslav would live and grow, and fulfill my purpose.

At twelve, he was as strong and skillful as many a young man of sixteen. He dearly loved sports, especially hunting and archery. Much of his time, now, was spent out of the city walls in the company of Ruga and his young tribesmen. "Draga will love him," Ruga remarked on his slate. "Yes," I agreed, "you have made Boleslav a worthy grandson for Draga."

Secretly, I was not sure. Boleslav was strong, vigorous and hearty; but there was a softness in him. Sometimes he actually wept, not for his own hurts, but for the sufferings of others. He wept when he heard Ruga ridiculed. He wept when Yolann's fourth baby died. "Babies die," I scolded him. "Let Yolann weep. You go ride, let the wind clean your face. Ugh, Boleslav! You cry like a girl!"

With this strange softness, he was biddable. Like his father, he lent a willing ear to advice. This weakness I encouraged; for I meant to whisper in that willing ear when Boleslav ruled the city. Like Ludmilla I would dissemble, pretending innocence and sweet domesticity, and ruling the city with a whisper. And no bishop would rule me! Often I sat smiling, thinking how different life would be then for all in the city, from high seat to dung hill!

I planned it all with Ruga on winter nights while the palace slept. Yolann sat with us, drowsy and silent. She never cared for these fictions of power; these stories men tell each other. To Yolann the only real value was life itself.

Boleslav was not included in these sessions. Like the rest of the palace he slept soundly through our whisperings. He was too open, too friendly to be trusted with secrets; and he sometimes strayed beyond our group. We trained Boleslav as hunters train a hound puppy. The dog knows nothing of its purpose, no one consults with it about its destiny. It is simply raised and trained for the hunters' use. Even so, like a great glossy hound our Boleslav ran and played and slept near the hearth, and never dreamed of the great hunt planned for the morrow.

* * *

On a frigid night in the fifteenth winter Yolann opened her door to a timid knock. Sophie stood there, shivering with cold, and with fear of us dangerous folk. Yolann brought her to me, where I sat mending at the hearth. "The king," Sophie managed to whisper, "he's dying."

My needle faltered. Hard upon Wendz's death would come my rebirth; and I felt strangely unprepared. Also, a slight melancholy moved in me. Too mild to be called sadness, it was a recognition that a long testing had come to an end; and I could never now make peace with that other lonely soul.

I sewed on. "The king has been dying for fifteen years."

"He . . . he . . . he calls for the prince."

At that I looked up. "*This* prince?"

"Prince Boleslav."

So Wendz had remembered his abandoned son. Hiding my surprise, I nodded toward Boleslav's bed. "He sleeps behind that curtain. Rouse him."

"Lady. . . ." Poor Sophie struggled for speech. Coldly, I watched her. "The king . . . calls for . . . you."

"Fool, you are mistaken."

"No mistake." The frightened voice trailed off. The stupid eyes entreated. I considered. I would like to hear what Wendz might say to Boleslav. And even if Sophie were indeed mistaken, there was little chance of an angry, humiliating scene at his Christian deathbed! I folded up my mending.

Wendz reclined almost upright against stiff pillows. A harness held his ribs up to ease his harsh breathing. In the soft candlelight his white face appeared shrunken, his nose sharpened, the lips cracked. His skeletal hands lay limp upon the quilt, and one of them was covered by Ludmilla's hand. She sat by his head, dry-eyed and erect. With surprise and grudging admiration I observed her composure. If Wendz was at last going to Heaven, she was willing to see him go. At the foot of the bed Wendceslas knelt, his face hidden in his folded hands. The holy man, Wendz's confessor, presided at the bedside like a kindly angel of death.

Entering, we passed Bishop Niklas leaving. He had given Wendz the Sacrament, and still carried the patten in his thick hands. Candlelight glanced across the golden surface. Out in the hall the servants knelt, though the patten was empty, and a chorus of monks raised mournful melody.

· I pushed Boleslav in ahead of me and closed the door. In silence we came to the bed, walking respectfully; for we could feel the presence of death. Tears slid down Boleslav's cheeks. He hardly knew Wendz, but the sight of suffering unnerved him. Ashamed, I looked away.

Wendz cracked open his eyes and croaked, "Come to me . . . Son." Boleslav knelt by the bed. "Take . . . my hand." Boleslav grabbed the king's hand with the impulsive, passionate strength of youth. I heard bones crack; but the dying man never winced.

Wendz studied his unknown son. Dimly his glazing eyes wandered over Boleslav's good-natured,

143

bronze face. Maybe he saw the tears. He smiled. "Good lad," he whispered. "We will be friends . . . hereafter. My son; I regret. Regret."

Wendz gasped. Candles spluttered. Boleslav's tears dropped on the transparent hand he held. Wendz whispered, "Marya."

I thought he prayed. Again he drew pained breath to whisper, "Marya." Ludmilla frowned at me. Wendceslas raised a tear-slimed face from his hands to look at me imploringly. Startled, I understood: Wendz was calling me.

Death stood there in the room. Death watched me from the gentle eyes of the old confessor. Not even I could maintain proud anger in the face of this death. I bent to Wendz and answered, "This is Marya; I am here."

Wendz gazed up at me, unseeing. His eyes were glazed. He barely mumbled, "Forgive."

He asked too much. The comforting answer lumped in my throat. Bitterly I thought of all I was being asked to forgive; my betrayed youth, my stolen child, myself, what I had become. I could find no answer.

Wendz's eyes slid shut. Once more, with extreme difficulty, he murmured, "Forgive." I felt Ludmilla's frown; the quiet gaze of the confessor, the earnest gaze of the young prince. Boleslav touched my sleeve.

Within the hour Wendz would die. Then for me a new life would begin. This was the beginning of victory for me; of glory and freedom. What difference would a word make to me?

It was not Ludmilla, asking forgiveness. That I

could never have granted! I knew who were my enemies. I knew that the dying man had been their tool.

I sighed. I fetched a deep breath, harsh as Wendz's own. And I let that foreign woman who still lived in me answer Wendz for me. She said "Wendz, I forgive you."

Wendz smiled. Boleslav seized my hand and squeezed hard, boyishly pleased. The confessor smiled at me gravely, and Wendceslas shot me a grateful look before wiping his face on the quilt.

Ludmilla whispered harshly, "Please go now. He may rest."

"I am glad, Mother!" Boleslav exclaimed as we entered our apartment. "I feared you would make no answer. I was so afraid you could not forgive, and he was pitiful! Uncle Ruga, do you know the king is dying?"

Ruga squatted by the hearth warming his hands. Half-turning, he nodded to Boleslav, and shot me a pregnant glance.

"I sent for him," Yolann explained.

Ruga had no need to produce his slate, nor to resort to finger-talk. He spoke clearly in my mind: "It is time," he said, "Unleash the hound."

I turned to Boleslav. "Son," I said firmly, "sit down."

Boleslav began to answer excitedly; but my eyes and the silent regard of the others quelled him. He sat down. I sat between him and Ruga, and Yolann hovered. Even now, at this high moment, the culmination of fifteen years of work and planning, half her attention was bent upon her newborn in the cradle at our backs.

"Boleslav," I began, "we have never told you. I do not think you guessed it, either. But you must have suspected that your uncle did not train and teach you all these years for nothing! Believe me, he did not. He had a lofty purpose. We have all three had a lofty purpose."

Boleslav's mouth slackened. His dark eyes opened wide, innocent and startled. Their astonished gaze touched a wound deep within me, a wound I had thought long healed and forgotten. Very vividly I saw myself, a girl of about fifteen, listening to Draga outline my glorious future. "You are a princess," he told me, laughing. "Know what that means?" Soon enough I learned what it meant!

"Boleslav," I went on more gently, "you are to be city king."

Boleslav shook his head. Confidently he corrected me. "No I'm not. That is Wendceslas' fate— you know that, Mother."

"I know that is Ludmilla's and Niklas' intention. Our intention opposes theirs. Ruga has taught you, and I have raised you, to be city king. We believe that you, who are a true grandson of Draga, will make a better city king."

Mildly sympathetic, I watched Boleslav's reactions sweep broadly across his honest face. Blank astonishment was followed by pride. "I, a grandson of Draga! I, a better city king! Aha!" But pride in its turn gave way to doubt.

Ruga scribbled Boleslav a note. He glanced at it, and his bronze face turned gray. "But why would the tribesmen gather for *me*?" he asked, quavering. "They do not know me. To them, I'm just a boy!"

"They know Ruga," I reminded him. "They know Sorbal. And they have waited long for this night. Ruga has only to send a message."

Ruga signaled, "It is sent."

Boleslav cried, "You should have told me!"

Frankly, I asked, "Would you have kept the secret?"

"I don't know," he admitted. "I don't know, but. . . ."

"We thought best not to tell you till the time came."

"Well, let me ask this: If I become city king, what becomes of Wendceslas?"

Ruga's brisk fingers replied.

Boleslav went from gray to white. "But Wendceslas has never harmed me!" Indeed, we had worked hard to keep the lads apart. Without our constant watchfulness they might have been close friends.

I soothed Boleslav. "Perhaps it need not come to that. Wendceslas is not like you, my son, hardened and trained for action. He may very well fly to the monasteary at the first sound of battle. Then, you can leave him there."

Boleslav looked at me suspiciously. My glossy young hound was learning fast! I asked him, "When have I lied to you?" I asked it freely, without dread. I had never lied to Boleslav. Always till this night he had trusted me with good reason.

"You have never lied to me, Mother," he conceded slowly, "except by not telling me this."

"Well, now that you know, I hope to be very proud of you! All your life I have waited to see you ride a war pony into battle!" I went on to describe the glory, honor, and power that would be his; and as I talked I watched the dusk creep slowly back into his cheeks. His eyes brightened. "You see," I pointed out, "already it does not seem so strange to you! You are a prince, Boleslav. You have always known that you might be city king; and you are well trained for it." Boleslav was beginning to believe me. I saw him beginning to imagine himself city king, free and powerful, able to reward friends and command service.

Ruga wrote a note. Very reluctantly, Boleslav nodded. "If I have to," he said. "If I have no choice. But if he flies to the monastery I will not pursue him there." Ruga scowled. I signaled him. The matter of Wendceslas could wait. Deceit is the norm in government, and a young king might well be deceived for his own good by his trusted advisors. Meanwhile I wished no cloud upon Boleslav's growing excitement.

The next morning I stilled my own growing excitement, and went quietly, decorously, to view my dead husband in the cathedral. Breathless and flat, Wendz lay in the rich, ornate coffin ordered months before, lit by the steady flames of a hundred tall white candles. Whiter than the candles, his sharp face was quiet, now, unmarred by pain. The deep scars of fifteen years of illness hung slack in his cheeks, mercifully relaxed. In the shadowed stalls the monks chanted, bowing back and forth and to the altar. Incense drifted in the still air. Unsuccessfully, it sought to mask the strangely sweet death scent.

Almost moved, I gazed down into Wendz's final

148

face. Now I was glad of my grudging, hard-wrung words of forgiveness. That much peace I was glad to have given him. Wendz had never been truly hateworthy, he was only a fool. I glanced up at the wooden St. Peter, and the golden key he held; briefly I wondered if that key had actually turned, unlocking for Wendz the heaven he expected; or whether he had been surprised by something quite other on that side of stillness; or whether he had sunk into nothingness. I was not to know. Wendz could never tell me. Not even deceitful candlelight could lend life, or the semblance of expression to that face.

Turning away, I found a cowled figure at my elbow. I stepped aside to let the monk come to the coffin, and glimpsed the face within the cowl. Thus disguised, young Wendceslas drew no attention. He could mourn here, he could even weep, and none would know or remark it.

Under cover of the monks' chant I spoke to him. I will never know what motive urged me to speak, breaking our silence of eighteen years. Never had I stood so near him before, and I believed I never would again, for we were agreed upon his death. But I found myself speaking to his red, grief-hard eyes. "Your father is relieved," I murmured. "He is at rest. The city crown was a heavy burden for him."

From his cowled darkness Wendceslas watched me, silent. The years of silence, of withdrawal and suspicion flowed between us. I remembered the golden-haired toddler who stared at me with my mother's eyes. I remembered the young boy in the garden, watching me yearningly across our invisible barrier. Almost, I remembered the small, warm infant with the rosebud mouth, whom the wolf-bitch snatched away.

This must have been why I heard myself say, "Be wary of that crown, Wendceslas. You, too, may find it heavy."

I passed him then, and left the cathedral; wondering mightily at myself, and at the unwilled words of warning that had spoken themselves through me.

Before dawn I sat sleepless at the hearth. Neither Draga nor his tribesmen had been seen near the city. Even Ruga had not set foot in the city since the king's death. There was nothing to do now but to follow our plan, and trust others to do so. If only I could have spoken with Ruga! If only I knew where Draga was at this moment!

Again and again I imagined it all taking place exactly as planned. At the right moment the right horseman rode around the corner. The right bow was drawn, the right signal sent and seen. "Such a simple plan," I muttered to the flames, "can hardly go wrong." Unless Sorbal decided to go hunting; unless his men were drunk (I knew my free tribesmen!) or a prosperous nearby village proved too tempting, or Boleslav. . . .

Boleslav was my deep anxiety. Our young hound was imperfectly trained after all. I thought of his shocked, astounded eyes. "Me, kill Wendceslas? Oh, no, please!" "He won't betray us," I muttered. Certainly not. Loyalty was born, not instilled, in Boleslav's young heart. But he might fail at the crucial moment. Well he knew how to handle sword and bow—Ruga had trained him. But he had never actually used these weapons against a human enemy. Boleslav had never killed a man. I shivered, realizing that hideous gap in his education.

Ruga was aware of it. "Not sure," he had jotted on his slate; for Boleslav was untried. Such a trial had been impossible in Wendz's Christian city.

"Why do you shiver?" Yolann asked. "And do you know that you are talking to yourself?"

I swung around. I had not heard the door open, or footsteps approach. Yolann stood back in the shadows at the edge of the firelight. I saw her in the faint gray window-light, a fall of white linen with a baby hugged to its breast.

"Did you expect that I should sleep? Come, keep watch with me. With a jug of mead we two could be lighthearted as soldiers!"

"What made you shiver?" Yolann came and sat by the hearth with me. The baby stirred, muzzling against her breast.

"The thought that Boleslav is untried."

"Yes. It is like trusting a puppy to lead the pack. But you have little choice."

"*I* had little choice?"

"You and Ruga."

"Are you not in this too, sister?"

"No," Yolann said honestly.

"You have been in it from the beginning! And believe me, if we fail, you will suffer with us!"

"Oh, that is true enough!" Yolann's low voice grated bitterly. "I do not mind for myself, I mind for . . ." she nodded at the infant, and jerked her head toward the anteroom where the four-year old slept. "If only I could have sent them away with Ruga, like the others!"

Angrily I burst out, "Are you not ashamed!"

Yolann straightened. Her small, dark eyes glared at me somberly. But she answered quietly enough, "Dragamir, you are dealing in dreams. What matters the city crown, or who wears it? What matters religion or revenge? These are but stories men tell each other. All that matters under the sky is here." Once more she nodded at the sleeping infant. "And if through your doing, harm comes to her, I will never forgive you."

I scorned Yolann's thought, but I understood it. A door in my mind swung open and I glimpsed a landscape in which I had once lived . . . for a few hours. I stretched a hand to her. "I forgive you those words, now," I said.

She drew back; then she thought again, leaned, and took my hand. "Let us be friends," I said, "as well as sisters. You can be angry later."

"I hope," Yolann whispered, "I hope I will have time for anger!"

"What was that!"

"A man cried out." Yolann withdrew her hand and huddled down over her child.

"The watch?"

"Most likely. There's another cry."

I leaped up. I strode to the dark corner and seized the bow Ruga had given me. Stringing the bow, I hung my dagger at my waist.

"What are you doing, Dragamir? Are you going to join battle yourself?"

"I am going hunting, from this window. They will drive my quarry past." Now that the first shouts were sounding, all my fears fell away. Suddenly I was eager, action-ready, strung tight as the bow.

Gray dawn-light brightened at the window. From the square below more shouts rose, then a clatter of iron-shod hoofs; city horses. Red light streaked the gray.

I bounded to the window. Fire leaped in a back street. By its fitful glow and the slow-spreading dawn I saw the square filling with furtive figures. Merchants and monks, servants and beggars flitted from one alley to the next, seeking to hide. Behind the spired bulk of the cathedral, men were shouting, a horse shrilled. From the opposing street I heard whoops and shrieks, a plains wind blowing through the city.

I said over my shoulder, "Our brothers have come." I leaned the bow on the stone sill, with the arrow notched. Below me the surprised guards came running into the square, pulling on armor as they ran.

There comes to the waiting hunter a moment of intense beauty; the moment when the brown hare leaps from brown earth precisely where he judged it would leap; when the stag's antlers rise from the thicket exactly where he imagined it hidden. This moment came for me as Bishop Niklas himself rode around the corner of the cathedral, exactly where I had planned that he should ride.

He did not come mitred and robed, as I was accustomed to see him. The leaping brown hare appears in that moment as a flying clod of earth. The

153

stag's antlers are branches, lifting away from the thicket. So Bishop Niklas appeared suddenly as any fat man, naked under a hastily snatched cloak, riding bareback on a white charger. Even as he trotted around the corner he was buckling his sword belt. He shouted to the bewildered guards. They drew their swords and looked about, expectant now, no longer hopelessly confused. Their leader had come.

I drew my bow.

The bow was heavy, the range far. My arm trembled. Bishop Niklas' heavy paunch was the safest target. Aiming, I waited for him to ride closer. My target jiggled about under the loose-flying cloak. The charger trotted, paused, turned. The quarry was closer now, and my arms could no longer stand the strain. I let fly.

Arrow leaped, bow twanged. My aim was true, but the horse sidestepped. The arrow shot harmlessly past Niklas' belly and bounced brittlely off a paving stone.

Niklas wheeled the charger, looking up. Maybe he saw me, leaning in the window in half-light. Maybe he saw the bow. Barking an order, he pointed. Three soldiers ran toward the palace, glancing up to mark the spot.

Boleslav and the tribesmen should have come streaming into the square by now, but this had not yet happened. I had no time to wonder what had gone wrong—those soldiers ran fast. I dropped the bow and made for the door. "Out of here!" I cried to Yolann. From the corner of my eye I saw her leap up, clutching one brat, and run to wake the other. I did not wait. I fled down the hall. Like those furtive figures in the square, those pathetic beggars and monks, I glanced sharply, hopefully, from side to side.

A door cracked open. I whirled toward it. It was the door of the chapel; and an ancient, withered face, whiter than the veil that framed it, peered out at me. "Dragamir?" it whispered, "what is that uproar?"

The chapel would be the perfect hiding place! They would never look for the pagans in the chapel! I rushed and shoved Ludmilla back. She staggered and barely saved herself a fall. I glanced back to Yolann, who was running toward me—the infant stuffed, howling, under one arm—dragging the whimpering girl. I signaled her, and she dodged into the chapel beside me. Softly I shut the door, and was horrified to find that it had no bolts. I clapped my hands over the girl's soft mouth. "Shush! Not a sound!" Yolann jiggled and murmured to the baby. Its roars sank to cries, its cries to murmurs.

The chapel was dark, save for the eternal flicker of the sanctuary lamp. The small gold tabernacle winked in the gloom. Dimly I made out the wooden Marya in the corner, still smiling as she smiled the last time we met—when Wendz made his vow to me.

I rushed to the narrow window and cracked open the shutters. Ludmilla tottered after me. Her white head shook on her stringy neck like a flower on a wind-stirred stalk. "What is it?" she kept mumbling. "Is it the farm folk? The poor harvest was not our fault! Dragamir, you look so fierce! Is it—is it the horse folk?"

155

I thrust my head out over the sill. Below, the square was alive with tribesmen, fighting ponies, dodging soldiers. Some of these were learning—too fast—to attack the ponies rather than the men. Bishop Niklas, dismounted, was retreating backward up the cathedral steps, defending himself with surprising agility against Ruga. Sorbal held off his guard.

Directly below me, a white-robed, stocky young man walked calmly out on the broad palace steps. The first sunlight glinted on his bright hair. Unarmed, he held aloft a gleaming object—from above I guessed it was a crucifix. I gazed down on him almost proudly. That young man, serene in the face of tumult, spiritually armed in the face of bare weapons, could almost have been my son! At that moment I could have gladly acknowledged him as such. He was a fool, certainly, no doubt of that. But he was a grand fool.

Boleslav rode out of a side street. He rode a black war pony bareback, unbridled; guiding it expertly with his knees. In one hand he brandished a sword, with the other he managed a light leather shield, unpainted. Ready for business, Boleslav might have been taken for an experienced plains warrior but for his dead-white, terrified face. Under the leather helmet his eyes stared, frozen.

Annoyed, I mumbled curses. At my shoulder the old woman gasped, "That is your son!" She accused, pointing to him, "He rides like a tribesman!"

"Almost."

I could not see Wendceslas' face, only the top of his shining head. He hoisted the crucifix high—it gleamed like a sword—and called upon Boleslav. I did not catch the words. Boleslav swung the pony toward the steps. Intelligence flashed through the terror in his eyes. He followed the Plan. He shouted to the pony and bent low to its mane, holding the sword purposefully, and rushed upon Wendceslas.

Boleslav was fifteen years old, and untried. Besides the natural reluctance, which he had not had a chance to overcome, he had to combat a certain secret admiration for Wendceslas. I had fought down this admiration. I had scoffed and scorned, and taught Boleslav to laugh at the older boy's inferior skills. But I had noticed it yet flickering in his eyes, this admiration, when Wendceslas passed close by him in the hall; or when, passing the chapel door, we glimpsed him kneeling cruciform, unmoving, oblivious to weariness. In this quick, decisive moment, I knew, Boleslav would have to forget all compunction, and attack with a whole heart, as though he were hunting. He was, after all, an insatiable hunter. Anxiously I watched the war pony bound up the steps and bowl Wendceslas over. It proceeded to rear and kick and trample, as it had been taught. The pony performed well, much better than Boleslav. His raised blade never fell. The point gleamed, unbloodied, in the rising sun. Thankfully, the men in the square were far too occupied to notice.

Ludmilla shrieked. The dawn wind ruffled her veil and blew it across my face. "What is he doing?" she moaned. "He will kill his brother!" She turned to me, her bleary old eyes widened, horrified. "This is your doing!"

I smiled.

157

Ludmilla began to back away from me, toward the Marya. "What else should we have expected of you? I told my son what you would do, but he would keep the vow you forced on him! He never believed you would do it, but I was right. You have taught your son to kill his brother!"

I said, "My son has no brother. Have you forgotten? A wolf-bitch snatched away his brother."

Ludmilla raised trembling hands. Her head shook violently on its wobbly stalk. She saw the rage rising in me before I felt it.

I left the window. Slowly, purposefully, I followed her into the corner. "Dragamir!" Yolann called. I heard her as if she called from far, far away. I paid no attention.

"You were the wolf-bitch," I told the old woman softly. "I saw your soul leap in the window, a gray wolf. The cold wind rocked the cradle."

Ludmilla bleated, "Marya!"

I will never know if she cried to me, or to the statue behind her. But that cry doomed her. "Marya" was a young girl, love-ready, brim-full of the Goddess. When I heard her name called, her unforgotten pain flooded my being. A cold hand gripped my throat—the hand of the Goddess I thought I had conquered years ago. My unused breasts swelled and hardened with rage, as with milk. Buried memory rose, cold-shrouded from its grave, and fury with it.

This cowering witch was my real enemy. The dead king had only followed her instructions. The young king now sprawled under the pony's hoofs would have done the same. Not even the brutal

158

bishop, now dying at his altar, had injured me as she had injured me; this old woman, this werewolf who had leaped in with the winter wind.

Ludmilla shrieked. She turned to run; but her old legs would not serve her. Yolann bustled between us. "Dragamir—"

I thrust her aside and drew my dagger. Yolann cast herself upon me. I struck. I never saw Yolann at all, I was looking at the hated enemy face over her shoulder. It seemed to me that I struck Ludmilla, but it was Yolann who slumped against me. My dagger stood in her upper arm. I shoved her away. And now there was no barrier between me and Ludmilla.

Ludmilla straightened. Now she looked me in the face with startling calm. She stiffened like a wooden statue, her robe and veil arranged themselves gracefully, as though carved. Like a martyr painted in one of her books she raised dim eyes heavenward.

I lunged.

Eighteen years before I had searched the palace for my stolen child. Dagger in hand, I meant to kill any who came between me and my son. That day I found neither child nor enemy. The child was lost to me forever. But now I had the enemy by the throat.

I seized the white veil in both hands. I yanked and twisted, knotted and tightened. The wooden saint returned to momentary life. It made beautifully satisfying sounds of anguish; but not for long.

Struggling, Ludmilla sank to the floor. I knelt to finish the work. Only when I was sure that stringy throat would never draw another breath did I release the veil. The corpse lay still, a flat bundle of

159

white linen. One mottled hand, outflung, pointed to the wooden Marya.

Slowly, reluctantly, I rose to my feet. The chapel formed again around me, and I was back in this precious moment of time; this urgent moment. I glanced about for Yolann.

She leaned in the far corner, pressing her gown to her wounded arm. Blood had dyed the linen. Beside her, the little girl held the struggling baby, half her own size. Four black eyes regarded me with horror, and some fear. In the urgency of the moment I did not pause to grieve for this.

I asked briskly, "Is it staunched?"

Yolann nodded.

I stepped back to the window. My heart still pounded, my head swam. At first I did not believe what I saw.

Solid and broad, bodied in unhurt flesh, Bishop Niklas stood straddled on the cathedral steps. He pointed and shouted, and men rushed obediently hither and thither. Riderless war ponies galloped confusedly about the square. One bridled pony dragged its rider by a twisted rein. No mounted tribesmen were in sight. "Holy Mother!" I gasped, and leaned farther out to look down on the palace steps. No trampled corpse lay there.

Behind me, the chapel door burst wide.

I felt a brief, searing grief. "If we fail," I had told Yolann, "you will suffer with us." But I had not seriously considered failure. My vengeful passion had felt itself invincible, destined for sure victory. Now for the space of a sigh I mourned for Yolann and her little ones; for Boleslav and for myself.

Then I turned. Wendceslas stood framed in the doorway. He held a short sword now, and his white robe was bloodied. Muddy hoof marks printed it. But Wendceslas, proud and alert as I had never seen him, was clearly unhurt.

Quickly he took in the scene. His gray eyes, suddenly hard, roved from me, gaping at him in the window, to Yolann, huddled in the corner, to the body sprawled at the feet of the Marya.

In three strides he reached Ludmilla's body. Kneeling, he gently turned it. Blotched and heavy-tongued, the head lolled in his hands.

He did not sigh or shudder. Silently he looked into the dead face; and up at me. Silently, the chapel filled with his soldiers.

Yolann hobbled over to me. Still pressing her wound with her gown, she stood beside me. Silently I urged her, "Get away!" I know that she heard my thought, and she refused. Together, we looked back at Wendceslas.

Never taking his gaze from mine, he rose. His grave face turned to stone. His eyes were like gray pebbles. His full lips, still visible through the new beard, became thin. Watching him, I never saw the guard seize me. I only felt a hand heavy on my shoulder, a sharp point at my throat.

Instinctively I drew back from the shock of the cold iron. The blade came with me. I drew myself up, then, gritting my teeth.

But Wendceslas raised a slow hand. The blade wavered against my throat, and then drew away.

❋　❋　❋

161

That was a wise move. I was surprised to find Wendceslas so clever; and he had thought of it himself, unadvised, and in the heat of anger! Our immediate death in the chapel would have gone almost unnoticed; part of the general uproar. By making a public show of it Wendceslas would mark the beginning of his reign. The city would have no doubt who sat in the high seat; our fate would be ceremonial proof.

When Yolann and I had searched the palace nineteen years before, we had missed this place. I had never known of these long rock passages winding under the kitchens, under the earth, lined with dark stone cells whose wooden doors were barred and bolted up and down with iron. My cell boasted a stone ledge under a high, narrow window. A departing guard tossed me a tattered horse hide. Gratefully I huddled into it, for the cell was cold with the damp of a hundred winters.

I thought Boleslav must be imprisoned in one of these cells, but he was not nearby. I called softly, and knocked my knuckles sore on the wood, but with no response. For the sake of dignity I decided to make no more noise. Boleslav, like myself, would have to endure alone.

Crosslegged on the stone ledge I contemplated my fate while a winter day shone briefly in on the damp stones, and shadows deepened after noon. Slowly I enjoyed an evening mug of greasy broth. Doubtless it would be my last meal; I lingered over it, savoring its saltless, slimy texture. It revolted me, and nothing would ever revolt me again. As darkness closed in I listened eagerly to the rustle of waking, scurrying rats. My ears welcomed sound, any sound, while they still could hear!

At least I had hunted down the wolf. Licking the last broth from my lips I smiled at that. One victory I could enjoy, and that the most urgent one! Why waste sorrow on the fact that Wendceslas and Bishop Niklas would rule the city? Did I care for the city? Did I care if the church still reigned supreme? But I was sorry I could not stable Draga's ponies in the cathedral, as I had vowed.

Draga was wiser than I. Understanding well the risks of conspiracy he had chosen not to appear. On this very night he feasted, doubtless three days' journey from here; and Wendceslas could never prove his complicity. Suspect it he certainly would—I was pleased to admit the lad had brains—but he could never use it as an excuse to withdraw from Wendz's agreement with Draga. Coolly I considered all this, as though from a comfortable distance; as though it had little to do with me.

"You will suffer with us," I had assured Yolann; and now she would. I was glad she had sent the older children away. Probably tomorrow, she and Boleslav and I would die. I knew nothing of Ruga. He was most likely dead, but he might have escaped. He might be hiding in the city now, he had unlikely friends. He might be riding now to Draga.

For Boleslav I grieved. I had trained Boleslav as I would train a dog, and sent him, innocent, into the bear's den. Determined as I was to preserve dignity before Wendceslas' high·seat, I thought I might bend it a stiff finger's-breadth for Boleslav's sake. I might even plead for Boleslav—if he did not dis-

163

grace me and plead for himself. Thinking of the soft, pliant nature he had inherited from his father, I groaned aloud. I thought I feared nothing so much as disgrace. Yet fear leaped in my throat at the sound of footsteps in the passage.

They echoed hollowly from rock wall to rock wall, rapidly drawing nearer. A torch gleamed outside the cell door. The shot bolts clanged.

Fright-chilled, I rose and stood proudly, facing the door. A sword winked in torch-light. Men's voices grumbled together. The executioners were making no effort at secrecy. "Let them come quickly," I prayed. For a few moments, pride could hold my awful fear in check.

A familiar voice ordered, "Withdraw a good distance. I am to confess her, and our conversation must be private."

"Yes, Your Holiness," an ignorant guard muttered. Another added, "Yes, Your Piety."

Bishop Niklas himself took the torch and entered my cell. The guards banged the bolts to and departed, echoing away down long rock corridors. Haloed by the flaring torch, Niklas came up to me. Now he wore stiff ceremonial robes and his high white mitre. As the threat of immediate violence retreated to await another hour, my terror ebbed. "I am glad to see you dressed," I mocked. My voice came out high, almost shrill. Controlling it, I remarked, "This is not the season for riding in the streets half-clad!"

Niklas growled, "Do not laugh." He turned aside to set the torch in a wall sconce. Its mad light hissed through the cell. He came back and stood before me, breathing hotly in my face. His big hands were tense at his sides. I edged away from him, back toward the stone ledge. I thought how this man's lust had reached out with invisible hands to seize a young girl's mind. I felt it grasping for me now; but I was no longer a young girl.

Why had Niklas come to me? If not to kill me, surely not to confess me! Puzzled, I smoothed my gown to cover the knocking of my knees. This must be part of the morrow's ordeal, beginning early. I must meet it accordingly. I lifted my chin high.

"Do not laugh," Niklas repeated slowly, "If you hope to see tomorrow's sunset—"

"I do not hope."

He paused. Then he asked, "What would you give to see tomorrow's sunset?"

"Why do you ask?"

"Because I might save you, woman! You know that your son listens to me."

"My son? Where is he imprisoned?"

One tense hand jerked. "Oh, come now! Wendceslas listens to me."

"Yes, I know that. He listens to you as his father listened. I have long known who ruled this city! I know it was you, Niklas, who brought me here out of freedom, to bear Wendz a Christian heir. And when the heir was born, you stole him from me. What do you want of me now?"

Promptly, shamelessly, Niklas replied, "We understand each other well. For years you have watched me watching you." His nostrils suddenly flared. His deep voice trembled. I noticed his fists shaking against his robes. "I have long respected your intelligence; perhaps not quite enough. When you struck you took me by surprise. I thought you would wait to strengthen your forces. I did not expect you to kill the old lady with your own hands, either. Why her? You know your true enemy. You should have killed me!"

"I tried."

"That you did; and again, with your own hand. Another mistake. At that range you would need a man's arm. I have respected your intelligence, and your determination; but I have long admired your softer qualities, as well." His voice gentled. "Perhaps you forgot that you had softer qualities? I did not." His hot gaze left my face and slid downward. "I have long dreamed of the soft breasts under that stiff wool." He grabbed for me.

With a sharp cry I struck his hands away. I found myself crouched like a cornered cat, snarling up into the close, oily face. "I can yell," I warned.

Niklas smirked. "Who would hear? The guards have piously withdrawn. Suppose they heard, would they come? Suppose they came, would they believe your story?"

"Yes!" I retorted desperately. "All the world knows of your lechery!"

Niklas' smile was gentle. "The world may know it; but who believes it? We all know things we do not believe. You, for instance, know full well that Wendceslas is your own son. You bore him nineteen years ago in my own sight; and if I have not forgotten, you surely have not! But you refuse to believe this. So is it strange that Wendceslas, seeing that I love women more than God, does not believe it?

"He cannot believe it. I am his bishop, his mediator with God. Surely, then, I must be at least as pious as Wendceslas himself! I assure you, Wendceslas will credit no accusation against me." Niklas extended a cautious hand toward me. Carefully he advanced a step, as toward a trapped wild animal. "Now, consider; what I tell the king, he believes. My judgment weighs heavily with him. What advice do you wish me to give him tomorrow?"

Still retreating, I pressed against the stone ledge. "I have murdered his grandmother with my own hands," I reminded him. "Have you *that* much weight with Wendceslas?"

"Indeed, yes." Niklas followed me watchfully. He was now very close. His lust-hot breath fanned my face. "The truth is—perhaps I should not tell you this—that Wendceslas is very like Ludmilla. Her teachings flow in his veins like blood. He would doubtless be relieved to hear me advise mercy. Now—"

He seized me. He swarmed over me, bending me back across the ledge. Repulsed and horrified, I felt his sweaty fat engulf me. His incense-permeated robe flapped in my face, choking me. I was pinned under his vast weight.

Surrender never occurred to me. I believed not a word Niklas had said. I was reconciled to death on the morrow; my only concern now was for my pride. Niklas attacked my pride more than my body; and as the body weakened, pride rushed into battle.

His weight shifted as he wrestled with his robes. One seeking hand landed on my shoulder. I turned and bit it.

Niklas started, releasing me momentarily. With both hands, catlike, I scratched down his face.

Crying out, he leaped away. I drew back against the wall, ready to ward him off again. But Niklas swayed where he stood, pawing his face. His hands came away bloody. He gaped at them, holding them to the fickle torchlight. "Blood!" he gasped. "Holy saints, woman, you drew blood!"

I snarled, "So you can bleed!"

Panting, he glared at me, quivering with rage. The cell rang with my laughter. This much revenge I could take! But even as I laughed I noted that Niklas had spoken truth—we were alone. No guard came to investigate the uproar.

Niklas was a large and powerful man, and now he was angry. I saw him considering revenge. His black eyes glistened thoughtfully as he rubbed his wounded cheeks. I purred, "No pleasure in it, Niklas. I can see to that."

He said, "I believe you. You are a witch, after all."

He picked up his fallen mitre, dusted it off, and placed it carefully over his greasy curls. Vain as a woman—and as eager to allay suspicion—he smoothed his robes. Majestically, then, he lifted the torch from its sconce and moved to the door.

Slowly, from far away, the guards responded to his shouts. We heard their steps echoing toward us up the long rock hallways. Niklas turned back to me, lifting the torch to glare in my eyes. "I shall always remember you with regret," he told me quietly.

168

"Nevertheless, be sure the king shall receive just and sound advice from me."

The door opened for Niklas and slammed behind him. The heavy bolts clanged. As he departed I heard him say, "Should the king ask, tell him the lady is unrepentant."

I leaned back against the cold stone wall and trembled and shook. This once Niklas had spoken truth! I was indeed unrepentant. I ground my teeth, rejoicing that I had at least avenged my sorrows on cruel Ludmilla. If only I could have shot Niklas! How had Ruga failed to kill him? Had Niklas possibly killed Ruga? Ruga was a beautiful, skilled fighter, hardened, and carrying far less bulk than Niklas. Yet, fighting on the cathedral steps, Niklas had shown quite surprising vigor. He might, conceivably, have won.

Briefly my pained thoughts touched upon Ruga, upon Boleslav, upon my loyal sister. I had last seen her beside Ludmilla's corpse, pressing her skirt to the wound I had given her; while the little girl, clutching the infant, cowered against her.

I would have grieved for Ruga and Yolann, but I had no time. Soon Boleslav and I would join them. I had time only to compose myself, to collect all my pride and courage.

Shivering in the cell's cold damp, I drew up the thin horse-hide the guard had left me. Huddling exhausted, I loosened my mind. "Go free," I told it. "Imagine. Remember." Thus I hoped to live my final hours; thus my life might become real to me, and in some way complete.

I drifted. Bright plain, wide light. Spring flowers reddened the rolling land, which bumped and bounded under Belatruz's pounding hoofs. I saw small hands tangled in his mane; they were the hands of a little girl. They were my hands. My little heels drummed the pony's sides. Safely circled by strong-sinewed arms I laughed, and leaned back against Draga. Boundless light poured from the far-arching sky. Red and purple and brown the boundless plain reached to embrace the light.

The vision paled and faded. Amazed, I knew I had dreamed. How had I dared to sleep? I jerked upright. Huddled on the ledge, shivering under the tattered horse-hide, I saw cold, new light brighten into my final day.

Watching the slow dawn I pondered; how had I come to this last winter dawn? What angry fate had led me, step by step? I was too proud to blame others, though it might have been easy. I thought of Wendz, that sickly married monk. I thought of the father who had abandoned me. I even remembered Marya Whore with angry sorrow; that far back my thoughts wandered, inviting long-forgotten scenes to flicker brightly through my brain, till a distant clank and echoing, coming footsteps recalled me to the terrible moment.

Boleslav slumped between his guards outside the door of the audience hall. At the sight of him my heart softened, my eyes came near filling with tears. In that moment I almost regretted having used Boleslav as a weapon in my war, having borne him to be a weapon. I had considered him a tool, and little more. But he was in fact a healthy young boy, a fountain of life springing higher day by day; and now, by my doing, his days had come to an end.

"Come now," I warned myself, "this is no time for regrets!" I blinked away the forming tears. As I approached with my guards, Boleslav's fear-tight face relaxed a little. Childishly, he felt that Mother's coming meant relief. I gave him a hard look and lifted my chin. Then he understood. There was no relief, no help. Pride was our only defense. I was glad to see him straighten his shoulders, and firm his too-mobile features. I hoped that he would not disgrace me.

The great door opened. Our guards would have taken hold of us, but my cold, regal stare pushed them away. They left us alone, and we walked freely, side by side, into the audience hall.

The huge hall was packed. Soldiers, monks, nuns, and citizens jammed the outskirts. They opened a path for us, drawing away from us as from contamination. Nearer the high seat, nobles and rich merchants formed the crowd. Moving slowly, head high, I felt cold dread and anger from all sides. Hatred was a mist in the room; we moved through hatred as through a thick fog. The hate-fog did not frighten me. It was only a thickening of the mist in which I had passed my life. But I feared for Boleslav. Hatred can strike almost as hard as violence. I glanced at him. He paced quietly beside me. The glossy bronze of his face had paled to gray; his eyes were fixed and unnaturally dry. But he walked calm and erect. Boleslav would not disgrace me.

The crowd no longer moved from our path. We

came to a halt and stood gazing into the hate-fog. My heart drummed, my ears gurgled strangely. Faintly, at first, I saw the high seat before me, and the young man seated there, straight and tense as we. Beside him stood Bishop Niklas, broad in his heavy robes, mitred and somber. In his steady gaze all the hatred in the hall was concentrated. Seeing him, I woke with a start. I had been walking in a trance. Now I understood that all this was real, it was all fact. A moment more, and Wendceslas would speak. Another moment, and the guards would act. And there was no holding back the advancing moments.

It was Bishop Niklas who spoke. Gently, with admirable control, he broke the silence. His words struck my ears, but wakened no understanding; it was as though he spoke a foreign language. I knew only that he was listing charges against us. "Insurrection," he said mildly, "Murder, witchcraft." I turned my numb gaze to Wendceslas' face.

It was the same face I remembered from his childhood; smooth, composed, serene. It stared back at me thoughtfully, with the shallow gray eyes that were my earliest memory. No anger furrowed that brow, no hatred hardened it. And this surprised me mightily; for Wendceslas was only eighteen. He stared, and stroked his new beard with a slow, deliberate hand. Where had he learned this cold discipline?

At last Bishop Niklas fell silent. Silence boomed in the crowded hall. Wendceslas bowed his head, his hand paused upon his beard. He considered.

Faintly, silks and linens rustled. The crowd breathed. Far to the back a soldier drew his dagger half out of its sheath. The whispering rasp could be heard throughout the silent hall.

Beside me, Boleslav began to shake. But I did not think he would disgrace me. I did not tremble, though my breath came shallow, and I felt deathly cold.

Wendceslas looked up. His gray eyes met mine. He spoke quietly. Desperately I strove to understand his slow words, but my brain was numbed. I caught names: "Ludmilla . . . Christ . . . Marya." I understood "Sin . . . judgment . . . salvation." Mother Earth, he was preaching! I almost smiled. I did laugh inside, and this laughter cleared my head. Now I heard him.

"I know what she would say if she sat here today," he said. "My soul hears her soul speak, and I obey her gladly." He rose and stood, facing us. He made no eloquent gesture, he did not raise a hand. Quietly he turned away from me, to Boleslav. "Brother," he greeted him.

Boleslav gasped. The crowd gasped. Dazed and dumbfounded, I heard Wendceslas continue, "Swear to me now that you will henceforth uphold our Church and faith (Niklas muttered in his ear)—and my rule."

My heart swelled. I feared I might weep. My poor child—for that was what he was—my poor child would live! Wendceslas' folly was unbelievable, he would certainly not rule for long; but I would not complain of that!

173

Bishop Niklas stood forth, obviously disapproving; yet he spoke the vow, nodding to Boleslav to repeat what he said. Boleslav cleared his throat twice, then haltingly he spoke the words. His voice broke once, and he squeaked. A monk brought forward a huge gold-chained Holy Book for him to kiss. Not turning to look, I felt him bend to kiss it, and then abruptly leave my side. He walked shakily up to the high seat, took Wendceslas' hand and kissed it. The crowd muttered.

Wendceslas motioned Boleslav aside. I rejoiced to see him step into the crowd, out of the center of dangerous attention where I stood. He turned a gray face to me, the eyes still glazed. His mouth framed silent words, but I could not ponder them. Wendceslas was turning back to me.

"Mother," he said. This was the first word he ever spoke to me. I gaped at him, unbelieving. The day before, when he faced my tribesmen armed with his crucifix, I had reluctantly thought him my son, after all. I had seen my best self in him, and even something of Draga—though he was not of Draga's blood. Now, in this astonished moment, I withdrew that judgment. He was Ludmilla's grandson, not Draga's. He was a fool, a Christian saint. The heart of greatness was not in him.

"Mother," the fool said, "swear to me now that you will henceforth uphold our Church and faith . . . and my rule."

I trembled. Salty sweat dripped down my face. The moment had come and passed over, a sword witheld. I was to live. Holy Mother Earth! I had lost only a battle, not my war!

174

Niklas glared. Hastily he dropped his eyes; but he could not conceal his fury. His fat hands shook, his voice shook as he spoke the vow. Dazed, I repeated his words.

I kissed the Holy Book.

I did not kiss the young king's hand.

5

The Cathedral

The little page who built my fire reminded me of someone. I lowered my mending to my lap and watched him. The slump of his young shoulders seemed familiar; his sturdy build and scuffing tread; and when he turned his profile, the black eyebrows curving down toward the childish, tipped nose. . . .

Breaking the silence I asked him, "Are you a son of Bishop Niklas?"

The child started. He dropped the faggots and whirled to face me. He looked perhaps seven years old. He drew his hands behind his back, and I knew the stubby fingers were crossed to ward off my evil. I asked again, "Is Bishop Niklas your father?" He bobbed his head. Unkempt black hair swung across his dark face.

I knew that Niklas had children all over the city. He made no secret of his sins; he confessed them publicly, and provided for his children, not, I had heard, from Church funds, but from his own—"his booty," as Yolann had put it. The daughters he failed to marry off populated the convent. "You'll find Niklas' sons in strange employment," Yolann had told me. "They serve as stable boys, kitchen help, bodyguards, all over the city. That way, Niklas has a spoon in every dish."

And a spy in my chamber! But this spy was only a child with wide, innocent black eyes. Softening my voice I asked him gently, "Do you tell your father about me?"

"Yes, lady," he assured me, bobbing till his hair flopped, "Every night. I tell him about Prince Boleslav, too. My father watches over you."

I smiled. "Does he pay you?"

The child was silent.

"Does he give you money when you tell about us?"

"Oh no!" He shook his head, black hair spun about his face. "Sometimes he gives me candy. We all get candy when we tell something important."

"I see. What about tonight? Will you get any candy?"

The black eyes sparkled. "I'm sure I will!"

"Really? But what can you tell him about me? I sit here mending all day."

"Not you, lady."

"Oh. Has the prince done something exciting?"

"Not him. The Saint."

"And what has the Saint done, lad?"

The child looked down and scuffed the hearth-stone.

"I haven't any candy, but . . ." I laid down my mending, went to the chest and brought out a coin. "Look, this is money. With this you can buy candy. Now tell me, what did Wendceslas do today?"

He muttered, "I only tell my father so he can watch over everybody."

I said quietly, "They say I am a witch. They say rightly." The child glanced up. "I can bewitch you, my lad. I can turn you into a salamander. Would you like to be a salamander, and live in my fire?"

He glanced back at the fire, and shivered. But he whispered bravely, "My father would know. You can't bewitch my father."

I smiled. "Maybe not."

He said louder, "You can't bewitch the Saint, either. God is stronger than the Devil."

I laughed softly. "What is your name?"

"Nikodem."

"Nikodem, let us be friends." He shot me a cautious look. "I used to have a little boy like you. He's gone, now. I used to have a sister to talk to, and she's gone. And I am very lonely, sitting here. I would dearly like your friendship. Wouldn't you like mine? How many boys have a witch for a friend?" I held the coin toward him again. "Come, tell me what your Saint did today. I promise I won't turn you into a salamander."

Very slowly, Nikodem came to me. To be less frightening I sat down in the one chair, and he stood at my knee. "He carried a bundle of faggots to a poor man," he whispered. "I helped him."

"Nothing very wonderful in that, Nikodem. He does things like that every day."

"Yes. But this time . . . it was snowing." He brought his hands out from behind his back to gesture the falling snow; and I saw that the small fingers were indeed crossed. "It was cold. Awful cold. I couldn't walk any more, the snow was too cold."

"Yes?"

"I had to tell him. I yelled to him, 'I can't go on any more.' I had to yell, he was way ahead."

"So then he turned back." Wendceslas might well turn back for a distressed child.

"No, he didn't come back. He yelled at me, "Walk in my footprints!"

Nikodem stopped. I nodded encouragement. "Go on."

"So I walked in his footprints. They were big, like this." He strode widely around the room. "And they were warm." He came to my knee. "Warm. The snow was warm."

"Let's see your feet." I made him sit down and take off his boots and wrappings. His small feet emerged, dirty and perfectly healthy. "They're not frostbit," I said, wondering.

"No, no lady, you didn't hear me—"

"I heard you. The snow was warm."

"Yes, and I was warm. I warmed up all over, as long as I walked in his footprints."

"Hmmm."

The black eyes glowed. "He's a Saint, like a statue in the cathedral!"

"That story should be worth two candies from your father."

"Oh yes, he'll want to hear it!"

"It's worth my money." I gave him the coin. He held it uncertainly, probably wishing it were candy. "Tell you what, Nikodem. For every story you tell me, I'll tell you one."

"You know stories?" The young face lit up.

"I have not sat prisoned in this room since forever! Certainly, I know stories to curl your hair!" He started; I laughed. And slowly, he laughed with me.

So every day when Nikodem came to build my fire he told me a story. From his eager lips I learned of Wendceslas' holiness. Miracle tales Nikodem spun for me; a sore throat was cured by a distant glimpse of the king. His touch calmed a baby's convulsions. And many were the tales of beggars feasted at his table, and clothed in rich garments newly sewn for them. I learned that Wendceslas slept always alone; thereby, I thought, he won the power to heal, and to walk barefoot in snow, as Nikodem said he did. "Every night he walks barefoot to the cathedral to pray. He doesn't care if it rains or snows or hails. He prays there all night."

"And how do people feel about all this?" I asked him once.

"What people, lady?"

"Well, how do the nobles like this praying king?"

"They love him. Everyone loves him 'cept. . . ."

"Except. . . ."

"Some of the merchants are secret pagans. They don't like to have to pretend Christian."

"Aha!"

"And sometimes my father frowns."

"Why does he frown?"

"Well, the king lowered taxes. It helps the poor people. But my father says it doesn't help the church."

"Aha!"

"Now it's your turn to tell a story."

181

"Certainly. Come, sit closer." My stories opened a wide world for Nikodem—and for me. Telling my life, I relived it. My prison walls faded, and I saw again the bright, generous light of the plains. Again I rode Belatruz, safe in the circle of my father's arms. I told Nikodem of the snarling dogs that scattered before Belatruz's flying hoofs; of the flickering rumps of fleeing hares, and the carpet of flowers fading to the far horizon.

Nikodem loved to hear how Draga gathered his tribesmen and rode among them; how his proud plume waved above the leather helmets, and his eyes glittered like spear points. I told him but once of the destruction and death that followed these glorious moments; he did not wish to hear it again. "Your father will go to hell for sure," he told me sadly. "He's not just a pagan, he's a *wicked* pagan!"

"I suppose so." From a Christian point of view, certainly. "But he was good to me, Nikodem, as your father is good to you."

"Oh?" Nikodem looked doubtful. Nikodem was a love-hungry child. His mother was dead; his father used him—as I did. Gradually he drew closer to me. One day he laid his small hands on my knee. And after a while I dared to rest my arm gently about his stooped shoulders. I did not care about Nikodem, I told myself sternly. I had vowed never to care about anyone. But after three years of solitary prison, my heart was hungry, too.

For three years I had lived alone, under the dour watch of nun-guards. Two at a time, they slept in the anteroom that had been Yolann's. There was no talking with them, they were constantly praying;

and if I spoke to one who was not praying, she quickly began to pray. Their looks were hard and fearful. They regarded me as a witch, marked for their hell; and if the king's touch could heal, mine might damn.

For company I had my thoughts; for occupation, all the mending and sewing I could beg from the nuns. Spinning was not allowed. I never laid eyes on wool; it was thought to be a pagan connection. For this reason, too, I might not drink mead, but only pale city wine; nor eat mutton, but only heavy meats and soft bread from the palace kitchen.

In this loneliness a recurrent dream came to comfort me, often at the end of a restless night. Young and small again, I would cuddle in the arc of Draga's arm. We would sit together on a white horse hide, under the curving wall of a tent; and he would converse over my head with shadowy figures of dark, scarred men.

Once, I remember, I felt his shoulder tighten. Startled, I glanced up to see his eyebrows twitching—or rather, writhing like snakes. Cold terror gripped me. Very slowly, careful not to draw his dangerous attention upon my small self, I withdrew from his arm, from his side, and crept away under the tent-wall. His men saw me go and took their cue. All eyes fixed upon Draga and his twitching brows, silence fell in the tent. In the silence I heard my heart beat.

Then Draga laughed. Good-humored laughter burst out of him and he swung a long arm to snatch me back against him. Once again I rested safely under his arm, warm and loved and triumphant. Only,

I could still hear my heartbeat. It was, in fact, the first morning hammer sound from the cathedral, waking me to another lonely day.

My son was allowed to visit on Sundays, while sand flowed once through an hourglass. Even for this brief time a nun sat with us, sewing. In summer we could move away from her, for then we were granted a turn in the garden.

Boleslav's imprisonment was lighter than mine. Kept close for a season, he was then set free within the palace. Another season, and he had the run of the city. He might have been free entirely if he had accepted baptism. I feared he might do this out of sheer lazy good nature, but Boleslav was loyal. He told me, "While you are a prisoner I will be pagan."

Because of this pagan status he could not approach Wendceslas, or come to know him. And I was glad of this; for I noticed uneasily his growing admiration for the king. "He is like the shamans you tell of," he said once. "He is not like other men. He does not ride or shoot, this is true. But he can look at a man and see his soul."

I replied, "It is well to understand your enemy. You should know his weaknesses and his strengths." I thanked all the gods that Boleslav could not fraternize with Wendceslas; for I knew I could never persuade him to kill a man with whom he had dined.

One spring morning in the garden, far from the watchful nun, I asked him, "Would you say there were many of us pagans left?"

"There must be a hundred pagan merchants in the city," he told me, "and hundreds more in the bigger villages. It is said they conspire with Uncle Ruga."

Ruga had escaped the city, during or immediately after the short battle. Lying alone in my isolation I dreamed of him. I saw him riding, and I seemed to ride with him, clutching his braided belt. I saw him stoop to enter a tent. I watched his nimble hands gesture in his silent speech. Waking, I often wondered if I had dreamed, or if my soul had indeed traveled abroad with my brother.

"Yolann has sent word," Boleslav muttered in my ear.

"Tell me!"

"She has married a chief, I forget the name; one of those with Draga."

"That is a good word!" I stopped on the path to breathe thanks to the air, to the spring sky, to whatever god might hear.

Consistent in his folly, Wendceslas had banished my sister, allowing her to leave the city with all her goods and children. Naturally, she had returned to Draga; and now, with her booty she had snared a minor chief into marriage; a chief who would now follow Draga even more loyally, in peace and in war! Truly, this Christian king was his own worst enemy!

"Listen, Nikodem. Can you approach the king?"

"I build his fire, lady!" Nikodem assured me proudly. I considered him. He was shy and retiring like any wise orphan, like myself; but he loved Wendceslas even more than he admired him. And I thought Wendceslas might be fairly easy for a child to approach. If you were poor, weak or helpless, Wendceslas was your friend; for that was the teaching of his cursed grandmother, and his cursed religion.

"Will you take the king a message from me?"

Nikodem looked doubtful. I thought of showing him a gleaming coin; but greed was not his weakness. Instead I appealed to his sympathy. "I never see him but from my window, as he walks across the square. If I could only talk to him, who knows? We might make peace."

Nikodem brightened. "Then you would be free!"

His friendly joy touched my heart. "Well, if you would like that, speak to the king. Tell him I crave audience."

"I will try. That is, if I do not find him at prayer. When he prays, no one speaks to him."

I believed that. But fortune was with me— Nikodem found the king between prayers. "I told him!" he reported triumphantly.

"And what did he say?"

"Why, that he will see you tonight!"

"Would you like a coin, Nikodem? You've earned one!"

"Oh no, lady!" The lad backed away from me, lest I push the reward into his pocket. "If I took your coin I would get no reward in heaven."

"I see. The king has been talking to you."

"Yes, he told me about heaven, and how God rewards our good deeds there, if they are not rewarded here on earth. From now on I mean to do good deeds every day!"

"But if you take no earthly reward you will be poor. Your father is not poor. He takes his rewards here on earth."

Wrestling with this thought, Nikodem scuffed the hearthstone. He looked so confused, I relented. "Would you like to hear a story, then? That payment would be so small God would never notice it!"

"Oh, I would like a story! Tell me . . . Tell me. . . ." He settled on his favorite theme. "Tell me about Black Belatruz!"

When Nikodem left, I took my mending to the window. The level light of a late spring evening gilded the square below. Pigeons fluttered blue in golden air. Merchants put up shutters in sidestreets; monks filed down the cathedral steps. One by one the builders laid down hammer and chisel. Their silence blessed the square.

Directly below me a band of urchins played hide and seek in and out of alleys, up and down the cathedral steps, around the pillars of the porch. They were betrayed by their dogs barking after them; wagging, friendly dogs, evidently used to Christian treatment. I let the mending lie on the sill; I leaned over and watched the world below; not with yearning pain, as when I was first imprisoned, but idly; as though it were a mummers' show, nothing to do with me.

I was listening for the clank and tramp of guards come to hustle me out and down to the high seat. I should be combing my hair now, they would give me no time; but I did not believe Wendceslas would send for me. He might have said that for the child's comfort.

Listening for the noise of arrogant power, I paid no heed to the quiet opening of the anteroom door, or the surprised voices of the nuns. When my own door opened I did not turn around. I was used to the nuns looking in. I continued to stare down into the square, watching the children run off to their suppers, the dogs frisking at their heels.

Behind me a man spoke. "You asked to see me."

I whirled. Unexpected, like a bear in an evening forest, a stocky young man stood alert in the gloom. He wore a gray homespun cloak and farmers' boots. His fair hair and beard flowed free, uncrowned, unadorned. No jewel glinted anywhere upon him. Only his gray eyes glowed, wide and serious.

I gasped.

"I hastened," Wendceslas explained, "hoping to hear a good word from you."

So that was it! He thought to find me repentant, perhaps ripe for conversion! Indignation restored my poise.

"Sir, I never expected you here! I have no high seat here, you must content yourself with this chair by the fire." I swallowed the nervous lump in my throat and smiled. Graciously, like a hostess, I seated him in the one chair. He glanced about for another. I plunked down cross-legged on the floor, not at his feet, a little removed, and relished his startled look.

"Remember, sir, I am a savage; my natural home is a tent. That is why I requested an interview. As a savage, I hope to serve you."

Wendceslas' eyebrows arched.

"As you decreed, I have little contact with the world. Yet, news finds its way to me." I paused, willing him to ask me how, so that I could deny him the information. He did not ask; he only watched me curiously from under his stiff-arched brows. I went on: "I gather that my tribesmen are giving you trouble."

Wendceslas nodded. His eyebrows sank. Suddenly, frankly, he told me the whole story; all the facts my little spy and Boleslav had told me, and more. He described the wrecking of rich trade caravans, the burning of villages and even towns. "I fear," the fool concluded honestly, "Draga the Savage may actually attack our city! He is strong enough. How do I deter him? His revenues have been paid and increased already. What more can I offer him?" He leaned forward. "Do you know what Draga wants?"

I nodded wisely. "Ah. Aha. I see that I can indeed serve you."

"What do you suggest?"

"I suggest that you send me out to make your peace with Draga."

One eyebrow rose.

"I also suggest that you send my son Boleslav with me. He could be a most useful liaison between you."

"True, he could. I need men to speak the language." Wendceslas bowed over, leaned his head in his hands and pondered. I waited patiently, remembering the last time I had seen him ponder. That time he had spared my life. Wisdom was not in the

189

man. A pulse fluttered in my throat. Sternly I held a smile off my lips. Freedom was only a fool's thought away!

Wendceslas looked up. "Once free, would you return?"

"If you wish it."

"I have no wish in the matter. But suppose you do not make our peace, but incite Draga against us! You might guide his forces clear into the city!"

I had a prompt answer for that gem of suspicion. "Indeed we might. But remember, sir, that we have both sworn on the Holy Book to uphold your rule."

And that ridiculous answer swayed him! Incredulous, hugging myself, I watched his troubled face clear. He bowed over again; but I knew he had made his decision, and only prayed for his god's blessing on the outcome. Laughing inwardly, I kept a solemn face when he raised his head and fixed me with my mother's stare.

"Very well. I accept your suggestion. Well escorted, you and my brother shall go to Draga the Savage. I trust your vow, lady. I trust you to make our peace with your father."

Now my barely suppressed smile broke out. "With your grandfather, sir!"

Bleakly he shook his head; then vigorously. "No. No. No! In the way of the flesh, I admit that Draga may be called my grandfather. But in the spirit—" his voice rose. Firm and arrogant, pompous as his father Wendz, he proclaimed, "In the spirit I deny any connection whatever with Draga and his savages. I acknowledge as my true ancestors the blessed

190

Ludmilla; Wendz the good; and a long line of city princes; civilized, earnest men, even if they were pagans. Those ancestors I acknowledge and revere; and I pray to be worthy of them." Wendceslas' gray eyes flashed now with unsuspected passion. I remembered how he had first appeared to me like a bear in an evening forest. Like the bear, he was unpredictable.

Cautiously I swallowed my amusement. I would have much enjoyed reminding him that pride is a cardinal Christian sin. I would have loved to tell him the truth about his precious ancestors! "Wendceslas," I ached to say, "let me tell you a true thing. You think that half of your ancestors "in the flesh" were free-riding horse folk? You are mistaken. On my side, your ancestors were farm folk; dirt grubbers. They were cruel without courage, ignorant without loyalty. Your grandmother was the village whore." How I longed to say all that!

Shuddering with secret laughter I bowed my head submissively. The bear rose heavily from the creaking chair and shuffled away, mumbling to himself. Maybe he scolded himself for his unChristian pride! Maybe he congratulated himself on his Charity. He left the doors open; and the nuns who came in found me prone on the floor, shaken by sobs; whether of joy or repentance—or laughter—they could not tell.

Bright plain, wide light. Spring flowers reddened the rolling land. Red and purple and brown, the boundless plain reached to embrace the light.

Slowly, dreamily, I rode through sunshine; through soft-swishing grasses and clinging weeds. I loved the mare's shifting movements, and the soft thud of her hoofs on brown earth. I savored the scent of wild herbs crushed in her passing. With a full, happy heart I watched a brown hare streak for cover, and laughed when the mare shied at a whirring, rising partridge.

Every unaccustomed muscle ached. My wrenched back jarred with every lift of the mare's haunches. My stretched thighs throbbed. These pains cheered me; without them I might have believed myself asleep and dreaming; and feared to wake, and look once more at stone walls, piled mending, and the cold face of a silent nun. Sometimes I thought I glimpsed stone walls from the corner of my eye and, turning quickly, was overcome by relief; seeing instead an expanse of sun-drenched plain, as real around as before me.

Behind me rode the guard; five soldiers leading pack horses; and Boleslav, excitedly riding his first big, city charger. At last Boleslav was seeing the plains of which I had sung to him as he lay in his cradle. For the first time in his life he was entirely free of the city; no town smudged any horizon. I rode ahead alone partly to savor my freedom; and partly to escape Boleslav's boyish enthusiasm.

Behind me now, a soldier shouted. Hurrying hoofs rumbled. Glancing back, I saw the guard galloping to catch up with me. The soldier pointed, jabbing eastward with his sword. Far off, near the hazed horizon, a dark cloud spun rapidly toward us.

Naturally we had been watched. No party of

seven, with pack horses, could penetrate the plain without being reported to Draga. His spies had probably been galloping back and forth below the horizon for days. Now came his response to this small invasion; a band of scouts sweeping toward us. Already their far yells shattered the hot silence of the plain. Mingled with the mens' cries I heard the shrills of excited war ponies; and now their hoofs rumbled like distant thunder.

The guard rode up around me. Uneasy, the city horses sidestepped; weapons, nervously handled, scratched scabbards. The soldier barked tensely "Show no iron!" The soldiers' stiff faces had turned whiter than palace bedsheets.

Boleslav checked his pawing gelding beside me. Behind his grin I spied fear. Boleslav spoke the language of the tribes; he shared their skills and interests. But he had never met his tribesmen on the open plain before. He had met them two or three at a time, with Ruga beside him. He had hunted with them near the city walls, surrounded by city youths. Now, as the screeching mob pounded toward us, even Boleslav paled.

I straightened my spine. "Wipe off that foolish grin!" I advised my son. "Remember who you are." I kicked my mare up beside the soldier. "Let me meet them." Nearer sounded the barbarous uproar. Oncoming hoofs trembled the earth. The soldier licked dry lips, and gave me a helpless look. I pressed the mare forward.

Now the dust cloud rose to dim the sky; and in its shade distinct figures emerged. The tribesmen were separating, spreading out, guiding their ponies to fling a wide circle about us huddled city folk.

Were it not for Draga's treaty, this would have been our end. Loosing a cloud of arrows, the circle would close. The brief clash would hardly raise an echo under the arching sky; and shortly the tribesmen would ride away with their take; while from far reaches of the sky the endlessly swinging vultures would slowly shift their direction toward our remains.

Thanks to Draga's treaty, this time we would at least have words before the circle closed. One of the warriors was galloping straight for me. He came on yelling, waving a short spear, guiding the unbridled pony with his knees. The hideous face leaning over its flying mane was familiar; familiar and beloved.

My heart surged. "Ruga!" I cried, and urged the frightened mare forward.

Ruga circled us, slowing the pony. At a fast trot he swung off, and caught me down from the saddle. We hugged. We smelled and rubbed and laughed and hugged. Delightedly I breathed in Ruga's welcome stink of sweat and grease and leather. Relaxed in his powerful arms I flung my arms about his grimy neck. I did not ask myself whether my excitement was sheer relief, or joy at the unexpected sight of him; or what sort of love it might be.

But gradually it dawned on me that our prolonged embrace might be unseemly. Slowly, unwillingly, I drew myself out of his arms. "Three years, brother!" I gasped. "Three years! And truly, I never expected to see you again!"

Ruga's darkly shining face showed me his answer. But he had to attend to urgent matters, and that without the power of speech. Vaulting onto his pony he trotted away around the circle, whistling orders his men understood, as Sorbal and his friends had understood years ago. The menacing circle wavered, and broke. Arrows were thrust into quivers, swords into scabbords. Our soldiers visibly relaxed. Boleslav rode out to me.

Boleslav had himself well in hand, now. He sat straight and held his head high; he greeted the curious tribesmen correctly. At first they were startled, hearing their own speech from this young city fellow; later, learning that he was Draga's grandson, they took him into their midst. By the time we reached Draga's camp, days later, they had adopted him. From a distance I could no longer tell him apart from them, save by the huge city horse he rode. He wrestled and raced with them, he hunted and gambled. At night he lay with them, boasting and gossiping.

Gratefully our guard turned homeward, leaving us alone with our tribesmen. Ruga and I rode together. We slept close together, Ruga wrapped in his sheepskins, I in my quilt. Often I lay awake, watching his sleeping face by starlight. Once the sheepskin drooped from his heavy-muscled shoulder. Reaching to lift it over him I brushed his shoulder with my hand, and found myself holding my breath. From my fingertips to my toes I felt the touch of Ruga's hard, warm skin like a shock. I had never felt more of Ruga's touch than his hands, or, rarely, his rough cheek. I longed to lay my hand firmly on his shoulder, and draw it slowly down the ridged back.

"Dragamir," I reminded myself, "This man is your brother." I drew my hand carefully away and turned over.

I felt definitely unsisterly. The rough ground under my city-soft body was not more disquieting than my thought. I wriggled and twisted, and smoothed the hard earth under me; and all the time my mind writhed, snakelike, around the forbidden image of Ruga.

Why should this man's presence so comfort and bless me? Never since my childhood with Draga had I felt so happily cared for, so content. Ruga reminded me of the Draga I had known, the ferocious protector. Suddenly, he reminded me of Belatruz. Smiling to myself, I remembered how I had fled for protection among Belatruz's legs. The fierce pony had given me his love; this fierce man might well do the same . . . but he was my brother.

"Naturally he is like Draga," I thought sadly. "Is he not Draga's son?" He was uglier even than Draga; and physically more powerful. If he had owned the common gift of speech he might by now have wrested the chieftainship from Draga; certainly he would have been his successor. As things stood, I supposed that would be Sorbal.

Restless, I sighed and rolled over. Face to face with Ruga, I found his eyes open and watching me. He was amused. "You have slept too long in a soft bed," he said.

I murmured, "Years and years too long." Then I started up. "Ruga! Did you speak?"

"I did not," Ruga said in my head. "With you I need not speak."

"Yes. That is how it is with us."

Ruga smiled his slight, grim smile. He stretched a hand across the ground to me; and I took it in mine. We lay like that, holding hands, like children. Warmth enveloped me. The earth softened beneath me, and I sank toward sleep. "Ruga," I whispered as I sank, "I wish I were not your sister!"

No answer pierced my drowse. Lifting my head, I saw Ruga's eyes closed. His mouth hung slack. Maybe he slept; maybe he pretended sleep. Unresponding, his hand lay warm in mine.

During those days my city life fell away from me like an ill-fitting cloak. I ached no longer. The clear plains light, the smell of horse, even the bite of fleas, recalled me to my true self—the young girl who had trusted Draga. The closer we came to Draga, the faster memory awoke. His absence had always been a dull pain in my heart. Because there could be no cure, I had ignored it; but now the cure was in sight, I allowed myself the luxury of longing. "Has Draga changed?" I asked almost fearfully. Ruga scowled, and shook his head. His eloquent hands fluttered signals, some of which I read; the rest I heard in my mind, as though he spoke. Draga would never change. He would die—he was indeed an old man—but he would never change. While he lived he would ride hard, command ferocious men like little children, gather gold. He scorned rich living, but he hoarded riches. He drank from wooden cups—or the skulls of his enemies—but he hung golden cups in his tent. He armed himself in leather, with bow and lance; but he piled up sabres, iron armor, heraldic shields. I remembered Belatruz's ornate saddle, kept for show. "He still rides bareback?" Ruga nodded.

Once, reluctantly, almost timidly, I asked, "Does Draga ever mention me?" Ruga shrugged, confirming my sad knowledge. I meant less to Draga than a golden cup hung up for show. I was but one of a thousand tools he had used in his long, ferocious struggle for power: men, ponies, dogs, women, weapons, daughters—he used them up and forgot them. Why should I hope to be remembered? But I would give him cause! I would show Draga a new weapon—Boleslav—and tell him a new plan. I would kindle gleam in those small, savage eyes! We came to close-cropped grass. Sheep and horse dung lay about. I thought, "We are near," and my heart leaped. Hours later we met the first herds; small groups of ponies, stallions on guard. They shrilled challenges to our mounts. The tribesmen laughed when Boleslav's charger tried to bolt.

When we rode through a flock of bleating sheep I knew we must be very near. Ruga pointed ahead. Rising steadily before us, the land dropped away sharply. Smoke eddied into the blue beyond the drop.

From the hill-top we saw the camp spread below us. Smoke curled from a hundred cooking-fires, blurring the spring sky. Hobbled ponies wandered among the tents, grazing sparse grass. Children ran and shouted, women chattered. Over the central tent Draga's silk pennants floated lazily on the breeze. All those years ago, coming home with my sack of roots and herbs, I would have seen almost the same sights. "Nothing has changed," I murmured. I checked the mare and sat looking, blinking an annoying warm mist out of my eyes. "Nothing has changed."

"It's all as you told me," Boleslav exclaimed beside me. "I might as well have seen it all before!" But he was flushed with excitement; he had not expected so large a camp, and neither had I. Several hundred tents spread across the plain, surrounded by huge herds moving leisurely, browsing in the distance. The farthest grazing ponies looked small as crawling ants.

"But there is a change," I noticed. Down in the camp they had seen us. Whistles blew, horns wailed. The gossiping women paused, and looked up at us. Children turned from their games, but only for a moment. No one ran for cover. No mother called her child's name. Lounging men drinking tea together barely lowered their mugs. Not one reached for his arms.

This was the happy result of Draga's power. These people lived calmly, in supreme confidence that no enemy dared even approach their far-flung borders. How eagerly I searched the crowd for a glimpse of Draga! He was old, now. Would I know him if I saw him? How could I not know Draga, the godlike old man who was father and mother to me, tribe and country! My eyes ached, scanning the camp. The white-haired warriors stepping out of tents all looked to be vigorous, ready men. But the central tent stood silent under its wind-whispering pennants. No hand stirred its curtains; though a crafty eye might well peep out between them.

He who rides armed and watchful may rest in camp. Safe in the shelter of a hundred shields he may hang up his own. Safe in the shelter of the central tent, my heart softened.

Outside, the spring night was loud with drums, pipes, quarreling dogs and children; and a far, constant bleating of sheep. The air without was heavy with dung-smoke, and the aroma of roasting mutton. Within, the tent smelled of smouldering herbs. Draga reclined alertly among silken cushions. Behind him the wall swept up and in, arching into darkness. The familiar round wall roused warm memories; unlike a square-built wall it comforted and embraced like a mother's arm. Between us a lamp fluttered, a moth of light beating at the dark.

Draga observed, "You are happy here."

I sighed, looking about. Indeed, I was almost happy! "I could be a girl again! So little has changed." If only I could unravel the years and be once more the open-hearted girl Draga had sold! "When I end my war I will return. That city will see no more of me!"

Draga chuckled. "We have changed somewhat—for the richer."

I studied him. He was old, indeed. Under that tough supple skin beat an ageing heart. His hair was white, his chin white-stubbled. His mouth was sinking in upon missing teeth. But I thought the lean hand grasping the skull-cup could yet lift me, and toss me clear across the tent. The small black eyes still snapped and sparkled. Draga had not mellowed. There was no softness in him.

"I noticed a change in you, Father, as I rode into camp. I was looking for you. I watched this tent, hoping for a glimpse of you."

"Hah! Yes. I watched you."

"When I was young you were always the first up and out."

Draga grinned. "Some of your city ways are worth trying. I learned this one from your lamented husband."

"You yourself do not appear at first? You leave all arrangements to lesser folk?"

"Suspense is effective."

"But surely not in battle?"

"No, you are right. The chief rides first in battle. But I don't remember our last battle." Draga drank from the skull and gestured me to drink. A moment I hesitated. The rich brown mead swam invitingly in someone's brainpan. I had grown used to drinking from more innocent cups. Draga watched me, twinkling. I drank.

Abruptly he asked, "And why have you come?"

Why does a child return at night to the hut, palace, tent, yurt it calls home? What love-magic calls across miles and years, drawing the adult homeward? Why does the hawk return in spring?

Calmly I answered, "Father, I have come for two reasons. First, to ask you a question that has puzzled me for twenty years."

"And what might that question be?"

"Did you know I loved you? Why did you sell me?"

He chuckled. "I meant to sell you, as you say, and for a good price. But I did better. I invested you; another good city trick. Here I sit in camp, and riches rush in to me. A river of gold and ivory and silk has been flowing in for years!"

"Twenty-three years."

"Even so. Look around, Dragamir. I like these old cups; but those up there are gold. Those bow-cases are inlaid ivory. These carpets are new, from the east. And every tent in camp is furnished like this! If I have a worry left, it is that our people grow soft! And all this I got for a gawky, gold-haired girl!" He gave me a fond, shallow smile. "Your hair is gray."

"That surprises you? You must have heard little of my life in the city."

"You are young, Dragamir. Take better care of your looks. When you end your war, as you say, you may want to re-invest them." Draga set down his empty cup to rock gently on the carpet between us. He leaned forward. The fondness faded from his shrewd eyes. Now he was serious.

"You brought your son with you."

"Boleslav."

"Seems a good lad."

"Ruga has taught him well."

"Has a kind of leadership. Undeveloped."

"He is young."

Draga laughed. "I have hundreds of good lads like that! I have fifty grandsons!"

"You have no other with royal blood."

"You mean to make him city king."

"With your help. That is the other question I came to ask. Will you help us?"

Draga leaned back. "Your Bola might make a city king, Dragamir. He would need much guidance."

"Which you could supply."

"Hah! One thing he lacks. It is a grave lack."

"What do you mean?"

"You must know it well. I could see it from a hundred paces! He lacks iron. The lad is soft."

Evading Draga's piercing glance, I looked down into the skull-cup. It had ceased rocking and rested, tilted my way.

Draga snapped. "Your Bola will never kill his brother!"

Automatically I answered, "Boleslav has no brother."

"Oh? And who is presently city king?"

I thought aloud, "The young man at the spring."

"Hah?" Draga snorted inquiry. "Hah?"

I looked up. "The young man your hound would not attack."

A small cloud passed over Draga's face, softening his glare. "So long ago, I had forgotten!"

"You said he had a magic."

"He was some kind of shaman, certainly."

"He is the city king." I left it at that. Draga could understand that. He could now comprehend what I was fighting. "Draga," I asked him bluntly, "Do you fight in my war?"

"No."

"I thought not. When you never appeared in the city battle."

"You sound bitter. Did you expect that I would throw away my . . . investment? You struck too soon. I would have had you wait."

"This time I strike prepared."

"Not if you rely on Bola Moss-Heart!"

"Draga, Boleslav is young, and pliant. Like his father, he is easily moved by a stronger will."

"Hmm. They say my friend Wendz was ruled by his mother; whom you killed."

"Boleslav will be ruled by me."

"Until someone kills you. You plan that his soft nature will serve your purpose, I see."

"I can firm the dagger in his hand for this one deed at least. After that . . . after that Boleslav will be city king. He will rule the city; Ruga and I will rule him. And you could rule us—if you help us now. Are you content with this loot?" I gestured contemptuously around at all the golden gleams in the shadows. "You little know the wealth of that city!"

Draga leaned back against the cushions and closed his eyes. He seemed to drowse; but his eyebrows twitched. Childish alarm prickled my scalp. In a faraway voice he asked dreamily, "Dragamir, why do you war?"

"For hate!"

"Not for riches?" Draga had sold me for riches. He loved riches. But he understood hate, too.

"For hate!"

"Dragamir, Wendz is dead. His mother is dead. Whom now do you hate?"

I hated the young man at the spring. I hated the victorious bishop. Most of all I hated the cruel Goddess. But I dared not mention Her name. I whispered, "I hate their god."

"You war with a god, not for riches. For hate."

"Draga, when I can stable ponies in his cathedral, the city riches shall be yours!"

Draga opened his eyes and laughed. He sat up and reached for the mead. "Drink with me, Dragamir."

"You will help us?"

"A small band of scouts might find their way to the city."

"Then—at the midwinter feast!"

"Midwinter is a farmers' feast. Do your city folk honor it?"

"For them it is the birthday of their god. The city will be sodden drunk." I laughed without mirth.

Draga poured the mead. Lamplight flickered softly up into his cragged face. "You could do it yourself, you know. Leave Moss-Heart out of it."

"He might turn against us."

"True. Your way is safer." Draga handed me the skull-bowl, brimming with brown mead. "I drink to you, Dragamir; and to your man's heart."

"It is your own heart," I told him. "Am I drunk?"

"Tonight you can be safely drunk, for I am not. Listen, Dragamir. Win your war; win me this wealth; and I will adopt you."

"What?" Over the skull-rim I stared at him.

"Ceremony. Feast. Drink for all. We mingle our blood, and I tell the world, 'This is my daughter Dragamir'."

"Draga, you have already said that."

"I have?"

"Twenty-three years ago you said it publicly, to the world. You told Bishop Niklas, 'This is my daughter, the princess Dragamir'."

"Hah. Yes. But then I lied."

The lamplight blurred. Horrified and humiliated, I knew I was weeping.

"I am drunk," I explained.

Draga ignored me. He went on calmly, "This time it will be the truth. You will indeed be my daughter if you can beat iron into your Bola's flimsy soul!"

"I can do that, Draga." I thought I could do anything in the world for the prize Draga offered.

Warm-welling tears rainbowed the lamplight. Through the watery dimness I saw Draga smile as he mused, staring down into the flickering lamp.

Boleslav said, "No."

Under Ludmilla's bare rose vines we stood close together. An evening wind whipped stray snowflakes across the bare brown garden. The wind lifted our whispers into the gloomy sky. Backs to the mossy wall, we watched the deserted paths and benches. No spy could lie concealed among the naked thorns—even had Wendceslas thought to employ spies.

"No," said my son. "Have you forgotten altogether? How can you forget?"

"Have I forgotten what, that he spared our lives?"

Nodding, Boleslav hitched his cloak higher.

"I'm glad you are ashamed to say it! What greater insult could he have offered us?"

Boleslav nodded again, but mumbled, "All the same, I am glad to live. Mother, do you know the people love him? And with reason! Never has there been a city king so tender to the poor, so careless of his own gain! His people love him as he loves his god! Do you think they would not avenge him?"

"Shhh! That shadow moved!" We huddled, silent. A gust of wind lifted a cloud of leaves from under the bench where once I had conversed with Bishop Niklas. Boleslav laughed softly. "That shadow has no ears! Mother, believe me, the assassin would not last the day. By sunset, his head would adorn a pike on the city wall."

"Ah, but first the assassin must be found. Listen: The city will waken drunk on Christmas morning, to an expected clanging of bells and bellowing of hymns. It will take a while for the news to spread that a funeral is in progress. Meanwhile, you yourself will organize the hunt for the assassin."

"And where do I find him?"

"Wherever you have an enemy."

"Suppose I have no enemies?"

"I have. Bishop Niklas would make a satisfactory assassin." I licked my lips.

Boleslav snorted. "Who would believe that!"

I admitted, "There are difficulties. Bishop Niklas will himself be found dead on Christmas morning. Let me consider. Perhaps Niklas killed the king, and was himself killed by an avenger, preferably yourself. Perhaps Niklas ordered the king killed, and did not pay; the assassin then killed him. I will think of something. Meanwhile, you need only keep the guard running about; conscript citizens; seize horses and arms. Our scouts will be trotting the streets, rousing terror. Their scarred faces are enough to keep the citizenry indoors! And when the furor dies down, you will be found in the high seat, naturally; of right; he has no son."

"He would be long remembered, Mother. One day a voice would rise—"

"A voice you would promptly silence. Look, Boleslav, you too can be a beloved king. It is not difficult; a matter of judicious gifts, low taxes, wide-open trade. And a king need not be a Christian to pity the poor!" Though it certainly helped! However, Boleslav seemed to inherit this weakness from his grandmother and his father. The poor were unlikely to make too much difference between his rule and that of Wendceslas. "Boleslav, the tribes wait for you. Your grandfather trusts in you."

"No one said so to me, out there."

"Draga never speaks unnecessarily. He spoke to *me*. Your companions were shy of you."

"Hah!"

"Yes, Boleslav. They do not know that here in the city you are only a pardoned criminal. To them you are a prince; yet still their brother. They look to you to open the gates of wealth for them. They see you as a real king—not like this pious fool who carries fuel to peasants with his own hands! You, Boleslav, will conduct the rightful business of a city king! You will see to the people's security and dispense true justice. Your power will enable merchants to trade safely, as they cannot now, with

Draga's harrassment. When merchants can trade, artisans can labor." I peered sharply into Boleslav's face. A spark had kindled; his brown eyes gleamed through the dusk. His full young mouth hung half open. Quickly I went on, "Boleslav, he is not worthy. Strength and wisdom are not in him. My little spy told me how he prayed at night—and it is true, I have seen it! From my window I have watched him cross the square to the cathedral, alone in the dark. He went in alone; and in the first light he came out alone, limping, fatigued with prayer. How can such a man pretend to rule a city?

"Consider, now, how he pardoned us, who were clearly guilty! Consider how he took us in when we came back from the plains! Would not the course of wisdom have been to banish us, at least? But now we are not even watched!

"All these are faults that show him unworthy of the high seat. They are rather charming faults, I agree, but serious ones. This city deserves better of its king!"

I rested my case. Boleslav hunched into his cloak. Dusk deepened into dark. Wind moaned, rattling the thorns around us.

"You have planned this for a long time, have you not?" my son asked.

"I have planned it for twenty years!"

"You were planning it before I was born?"

Recklessly I told him, "You were born for this plan!"

"Yes. I thought as much. Now you confess it." Boleslav sighed.

I could not sink deeper in my son's estimation. I

might as well profit by my confession. "You owe me this," I declared.

"If I owe you this," came the muffled reply, "I owe you nothing else. Nothing, ever."

Eagerly I cried, "I agree!" And glanced around fearfully. Nothing moved in the dark garden but blown branches, shaking thorns.

"But why do you need me?" Boleslav asked despairingly. "You can do it yourself! Ruga can do it! Why me?"

"I can kill, Boleslav, but I cannot rule. The city would never accept me. You must rule, you must give the city the gift it would not accept from me. And if you would rule, the deciding deed must be your own. Would you sit in the high seat that I had won for you?"

The wind sighed cold, the rose thorns clicked. Boleslav drew his cloak up over his head. He said, "I will pay my debt to you."

My heart suddenly loosened. A tight band fell away, and I breathed deeply. "I will do this one deed for you," Boleslav was saying, "but I will never do another. After this I will be free of you. Is that understood?"

"Understood," I promised quickly. I had little doubt that Boleslav would forget this bargain and come seeking my advice the moment the burden of government weighed upon him. Even if he did not, I could whisper in the right ear. "Understood."

Boleslav sighed, heavy and cold as the wind.

Exultant, I watched him burrow into the cloak. He was trying to hide from the wind, from me, from himself. My heart smiled broadly. For a moment, spring seemed to invest the dark garden. It might have been a spring breeze that tore my hair and lifted my cloak. Boleslav had agreed! Wendceslas' rule, Church rule, was doomed in the city!

In a bright, inward flash I saw Draga and myself mixing our blood in a skull-bowl. I saw myself brilliantly arrayed in red silk, veiled in cloth of gold. Over the dripping blood my arms gleamed with the soft glow of youthful beauty; my wedding bracelets sparkled.

The cathedral bells pealed the end of midnight Mass. Their festive clang was dimned by thick-falling snow.

The great doors opened. A brilliance of candles glared behind the Christmas crowd streaming out into the square. Some merchants climbed promptly into waiting sleighs and jingled swiftly away. All the side streets were loud with sleighbells; with the snorting and blowing of horses, and the farewell calls of friends. The horses' pounding hoofs made no sound in the snow.

The poorer townspeople stood about a while talking, stamping, blowing on their hands. Tired children tugged at their mothers' skirts. Wives laid reminding fingers on their husband's arms. "Ah, yes," they said at last, "Time to go. A joyful morning to you, friend. A good Christmas." And away they trudged, or rode, down dark side streets to their homes. Their holiday voices died away; at last the city lay silent under the snowfall; silent, and soon to sleep.

Now at last the great doors creaked shut. One by

one the thousand candles were extinguished. Now only the sanctuary lamp burned in the cathedral, bearing silent witness to the immediate presence of the god. In near darkness the cold cathedral awaited Christmas morning.

And now I stole into the cathedral porch and leaned against a pillar. Sheltered here from the fast-falling snow I huddled in my bearskin, shifting from one frozen foot to the other, waiting. I could see nothing, not even the pillar against which I leaned. With the departure of the worshipers the square seemed utterly deserted; but I knew that my friends were gathering. This deed would not need many hands. Only three of us would actually enter the cathedral. More would keep watch in the square; and beyond the city walls my tribesmen lurked, trotting their ponies for warmth, or building small fires in the lee of snowdrifts.

Faint through the curtain of snow a light appeared. I leaned around the pillar to watch it come. Small in the darkness, it bobbed slowly along the north side of the square from the direction of the palace. Nearer it came; and I saw the face above it; a young face, far too serious for its years.

My little spy had told me truth. Wendceslas was entirely alone. By the small, brave light of his lantern I saw him barefoot and bareheaded, as rumored. His hair and beard were feathered with snow. Mounting the steps toward me he lifted his naked feet high and carefully; walking with a strange grace, and none of his usual bearlike, shuffling gait. Over the lantern his eyes stared, huge and glazed. I saw that he was tranced, like a shaman. I remembered shamans treading snow with naked feet that felt no cold. If Wendceslas saw me now, I thought, he would not realize what he saw. Even so, I shrank from the light, back around the pillar. Wendceslas passed close by me. I could do it now, I thought, and spare Boleslav. But the thought came too late, Wendceslas was already half through the creaking door. And this was as well, I told myself. It is always best to follow a well-knit plan.

The lantern vanished in darkness. The great door thudded shut. Long moments later a torch flared in a side street.

Ruga whirled the torch around. Whirling snow-flakes shone silver in its light. Into this light moved faces: pagan merchants, fur-wrapped; grinning tribesmen in sheepskins; Boleslav.

Boleslav's young, round face was drawn thin. His eyebrows met in an anxious frown. Not thus should a young man approach his first enemy! First blood should be drawn joyfully, with a high heart! A young tribesman punched Boleslav lightly, grinning in his face. Ruga watched him gravely. He knew, as I did, that encouragement now came too late. Whether in high heart or in dread, Boleslav must do this deed now, within the following moments.

The young tribesman took the torch and held it low, and the men gathered around it. Only a flickering beam now gleamed between their massed figures. I glanced about the dark square. No light flickered in any window. No guard challenged. Softly through the snow came Ruga and Boleslav, and mounted the steps beside me.

We spoke no word. Ruga creaked the door open

and we slipped within, I first, Ruga last, Boleslav between us. The cold in the cathedral was snowless, windless. Before us the long building stretched dark, then dim, to the sanctuary lamp by the high altar. Along the walls vague, half-glimpsed figures postured, wooden saints and angels. A wing protruded, a halo caught brief light, a finger pointed to the altar, and the flickering light that warned of the god's presence. It did not frighten me. I knew that god. His hands were nailed. He could not thwart me.

The sanctuary lamp illumined the gleaming tabernacle and the huge bloody feet nailed to the cross above. To the right, shadow drew a sharp line down the center of the Marya's painted face. We saw no sign of Wendceslas, but his lantern sputtered softly on the altar steps.

Silently we parted and moved forward; Boleslav down the center, Ruga and I along the walls. Creeping around saints' pedestals and monks' stalls, I kept a hand on my dagger. I was cold, and breathed shallowly. My vigil in the porch had numbed me. I caught fleeting glimpses of Boleslav, a shadow among shadows, gliding rapidly, now, down the center. I hastened to keep abreast. Once I glanced across and saw Ruga lean like a gargoyle into the edge of light. He stood by St. Peter's feet; and above him the huge golden key gleamed in the soft light from the altar.

Coming to the front, I saw Wendceslas. He had been lying prostrate and invisible before the altar. Now he rose to his knees and stretched his arms, cruciform. Rigid he knelt, looking to Heaven, as we three converged at his back.

I hardly breathed. Ruga's hideous face was impassive. He was here on a mission, which would not fail. Boleslav trembled and gasped convulsively. It seemed to me the cathedral rang with his gasps. And the sound finally pierced Wendceslas' concentration. Turning halfway, he saw me.

Astonished, he gazed on me. Swiftly, astonishment gave way to joy; pure, shining joy. "Mother!" He called me for the second time. "Mother, my prayer is answered!"

Rising, he held out a hand to me. His joy was like a third lamp lit. He raised both arms to embrace me.

I understood. Furious, I saw that Wendceslas believed I had come to repent my evil ways, and pray with him to his nailed god! He thought that of me!

From the corner of his eye Wendceslas saw Boleslav, poised behind him. "Brother!" He murmured; and opened his arms even wider, to embrace us both.

Boleslav stepped back. Gray-faced and shaking, he yet drew his dagger. Seeing how it trembled, I drew mine.

"Brother." Slowly, Wendceslas frowned. "Do you carry arms before Christ's tabernacle?" He was still half-tranced, slow to take meaning.

I told Boleslav, "Now."

Boleslav drew the weapon back, low and ready. "Brother," Wendceslas repeated. His open arms sank to his sides. But then Boleslav sank to his knees.

My throat fairly burst with uncried protests. Hot with rage, I lunged. My dagger struck cloth, then flesh, and stuck. I shoved it home. I heard a loud groan. It came from my own lips.

Ruga struck from the far side. Unangered, unhurried, he aimed with care, then yanked out his weapon. Blood welled, gushed and spurted from Wendceslas groin.

Wendceslas shuddered. Throwing back his head he raised wide eyes to heaven. "Father forgive," he murmured, and sank heavily upon Boleslav. Blood gushed upon Boleslav, and upon his unused dagger. He gasped louder than Wendceslas, and cried out.

Ruga looked to me, across the kneeling brothers.

"Boleslav," I whispered, "Now you must strike. You must strike now. Do you want to be king tomorrow? Holy Mother Earth, do you want to be a *man* tomorrow?"

Weeping loudly, Boleslav supported his brother.

I stooped and seized his hand that held the dagger. With both hands I shoved the dagger into Wendceslas' neck. I shoved; but it was Boleslav's hand that held the dagger.

Wendceslas slumped to the floor. He rolled away from Boleslav and crawled up the altar steps. My dagger in his side scraped the steps, Boleslav's stood out of his beard. Ruga's stroke was killing him. Blood pumped rhythmically now from his groin, staining his robe, dyeing the rich carpet. Wendceslas rose to his knees and raised prayerful hands to the tabernacle.

Ruga watched him with satisfaction, Boleslav with slobbering horror. I was drawn to follow him. I stepped up beside him and looked in his face, and saw it transformed. Joy rose in his face like a sun. Joy glowed in his glazed eyes. For a poised moment he looked like a child who sees his mother coming. Then he folded face-down on the altar steps and lay still; though for some time yet his life flowed, darkening the steps.

None of us moved. We stood like wooden statues. In the silence we heard the whisper of the sanctuary lamp. All about us the cathedral stood dark; the wooden saints stared, unmoved. Outside, endlessly falling snow entranced the sleeping city.

When the flow of life-blood ended I crouched by the corpse. I lifted a wrist in my hand and felt its stillness. No life pulsed within. I pushed at the hunched shoulder, meaning to turn the body. It sprawled too heavy, I could not lift it. Ruga pushed it over with his foot and the shoulder flopped away from the face. That weird joy had faded entirely, leaving only the prints of pain. I stooped closer, listening for breath. I bent my mouth to the slack, dead mouth. No air stirred there. The body, young and perfect as it was, was empty flesh.

Twenty-three years ago I had bent my mouth to this mouth, as I did now. But then it was a small pink mouth, the rosebud mouth of the newborn. Tearfully I had rejoiced to feel its soft, warm breath. Now it hung open, breathless; and I bent to rejoice at its silence.

I looked at the wrist I gripped, at the drooping hand. It was a firm-fleshed hand, built for strength, like a farmer's hand. It was the hand of a brave young man who had been stubborn in his folly. Moments ago, this hand had lifted to me in friendship. Twenty-three years ago, womb-soft, it had closed around my finger.

Now I knew what I had refused to know; that this body had been formed within my own. It was the gift of the Goddess, She who spins flesh in the secret dark. Men may tear and destroy this web. But only the Goddess can spin it, and only in the dark.

I looked up, away. At the edge of light shadow drew a sharp line down the painted face of the Marya. She watched me with one wise eye, and one half of her secret smile. "I have won," she told me silently.

It is always best to follow a well-knit plan. The plan gives one a thread-clue through the maze; in the midst one may become confused, or cease to care; but there is the plan to follow.

I no longer cared at all for the success of this conspiracy. I did not care whether Boleslav took the high seat or not. I did not care whether or not I kept my vow to stable war ponies in the cathedral. This first blow, this initial victory, was defeat enough for me. Yet, I followed the plan.

When I rose from my dead son's side, Boleslav and I were alone; except for a dimly felt host of spirits, saints or fiends—all one to me—crowding in to hover under the high arches. Ruga had departed, perhaps some time gone, faithfully following the plan. At this moment, I thought, he was probably baring his dagger at Bishop Niklas' bedside. The thought aroused no triumphant joy. At best it was part of the plan, which must be followed.

I turned to Boleslav. He still knelt, shuddering, hiding his face in shaking hands. I went to him and touched his shoulder. With a cry he jerked away.

I collected enough spittle to whisper, "The plan. We leave this place now."

Boleslav moaned, "What matter?" And I knew he cared as little as I for the high seat, the riches and glory.

"The plan," I urged dully. There was some reason why we must finish what we had started. Oh, yes. "Boleslav, there are men out there depending on us. Their lives hang in the balance, as well as ours." And one of them was Ruga. I had made one ghastly mistake; now I would make no more. While I lived, Ruga would come to no harm through me! "Come, we must go."

I tried to raise Boleslav, but he scrambled away from my touch and struggled to his feet alone. He lifted his face, but he would not look at me. I turned and led him, according to the plan, through the sanctuary and out the side door.

We made our quiet way through the dark to the palace. Snowflakes brushed our faces. Cold and pure, the touch of snow was like the touch of warning spirits.

I climbed the dark stairs first. My heart thudded, mounting the stairs was an effort. My body dragged. Yet I was careful to make no sound.

Turning toward my apartment I paused and waited for Boleslav to climb up beside me. I wished to feel that we were still together, that I still had a son. But when I touched his arm, he shuddered. We parted silently.

Boleslav had said, "I will pay you this debt, and then I will be free of you." Stealing blindly along the passage I thought, "I will let him go free. I am not worthy to rule him." In any case, my war was over. My enemies were dead. Ludmilla was dead, Wendz was dead. By this time Bishop Niklas must be dead. And my son was dead. My son was dead. My son was dead.

While Wendceslas lived I had not believed him my son. Now I knew the truth. The world around me was changed, now that my son no longer lived in it. It was like an empty house, where I would listen in vain for a familiar voice or footstep. My son was dead.

Leaden-hearted, I pushed my door open, closed it very softly, and stood in the darkness of Yolann's antechamber. Now I was alone. Now I could weep, if I had tears. I could stumble now, and no one would hear and remember, later, that the savage lady had walked abroad. Blindly I crossed the antechamber and entered my own room. "I am alone," I thought. I felt otherwise. I felt a presence there in the dark, waiting for me. My skin crawled. Cold struck my bones.

I was horrified, but not afraid. I had passed beyond fear. If the Christian god waited to avenge his servant, I would welcome his revenge. I moved toward the bed, where I felt the presence concentrated. "Here I am," I said softly, aloud, "take your revenge." My knees grazed the bed. Weakly I sat down upon it; and lay down, collapsed. I felt hot breath on my face. The bed bore the weight of two bodies; my own, and another.

I had thought I was not afraid. But now my hair prickled and my heart paused. I froze.

Softly, a familiar voice spoke in my ear, "I meant to say that to you; here I am, take your revenge. But I hope you will listen to me first."

When the voice ceased, I recognized it. I drew breath. My rising hair lay down limp again. Calmly I asked, "How did you come here?"

"It seemed the safest place, don't you agree?"

Pursued by his soldiers, I had once ducked into the chapel, thinking that the best sanctuary for a pagan. They would never think of looking for me there. And now, the pagan's bed offered the same sanctuary to the bishop! "But how did you escape?" How had the plan failed?

"As you know, lady, I do not sleep alone. When your dumb monster crept up, sword in hand, the girl screamed. She must have thought him a nightmare! I was only dozing. I leaped out, bare as I was, and fled. He did not know the passages as I did. So, for the moment, I escaped."

"I see." Niklas was still shivering; the bed shook. "Are you naked now?"

"Intending not the least disrespect. I thought of the vestments stored in the cathedral; for I assure you, the snow was bitter cold! I scurried in there, and saw . . ."

"Yes." He saw my dead son stretched before the altar; and the blood I had given him staining the rich carpet. "Are you under my blanket?"

"Regretfully. No disrespect."

"Wait while I cover myself." I sat up, pushed off

221

my snow-sopped shoes and pulled a quilt over me. Then, deliberately, I lay down once more beside my enemy. Carefully separate, not touching, we yet took warmth from each other. We lay like little children, almost like friends, relaxing slowly in the warmth. It seemed quite natural.

"I could not stay to find the vestments," Niklas continued. "Your servant might come at any moment, you yourself might . . . I did not know your plan. But I knew you were abroad. I had been looking for this since Wendceslas freed you."

"Which he did against your advice."

"Well, naturally. But on this holy night you took even me by surprise."

"As I have done before," I was almost happy to remind him.

"Ah, yes. Knowing you abroad, I slipped up here into your den as the safest possible hiding place." Niklas sighed. "And here I am naked in your bed, as I have wished for many years. But I never imagined it like this!"

He still shivered. I felt his huge, flabby trembling, and wondered if he were still cold, or whether he trembled for fear. I said, "Niklas, we are alone. Why talk? You can kill me." Why did I say that? I think I wanted Niklas to kill me. I think I actually wished for him to reach out his big hands and grasp my throat. Certainly, I was resigned. I lay still. And Niklas lay still.

"I thought of it. But surely your savages have taken over the city?"

"Yes."

"You see. The satisfaction would have been short-lived. I thought better to meet you here alone and try to talk. Will you hear me out?"

Frankly I told him, "I have no choice. Until the Christmas bells ring I have no guard to call. For this hour we are alone together. You are the stronger now. Tomorrow I shall be stronger. So talk on, Niklas, or kill me." I truly did not care which he did.

"I am here to talk. Listen to me."

"I am listening."

"Lady, I can serve you. I can be of great use to you. Let me show you how. Doubtless, you intend that Christmas morning shall find your Boleslav in the high seat."

"That is the plan."

"But I am sure you know that Boleslav is not like you. You had a better, more likely son in Wendceslas, had you only known! Boleslav's heart is not beaten out of iron, his will is a bent arrow. Frankly, your Boleslav is a weak young man, too easily influenced. Do my words offend you?"

I shrugged. "What you say is true."

"That young man will make grave mistakes! Neither will the people trust him. To them he is a half-savage, a pagan. Now, you intend that your father Draga shall rule through Boleslav; am I right?"

"Quite right."

"But what will happen then? You know, your horse folk are talented destroyers; but they create no wealth. They understand nothing of business, trade, investment. Within ten years—holy saints, within five years!—your city will be a ruin. You and your

223

Boleslav will be riding the plains with all your wealth in your wallets!"

Niklas little guessed what a lovely vista those words evoked for me! A momentary vision of freedom; of boundless light, of fresh, bright air. Oh, to be free of this city, these constricting robes, these plans and hatreds! For a moment I glimpsed spring flowers reddening rolling land.

"Lady," Niklas said, "I can save your city and your wealth for you. I can—"

"Advise Boleslav, as you advised his father?"

"Yes. I can serve Boleslav well. I can save you both much trouble. Look, here is a free sample, as a merchant would say. When the people find their king dead at the altar on Christmas morning, what do you mean to tell them?"

"That you murdered him."

"Ah? Oho! But they would not likely believe that! They would whisper, you know. And the whisper would grow to a murmur, and the murmur would mount to a tempest that would blow down your high seat!"

"Perhaps."

"Perhaps! Lady, I assure you! That is the most likely outcome. Now hear me; listen to counsel. The body must be removed instantly to . . ." Niklas was thinking aloud, "Yes! To the king's own bed. His servants must all be dismissed, all courtiers turned away, the door bolted. I alone will attend him; for he has . . . ah . . . plague. Only I shall be with him, and a doctor whom I trust."

I smiled in the dark. "A son of yours, perhaps?"

"Perhaps, yes. The king will be pronounced near death. Prayers and offices shall be recited in the cathedral, candles lit—"

"You would deceive your god, Niklas? Remember, he was there. He saw the deed done."

"Oh, no! I would deceive the people, lady, not God! No one can deceive God; I have never tried."

"And your god will allow you to deceive the people?" What could he do, his hands were nailed. But I was curious to hear Niklas' honest opinion.

"God," he said gravely, "seldom interferes on earth. His vengeance is reserved for the hereafter." Ah yes; like his rewards.

"And you do not fear this hereafter vengeance."

To my surprise, Niklas shivered violently. "Yes, I fear it! I dream of it. I know well that I dangle over hell like a spider over a fire, on a silken thread." Earnestly he added, "I came here to offer you a bargain; if you reject it, give me one favor: time to confess my sins to a true priest of God."

Well, why not? "You shall have that. But tell me Niklas," I had always wondered this, "were you ever a true priest of God yourself?"

"When I was young. When I first came to the city I was a wandering preacher. Then I was hot with holy zeal. My soul was a rich field for God. But then came the enemy in the night and planted weeds among the wheat.

"What enemy did that?"

"Power corrupts, lady. Wendz gave me power and worldly wealth, and the chance to increase them."

225

"So that now you dangle like a spider over hell. I see." I had made use of the lust for power and wealth that others felt, but I had never felt it myself. My own hungers were hungers of the heart and body. I wondered if I had missed some understanding; if I were perhaps less complete and real than Niklas, or Draga. "Well, continue your plan. The king has the plague."

"Yes. He will remain locked away for five, six days. At last he will die. His coffin must be closed, for fear of the pestilence. This will be easily believed, for the coffin will stink abominably. I will see to that.

"I myself will not, I think, officiate at the funeral. I will be abed, deathly ill. Yes. Ten days later I will emerge, thin and pale—and ready to serve the new king."

I laughed dully. "I can think of no better doom for you, Niklas, than to emerge thin!"

"Now do you see how I can serve you?" Rolling in the bed to face me, Niklas dropped his almost bantering tone. For the first time he spoke anxiously, pleadingly. "You need me! You cannot afford to kill me!"

"You may be right." Actually, I thought he probably was right. Boleslav wished to be free of me. He would need an advisor. If I wished, I could arrange now that Niklas consult with me before advising Boleslav; that way, I could still rule from behind the high seat.

But I did not wish to rule. My final, costly victory had freed me from concern for worldly things; "power and wealth," as Niklas had named them.

The fictional trappings of glory had never meant much to me; now they meant nothing. I was free, as I had been free in my girlhood; except that now I was also dead-hearted.

Niklas lay beside me in chains. The love of these unreal things confined him, weighed him down more heavily than the iron chain with which I could bind him. I recognized the hate I bore him as such a fetter; a slender chain, whose dragging weight I just now noticed. I cast it off.

"Very well," I decided.

Niklas heaved a sigh. Still anxious, he asked, "You will speak for me to Boleslav?"

"No need."

"And your servant? The monster who will come here now, at any moment?"

"That monster is not my servant. Why do you expect him to come here?"

"Why . . . I assumed . . ." Niklas fumbled. "I always believed he was your lover."

What a pang pierced me! Surprised, I discovered I could still feel grief. If only Niklas had been right! "Ruga is not my lover," I informed him unnecessarily, "He is my brother."

"Holy saints!" Niklas' amazement almost amused me.

"And he does not care if you live or die," I went on. "You are nothing to him. *I* am your enemy, Niklas. You know why."

"I do. But—"

"I do not forget it. Nor do I forget our last conversation before this. You remember that last conversation?"

"I do. But—"

"I do not forget these things. I only pardon them."

"You will be glad of it!" Niklas promised fervently. "I'll give you cause to thank the saints—"

"Here, in this world?"

"Certainly, here in this world! Neither of us has hope of reward in the next world!"

"Then begin now, immediately. The Christmas bells will ring within the hour."

"Instantly! Give me a robe, and I will manage the . . . corpse."

I got up and groped in my chest for the bearskin. "Here; this wraps me three times around, it should cover you. You will need shoes. Try these . . ."

I heard Niklas pant and gasp, pulling on the shoes. "Terrible small, lady. To wear them I must break them." For all his bulk, he moved swiftly. I saw him pass the window, a black shadow against dark gray. At the door he paused. "Come with me, in case I meet your . . . brother."

"You will not."

"Where has he gone?"

Almost I told him. Then I remembered that we were not co-conspirators. I had neither cause nor need to trust Niklas. "Trust me, you will not meet him. That is"—the thought struck me—"unless the girl raised an alarm?"

"Girl?"

"Your girl; who dreamed she saw a monster by the bed."

"Oh. No." Niklas breathed relief. "The girl is dead."

228

I heard the door shut, and, a moment later, the outer door. Alone, I sank down upon the bed. I rolled into the warm hollow Niklas had left; and pulled all the blankets over my head. Even so, cold invaded me. I began to shake uncontrollably, as though I lay once more in the grip of the Goddess. My teeth chattered. I squeezed my eyes shut, but haunting visions flickered through my darkness.

Vivid, clear as daylight, I saw a child's head strike stone. Blood welled over the stone.

I saw a small girl's corpse, pierced and trampled. Blood caked the earth under her head and open hands. Blood welled, dripped, stained sand; stained a rich-patterned carpet. Sharply before me, my son's corpse lay breathless and empty; watched by the flickering sanctuary lamp.

I struggled for breath. I was being muffled, shut away from air, bundled in straw; no, in blankets. I thrust my head up into the cold gray dawn; still I gasped, half-strangled. Relentless fingers drew a band of blanket tight around my throat.

"I am alone," I fought to remember. "No one is here to throttle me but myself." I yanked the blanket away from my throat, and heard my own wheezing. In the gray, snowy light I saw my hands, talons, yanking and twisting, knotting and tightening. I thrust the blanket far away.

Softly, muffled by falling snow, the Christmas bells clanged. Throughout the city their message woke children eager for festivity. Monks and nuns heard the bells and rose to their knees on cold stone floors to thank their god. Bishop Niklas, hastening up dark stairs bowed beneath his grim burden heard the bells; he paused to breathe, then rushed on headlong like an ogre seeking shelter from the light. Ruga heard the bells; and led our tribesmen ambling through the snow-soft streets. The bells called pious citizens out to the dawn service. They heard the soft, menacing jingle of bridle-rings mingle with the bell-tones, and saw, with disbelief and horror, painted, scarred savages patrol past their doors. Boleslav in the high seat heard the bells and moaned, and hid his wretched face in guilty hands.

I heard the bells. "God's son is born!" they announced triumphantly. "God's son is born! Your son is dead. Your son is dead. Your son is dead."

6

The Shrine

Old Draga, chief of the horse folk, had a new war pony; a well-taught bay gelding, sleek and swift. Drinking with friends on a spring evening, Draga offered to race him against high stakes. Ivory bowcases were staked, slaves, fine ponies; and next morning the whole camp jostled to watch the race.

Red flags marked the track. The ponies pranced and pawed, jingling gold and ivory bridle-rings. Only Draga's bay still wore bone and wood rings. They clicked as the nervous pony shifted and circled.

The racers were old men, or men in their middle years. The ponies were young and vigorous. At the signal they tore off along the track, raising a whirlwind of dust that darkly hid the flags.

From afar the cheering crowd saw only the dust-cloud rushing, with the head of the foremost pony—Draga's gelding—and the tail of the hindmost. Swinging around the last curve, the rushing dust-cloud left a dark shape on the ground.

The race slowed, the dust cloud sank. Now the crowd saw the riders fighting unwilling ponies, tightening reins and looking back, circling to return.

The crowd broke, mumbling. Here and there men ran out to the dark shape on the ground.

So Draga died, racing ahead of his friends. Conflicting stories were later told and sung; that he had died without warning on the gelding's back; that he had fallen and been trampled; that he had leaped off and was trampled. This last was the most popular version. No version could ever be proved.

The festive crowd became a mourning crowd. Groaning women tore hair and garments. Men slashed their cheeks. Draga's flattened corpse was washed and dressed in silks and laid upon embroidered cushions in a painted wagon; and the whole camp followed the funeral wagon on its slow, creaking course from tribe to tribe across the plain. Where the wagon passed it left a trail of destruction. No living creature and no unbroken object was left in its wake. Men who saw it coming, accompanied by cries, moans and drumbeats, snatched their children and goods from its path and fled. Closing in behind, they joined the mourners; tearing garments, clawing their faces, and adding their voices to the dismal din.

On the plains the news traveled scarcely faster than the funeral wagon. We in the city heard nothing of all this. At this time I was packing for travel. I packed few goods; a red silk gown for the ceremony; my wedding jewelry; two cloaks and my bearskin; for inevitably returning winter would find me on the plains. I intended never to return to this rock-tomb; this man-trap; this city of sorrow.

Packed, I sought out Boleslav. I found him pacing the audience hall behind the high seat, lending a restless ear to Niklas' murmurings. At each window he paused, looking out despairingly. Thought was harder for Boleslav than any physical action; and that bright, windy morning was a morning for hunting, not for listening to this fat merchant of political wiles!

I sympathized; and felt the beginnings of delight; for I myself would shortly be riding into the spring wind.

Niklas could hardly keep pace with the impatient young man. His penitential thinness had been short-lived! As I came up to them I heard him panting.

They stopped. Niklas wiped sweat from his forehead with a furtive sleeve. Boleslav turned slightly gray. I had noticed this of late; my presence actually paled his bronze cheeks. Also, he never looked straight at me, but sideways; glancing away if I sought to hold his gaze. Long familiar with hate, I knew the symptoms. I thought Boleslav would be vastly relieved to see me go.

Abruptly I told him, "I am going away."

As abruptly he asked "Where?"

"To Draga; to celebrate my adoption."

"*What?*" Both men stared at me. "Your adoption as what?"

Almost enjoying myself, I tossed caution and propriety to the spring winds. "Draga has promised to adopt me as his daughter."

"But why . . . what . . ." Boleslav's eyes were on me now, baffled and puzzled. With those quick words I had stripped away his cherished heritage like a stolen cloak. He shivered, feeling colder air. "Mother, what do you mean?"

Niklas suddenly bowed his head and turned away from us. I saw his fat shoulders shaking with repressed laughter. I smiled, explaining away the deceit of years as a trickster might explain away cheap magic, backstage. "I was not born Draga's daughter," I calmly told the young man who thought he was Draga's favored grandson. "I never knew my father. My mother was a woman of the farm folk. I was very young when Draga snatched me away."

Boleslav gaped fishily. His face had gone completely gray. More gently I told him, "I did not coldly deceive you, Boleslav. Often I forgot the truth, and thought of Draga as my father. But now, in a few days' time, I shall become Draga's true daughter. Then you will be his true grandson."

Niklas half-turned toward us. "I think I should leave you now," he said, barely stifling his laughter. "Already I have heard far too much."

I detained him. "Before you go, Niklas: My brothers will escort me to Draga, the city need take no thought for that. But I would like one city attendant to go with me."

I myself did not know why I wished the burden of a child. I had meant to be free, unencumbered for the first time in many years. I could hardly wait to feel the plains wind in my face, to look to a far-circling horizon clean of walls. Yet I felt that I could best enjoy freedom by sharing it. I remembered how Nikodem's eyes had glistened at my tales. Patiently he had returned to his labors, content to dream, to know that there was in the world a place unwalled, without rule. Now I longed to show it to him; to see his black eyes gleam again.

"You mean," Niklas said, "my young son."

I smiled. I refused to be surprised. "You are always informed, Niklas."

He bowed courteously. "My son will be glad to go."

"I should tell you, I do not mean to return soon."

"Send the lad back when you like." Niklas bowed again and departed, barely suppressing his laughter with a fist pressed against his mouth. Boleslav stared after him. Slowly he turned back to me. He looked shocked, like a shaken child. So recently he had been a child, I raised instinctive, comforting arms. Quickly he stepped back from me.

He said haltingly, "If I understand right, you said your mother was a farm wife?"

"Not exactly. She had no husband."

Boleslav groaned. "Your ancestors were farm folk? Dirt grubbers since the days of Adam?"

"Yes." I saw that it was almost too much for him. "But you must remember you have your father's blood, too." That, at least, was all he thought it; civilized, Christian, royal.

"Oh, I will remember that! Before Heaven I will!"

I looked curiously into his slack, gray face. "You use some odd language, son. Heaven? Adam? What talk is this?"

"Christian talk, such as my father used." Boleslav thrust out a stubborn chin. Suddenly, he looked like Wendz. "When you came the bishop was planning my baptism."

It was my turn to step away. But I should have known. Had I been less sunk in my private misery, I would have noticed Niklas' steadily increasing confidence, amounting lately to insolence. One example after another flashed now across my awakened mind. So—Niklas had won again! Like myself, he was persistent. He and I were like those lizards that, caught by the tail, tear away, later to grow new tails.

Mentally I bowed to Niklas. I did not care overmuch; it no longer mattered. Calmly I asked, "Did you settle the details of the ceremony?"

"Yes, we did. It takes place at Christmas time. I hope," he said stiffly, "that you will honor me with your presence in the cathedral."

"At Christmas time I shall not be here, Boleslav. I do not mean to return here."

"I see." We faced each other, unbending. Shame and anger were driving the shocked pallor from Boleslav's cheeks. His black eyes snapped defiance. I had never seen him look so manly.

I sighed, and turned to go. He stopped me with a gesture. "One question, Mother. I see now that you are a fine mistress of lies." I did not blink. "I must know. Forgive my rudeness, but you see I must know. Tell me truly—we are alone—was Wendz my true father?"

"Yes, he was."

"Are you my true mother?"

"Yes, I am."

"You would swear to those statements?"

"By the Goddess!"

"You are my mother. I am sorry for that."

"Boleslav . . ." I grieved to leave him so. I thought I had never loved either of my sons. One I had disowned entirely, the other I had used like a weapon; and now his use was over. But lately, to my sorrow, I had learned something of the mysterious ways of the Goddess. Now that the world no longer echoed Wendceslas' awkward footfalls, it had become for me an empty palace. I had thought I hated the sound of his soft voice. Now that it was silenced, I cherished every rare word it had spoken to me. Unwilled ties bound me to my dead son. Was I bound, also, to the living one? Far away from here, free on the winter plain, would I wake to wonder if Boleslav slept warm? I feared this might be so.

"Boleslav," I said quietly, "I am not sorry that you are my son. I am proud."

Boleslav curled an angry lip. "Will you be proud of a Christian son?"

"Yes. I will." I thought of my father, that laughing, ferocious pagan whose love I had always sought. I thought of his people, the brave wanderers who had taught me to live. Then I remembered my mother, and her ancestors, "dirt grubbers since the days of Adam." Horse folk and city folk alike might scorn them, but I knew their strength, their pride. They scorned the free nomads, who did not know how to work. They derided the city folk, who dreaded to dirty their hands. In their own world of soil and sweat they were supreme; ox-shouldered gods, moving the earth. And now my son looked at me defiantly; and I seemed to see a crucifix in his left hand. The right would always hold a sword. "I have a strange, far-flung family," I told him. "And I am proud of every part of it. Your father told you that in his Heaven you would be friends. Boleslav, I tell you that you and I will be friends yet; and here, in this world."

"That will need time," my son warned me.

"I know it will. I hope to have the time."

That same windy morning we rode away from the city walls. Gladly I left them behind; those gray stone walls that for twenty-four years had marked the boundaries of my life. Gladly I rode into the warm spring wind that cleaned my face and lifted my hair. Near the city it brought me the scents of ploughed ground and spread dung. I felt free when the wind exchanged these warm farm scents for those of fern, herb and flower; when we left the farm country behind and entered the plain. I felt, then, that the wind carried my past away with it, back upon the city; my past, and all its misery.

I rode free. The slight baggage tucked under the saddle constituted my worldly goods. I had braided my hair into one long, gray plait, and left it unveiled. "Nikodem," I said to the child beside me, "I feel young! Almost like you!"

The little boy turned a surprised face toward me. This was his first time on horseback. His mount was carefully chosen, placid and elderly; even so, keeping his seat took most of his attention. Yet his predominant expression was one of surprise and unbelief. "My son will be pleased to go," Niklas had said. Nikodem was not pleased—he was radiant. Never had he thought to see with his own eyes the wonders of which I had told him! Amazement had been his first reaction; then delight, then doubt. "Will we have to hunt our dinners?" he asked first.

"I suppose so."

"What if we meet horse folk?"

"We intend to meet them. Do not look so alarmed! They will be our friends and brothers."

"It's the dogs worry me!"

"Ah. But we are armed." My dagger thumped my hip. The bow Ruga had given me swung from the saddle. "And my brothers are even better armed."

Sorbal rode ahead, watching all horizons. Ruga brought up the rear. Glancing back, I caught his somber eye; and warmth surged through me. "In such company," I had told Nikodem, "you are safer than at home." It was true. With Ruga alone I would have felt safer on the wide, spring-reddened plain than within walls.

And now the reason for my journey took on reality. I was really going to Draga. I really would be adopted. I had as yet given little thought to what might come after; but I felt that I would be reborn, even as my son would be reborn at his baptism. I believed that I would become a different woman; a woman free of hate and remorse, open to freedom. "Freedom" was the name of my future. The wind sang "Freedom" in my ears. A high-circling hawk cried "Freedom!" Much as I loved my father, I would never let him re-invest me. I would live for my own interests, and never again for his.

As the spring sun dropped, Sorbal pointed, and turned south. We followed without question. "Lady," Nikodem whispered, "I ache so!" I turned to him. Excitement had faded from his round, dark face, giving room to fatigue. He bit his soft lip, and hung onto his nag's mane. The horse plodded steadily, following Sorbal's mount. "Lady, when do we stop?"

"I think very soon," I encouraged him. "I think Sorbal is heading for that smoke on the horizon."

The smoke smudge grew—rapidly for me, much too slowly for Nikodem—and became turf roofs and stone chimneys. We rode along a beaten track between ploughed, hedged fields. "See," I comforted the boy, "it's a village. You may even sleep in a bed tonight!" Silent, Nikodem hung on.

Sorbal grunted, and pulled his pony to a stop. "Others coming," he flung over his shoulder.

I left Nikodem, and rode up front. Two fields away, three shaggy ponies were trotting toward us, straight across the ploughed land. They bore swarthy riders in flapping rags. The foremost lifted a hand to us. "They don't know enough to keep to the track!" I muttered. "They will anger the farm folk." Sorbal shrugged.

The foremost rider raised himself to look at us. Abruptly, he kicked his pony into a gallop. It pushed through the hedge and pounded toward us, sending clods flying at every step. The rider dropped the reins to fling plump arms wide, as if to embrace us all. She came on full tilt, skirts billowing; and as she neared us the clink of heavy jewelry mingled with the clank of bridle-rings and the earthy thud of hoofs.

I kicked my mare. The startled animal took off awkwardly, half trotting. We met in the midst of the field. Hoofs sank in soft earth, a thousand seedlings died. Leaping down we rushed together. Laughing with tears, we embraced.

Yolann was larger, heavier than I remembered. She embraced me like Barax, like a minor goddess. Her arms strengthened, encouraged, consoled. She laughed down my neck, she blew wild onion in my face. I held her full-fleshed face in my hands and gazed into her joy-sparked black eyes. "I am home," I said.

"Home" was a circle of light on a dark plain. "Home" was a brazier where flat bread fried. "Home" was any unmarked spot on the unmarked plain where friends were found. "I have come home," I murmured into Yolann's grimy neck, and wept.

Holding me as she would hold her child, Yolann called to Ruga over my shoulder. "She must stop here. She must not go on." I heard him ride up to us, earth sucking at his ponies' hoofs. Yolann answered his signalled question. "Draga is dead."

The words rang in my ear. "Draga is dead." I buried my face in Yolann's shoulder. "Draga is dead." How could Draga be dead? We were alive. Here we stood, hugging, on rich brown earth under a spring sunset. The three of us here were Draga's children; and Sorbal; and Yolann's little girl, watching us from her saddle, was Draga's granddaughter. How, then, could Draga be dead? It was impossible. "What happened?" I asked.

The telling needed only a moment. In that moment the sun sank no lower; but darkness swept over my world.

When my son died my world became an empty palace. This surprised me, for till silence fell I had no notion that I listened for his voice. Dumbfounded, I wandered the empty rooms. Now, with this telling, the sun fell out of my sky. The empty palace darkened; and I was left alone in the dark.

I felt that I screamed like a child in a nightmare, and ran out of the dark palace upon a dark plain. Far, scattered fires beckoned. No stars shone.

I stood alone. I was no one's daughter, no one's mother, no one's wife. I had extinguished my fire; and now the sun had fallen. Holy Mother Earth, how dark the plain!

Those scattered, beckoning fires resolved themselves into sound. Voices near me argued and explained. Sorbal, Ruga and Yolann were wondering what they could do with me.

"No need to do anything," I cried to them. "I am not your sister!"

Smoothing my braid with a motherly hand, Yolann said, "She cannot go on to the strava. They would likely throw her on the pyre."

"Very well," I said, struggling. "That sounds fine." I belonged on the pyre, with Draga's rich booty. The thought held no terror for me. Life held terror now, not death.

"I know," Yolann said to Ruga, "Naturally you must go. Of course. I know you will be back!"

After a few more attempts I gave up trying to speak. They paid me no attention; and I did not mind if they burned me on Draga's pyre, or stored me away in this village, or simply left me. In my darkness, no dim shape could terrify or attract. One was like another. None mattered.

They reached some decision. We mounted and regained the track. We rode slowly on to the village;

Sorbal and Ruga and Yolann, her child and servant, Nikodem and myself drew rein at the head of the street. The snarling village dogs raced out to meet us. They circled us, growling and bristling; but at a safe distance from the plains ponies' hoofs.

Whitewashed cottages lined the one street. Some had blue shutters and outside benches. Their western walls glowed pink in the sunset. Sorbal nudged his pony and ambled gently down the street. "He will find you somewhere to stay," Yolann murmured comfortingly. I doubted it. The farm folk edged away from him. Children peeping from doorways giggled at the passing savage, and dodged back out of sight.

These folk were clean-clad. With a mild, dawning interest I studied the street. Many more pigs and chickens than I remembered rooted and scrabbled in the ditch. The Christian rule had brought prosperity and peace, even here. Down at the bottom of the street I glimpsed a respectable, whitewashed hut; surely not the home of the village whore.

Slowly, I turned.

The level light of sunset reaching in under the wattled roof of the shrine gilded the red and blue painting. Before the shrine three little girls paused in prayer. Their backs were turned to us; but they kept glancing back at us, very nervous of our presence. They were neat little girls, with smooth-braided hair and almost-clean skirts. Our headman's daughters had looked like them. But I thought these were more ordinary children, examples of the general prosperity.

They mumbled their prayer, and each child laid a

small offering on the shelf before the Goddess. They minced away, then, holding hands and giggling, watching us. Suddenly they broke and ran, laughing, down the street.

Their offerings glowed in the sunset light. I slid down the mare's side. "Hold her," I bade Nikodem. Bravely he took her rein; though he listed sideways, exhausted, gritting his teeth. Slowly I dragged myself across the space of beaten earth; and stood once more before the Goddess.

The children had left Her flowers. Humbly they shone, giving up their last fragrance in last light. Drawn against my will, I raised my eyes to my Enemy.

More than prosperity had reached out here from the city. Flowers were all the sacrifice this shrine would ever know. No Goddess of paint and straw looked back at me. No little straw daughter was plastered in Her arms, although it was full spring and all the fields around were planted. I looked into the quiet face of the Marya.

She was blue and red, like the Goddess, with gold. Golden paint touched sleeve and veil, and gilded her gown. In place of the straw daughter she embraced her son; a crowned son, infant-small but man-shaped, wise-eyed. He raised stiff arms cruciform, as if to embrace . . . or remind me.

Tenderly the Marya bowed her crown against His crown; lightly her gentle hands enfolded His form. Her dark, oval eyes watched me mildly; inviting, not insisting; accepting, not vengeful. Her gaze pierced me.

Around us in the spring air I felt the Goddess

hover. She was the air and the seeded earth; Her power haloed the Marya. Her power haloed me. Gazing dumbly, I knew myself the Marya; myself the Goddess.

But I had refused my own Being. I had torn down the empty palace of my Self, and now I stood alone on a sunless plain. Like a cool moon the Marya shone into my darkness. Her quiet rays searched me out. "Where are you, Marya?" She asked; and invited, "Even now, we might try again."

Might we? I had no ready answer for her. I was too weary, too baffled. Silently I watched the sunset fade from her face. The sacrificed flowers gasped incense. Night enfolded the fields, as the Marya enfolded her Son.

Behind me a pony muttered, a dog snarled. Slowly I turned back to the others. Shadows against a dim sky, they waited patiently as I walked toward them. Yolann was a husky shape, rugged as a ploughed field. Exhausted Nikodem slumped, still bravely holding my mare on a tight rein. A little apart, Ruga sat his war pony like a wooden warrior. He did not look at me. I saw his flat profile turned southward toward the strava, where tomorrow he must ride to burn Draga's corpse upon a pile of riches.

Ruga did not look at me; yet he awaited me. All these friends awaited me lovingly; though Yolann must be concerned for her husband and children, and Ruga for his position; and Nikodem was close to falling off his horse. Why did they wait? I was no concern of theirs.

I went first to Ruga. The war pony skittered, and

chopped warning teeth, but I laid a hand on Ruga's knee. Calming the pony, he looked down at me. "Ruga," I said, "You need not come back from the strava for me. You are not my brother. That was only a story we told each other."

Now we faced each other frankly. This son of Draga had no need to consider me. I was only his ally from a lost war. My friendship carried no value.

Clearly, Ruga answered in my mind. "I am not your brother, Dragamir. Therefore I will come back." Grimly he smiled his hideous, beautiful smile. Around us the ponies sighed, shifting, printing rich earth with tired hoofs; and the earth sighed to the evening as a million seeds stirred, seeking life.

Melissa Hepburne

Over one million copies in print!

MY ENEMY, MY SON

The cold in the cathedral was snowless, windless. Before us the long building stretched dark, then dim, to the sanctuary lamp by the high altar. Silently the three of us parted and moved forward. Creeping around saints' pedestals and monks' stalls, I kept a hand on my dagger. I caught fleeting glimpses of Boleslav, a shadow among shadows, gliding rapidly now down the center. I hastened to keep abreast.

Coming to the front, I saw Wenceslas. He had been lying prostrate and invisible before the altar. Now he rose to his knees, his arms outstretched, oblivious to us as we converged silently at his back. I hardly breathed. Boleslav, on the other hand, trembled and gasped compulsively, and the sound finally pierced Wenceslas's concentration. Turning halfway, he saw me.

Astonished, he gazed at me. Swiftly, astonishment gave way to joy, pure, shining joy. "Mother!" he called me. "Mother, my prayer is answered!" He rose and spread his arms to embrace me. He then caught sight of Boleslav, poised behind him. "Brother," he murmured, and opened his arms wider, to embrace us both.

Gray-faced and shaking, Boleslav drew his dagger. "Brother?" Wenceslas repeated as his open arms sank to his sides in confusion. But Boleslav sank to his knees.

My throat fairly burst with uncried protests of fury. Hot with rage, I lunged, fingers tight on my dagger. . . .